LOVE LUST AND SERENDIPITY

MIMI FLOWERS

Published by Windsurf Publishing LLC
Greenwich, Connecticut
Copyright © 2017 by M Mihailescu-Lagana
Cover design: Windsurf Publishing LLC
Cover illustrations: Shutterstock

ISBN: 978-1-936509-20-1 paperback
ISBN: 978-1-936509-21-8 hardcover
ISBN: 978-1-936509-22-5 ebook

Library of Congress Control Number: 2017955694

 Created with Vellum

*With gratitude and thanks
to God and the Angels,
family, friends, and those
who have shown me
laughter, light, and love*

CONTENTS

CHAPTER 1

HE WOODS

Steve Woods met his wife Kate when he was studying at Harvard Business School. Kate was from the affluent suburb of Chestnut Hill just outside of Boston. Her father, Robert Brevard, was a highly respected and successful plastic surgeon. And her mother, Lucille, wrote children's books for an international publishing house. Kate also attended Harvard. She majored in art history and finished her master's degree a year earlier than Steve. And while Steve completed his master's in business, Kate took a temporary job working for the Boston Arts Foundation. Soon after, when Steve finished his degree at Harvard, he proposed to Kate. They had a small wedding in Chestnut Hill. Then they decided to move to New York where they would live and work together.

Not long after they arrived in New York, they found an exquisite apartment on Central Park South that had panoramic views of Central Park. They also purchased a stately home in Greenwich, Connecticut. This brought them closer to Steve's parents, who also lived in Greenwich at the time. They afforded all of this with presents from their parents, family, and friends.

Steve's father, Malcolm Woods, had made a made a fortune in the stock market in his early years. He was also a very generous man. Malcolm wanted Steve to work with him at the Woods department store. He opened the store after his success in the stock market twenty-five years earlier. Steve was more than happy to do so. He loved being the heir to what he considered one of the most exclusive department stores in New York.

However, over the next several years, both of Steve's parents passed away, leaving him and his sister Stephanie their entire multi-million dollar fortune. Stephanie wanted nothing to do with the Woods store. So, she sold her ownership rights to Steve. Then she moved out to Beverly Hills, California, and married an entertainment attorney. Steve rarely saw or heard from her since. California agreed with Stephanie and she wasn't planning on moving back to the East coast. "I'm done with Manhattan forever, Steve. I love it out here," she told him decisively.

For a few years, Kate worked for Christie's auction house in the city. But when she got tired of working for Christie's, she decided to spend more time in Greenwich with her children who attended private school there. Kate was not interested in the

Woods store. She had always preferred the art world. The retail business at Woods just didn't interest her. Kate and Steve had two children together, a son named Mark and a daughter named Julia. She enjoyed spending her time with them so much now that she only occasionally collected pieces of art as a hobby.

Appearances though meant a lot to Kate. She worked continuously on maintaining a slim and youthful figure. Sometimes she would have the children taken care of exclusively by nannies while she jetted to some of the world's most luxurious spas. She wanted to look as young as she could for as long as she could. This conscientiousness was brought on by some vanity and the grueling competition between herself and the ladies at the social clubs in Greenwich and New York. Underneath it all, Kate didn't think that she was exceptionally gorgeous. But she was very attractive in her own way. Her large green eyes contrasted well with her chestnut brown hair and well-proportioned cheekbones. And her slim figure allowed her to wear a lot of tight fitting designer clothes. She still looked great in a bikini and people often complimented her looks. Sometimes she wasn't always sure to believe them, but she loved hearing the compliments anyway. To her, there was nothing worse than feeling completely unattractive in her circle of wealthy friends. That would be too staggering to her self-esteem. "You can never be too rich, beautiful, or lucky," Kate often told Steve, defending her overall outlook on life.

Steve, on the other hand, continued to focus on the Woods store primarily. But after both of his parents passed away, he changed a lot for the worse. He became more complacent with the responsibilities he had at the department store, started gambling more frequently, and began having sex with more women outside of his marriage. Naturally, he kept this hidden as best as he could from Kate.

 OLO GAMES

IT WAS SUMMERTIME AND ONE OF THOSE SUPER HOT AND HUMID days at the polo club in Greenwich. Anyone would wonder how the polo players and their horses kept cool enough to play. But the high temperatures didn't prevent Steve from having sex with one of the vendor's daughters named Samantha. Over the summer they were having sex on and off the polo field. She was many years younger than him and loved the attention he gave to her.

Before the polo match, they planned to meet during the game in a hidden area behind one of the horse trailers. Samantha brought a picnic blanket with her for them to lay on. When Steve got there, they started loosening their clothing so that they could feel parts of each other's bodies. Steve unbuttoned

Samantha's blouse while she pulled up her skirt and got on top of him.

"You've got all the right moves, Sam," he told her with sweat running on his forehead.

"You too, Steve. I'm so hot and excited. You always make me feel so good. I feel like I'm about to you know what," she said letting out a subtle sigh. Samantha had come. But she knew that he didn't yet. So she stayed on top of him until he came inside of her.

"You're just incredible, Sam," he told her, now feeling fully satisfied.

"I love doing it with you, Steve."

"Me too, me too, Sam."

The truth was that Steve loved having sex period. He was always hungry for some. And he liked it with Samantha because she had a fuller body and bigger breasts than his wife, Kate. This really excited him. He felt no remorse for his wife. He simply felt entitled to whatever pleasure he desired.

"Sam, we agree you're not going to tell anyone about this. Right?" he asked her as he did before in the past.

"Yes, of course, I promise. I just can't wait to see you again. You're the sexiest man I've ever met. Anyhow, if my father found out, he would kill me. He still thinks I'm a virgin and should remain that way until I get married," she told him. Then she laughed at that thought and felt relieved that that wasn't the case.

After Steve zipped up his shorts, he smiled at her with a pleased look. "I have to go now. Be careful getting back over to the other side of the polo field. I'll see you later," he added, picking up his cell phone from the blanket.

"Sure Steve, I'll miss you so much," she said, looking into his eyes one last time, feeling exasperated.

Then Steve's next big decision was how he was going to get across the polo field without being seen by Kate. He knew that she was somewhere on the other side near the announcers of the polo match. She had set up a private outdoor sitting area with tables, chairs, food, and champagne. Some friends from New York were expected to meet them there.

When Steve walked around the opposite side of the horse trailer, he noticed one of the field helpers giving water to one of the horses. Then he thought it best to make up a story so that he could ask him for a lift across the field. He speculated that Kate would probably not notice him getting over there that way. And he knew Samantha would take care of herself. She didn't concern him any longer. His own discretion and secrecy came first.

"Nice horse," Steve told the field helper while rubbing his left calf, pretending to be in pain.

"Thanks, he's really a runner. I think he's one of our best. Is there something wrong with your leg?"

"Oh, I happened to have tripped over a couple of wooden mallets. It's pretty sore. Do you think you could manage to give me a lift over to the stands on the other side of the field? I'll gladly pay you something for your trouble. I just don't want the pain to get any worse," replied Steve.

"No problem. But you don't have to pay me to take you," he answered politely.

"I insist," said Steve, following him to an old Ford truck nearby. "Oh, if by chance we run into my wife while getting there, could you keep this quiet? I don't want her to know how clumsy I am. She'll think I was drinking or something and wondered over here drunk. I only wanted to take a closer look at some of the fine horses that are playing today."

"Of course, I have a wife of my own," he said, laughing. "I hope your leg is all right though."

"I think it'll be all right, thanks. What's your name by the way?" asked Steve, both curious and relieved.

"Tanner Dobbes."

"Nice to meet you, Tanner. I'm Steve Woods."

"Steve Woods?"

Tanner was a local and had heard of his family name before. The Woods family was pretty well-known in Greenwich. Although, this was the first time he met one.

"I'm afraid so," answered Steve, looking for a good spot to be dropped off. "Just over there would be great. Thanks."

"I could get you a little closer," offered Tanner.

"Nope, this is fine. Thanks again. Here's a little something for you. I really appreciate your trouble," said Steve, passing him a hundred dollar bill.

"Hey, thanks," replied Tanner.

"Don't mention it."

Steve started searching the tents, wondering if anyone had

noticed him. While he was looking around, he saw another friend of his. It was Toby Barons, a steadfast fan of polo.

"Toby, nice to see you again at a game. We've missed you," Steve remarked on his way toward one of the bartenders to get a gin and tonic.

"Good to see you too, Steve. How's the action today? I notice Ascot Mews is leading so far and they're really progressing over the other team."

"Well, it's a little late for you and me this time around. I've already got something going with John Dillard. He's in New York today though. Why don't you see what some of the other guys are doing over there at the clubhouse," Steve told him.

Toby looked at him disappointed and replied, "Thanks, Steve. I think I'll do that."

"Don't mention it. Maybe next time we can do something together. Good luck," said Steve, thinking that Toby was really a waste of time for him.

Toby never bet big enough for Steve. And, after all, Steve already made his bets for the day. In his mind, Ascot Mews was destined to win. One of those bets was with John for two hundred and fifty thousand dollars. John was also one of his best friends. Then Steve thought that he better find Kate. So he walked around the tent stands to look for her until he spotted her.

When Kate saw him, she called out loudly, "There you are. I've been looking all over for you. Where on earth have you been? I want to introduce you to Nika Pagonis."

"Nika Pagonis. Any relation to Spiro Pagonis?" asked Steve,

relieved she hadn't noticed him crossing the field. He was sure to be questioned about it if she did.

Kate looked surprised underneath her Chanel straw hat and answered, "Yes, Spiro is her husband's name. They are from Greece and own the Pagonis oil tanker and yacht companies, among other things. In fact, they have one of their yachts here in New York parked somewhere along the Hudson River as we speak."

Steve smiled at her. He knew Kate loved to be among the super-rich. It made her feel like she was part of the world's international jet set crowd, whoever they were, and whatever they meant to her.

"He does. Well, I've already heard about his yacht at a party where I met him last month," Steve remarked, knowing it would annoy her because she wasn't with him at the time.

Her mouth frowned, and her eyes widened. "With who? When? And where was I?" she questioned him, with a somewhat alarmed look on her face.

"You dear, were away at a spa pampering yourself somewhere in the South of France. Don't you remember your trip? It sure cost enough. Anyhow, I met Spiro at a party at the New York Yacht Club. It was in celebration and honor of international yachtsmen from around the world. That was the reason he brought over one of his largest and most impressive yachts from Greece."

Kate looked like she had swallowed a bird. But after she calmed herself a bit, they both walked over to Nika Pagonis together. Nika was talking to Kitty Houghton. Kitty's husband had recently been written about in Forbes magazine. The magazine listed him as one of the newest wealthiest men in America. Her husband was a genius and had invented a new and unique computer chip that became very important to electronic companies around the world. It was an instant international success.

"Hello, Kate. I see you made it back to join us. Have you met Kitty yet? I'm rather disappointed that she and her husband will not be able to attend the upcoming party on our yacht," commented Nika.

Kate smiled at Kitty and said, "Nice to meet you. By the way everyone, this is my husband, Steve. Oh, and I'm sorry about the party, Kitty. It would have been great if you could have made it."

"So am I. But I'm sure there will be other parties in the future. You know, I've been shopping at the Woods store for years. It's great to meet you both finally. Oh, but I see my husband is waving at me to go over to him. Sorry, but I do have to run. Next time, perhaps," said Kitty, as she disappeared into the crowd.

"That was quick. Interesting lady though," observed Steve out loud.

"Yes, quite interesting. I hear she's starting a new magazine publication with some people. I hear her style is a bit flashy though and considerably nouveau. Nonetheless, I am wondering if the two of you can make it to our party next month. We're going to sail Infinity around Manhattan and Long Island Sound. I'm sure that my husband Spiro would be happy to have you both there," said Nika, with a genuine looking smile on her face.

"Actually, I've already met your husband Spiro several weeks ago at the New York Yacht Club. It would absolutely be our pleasure to attend," said Steve enthusiastically, as Kate simultaneously shook her head.

"Marvelous. We'll be in touch then. If you need to reach us in the meantime, we're staying at the Waldorf Astoria on Park Avenue. Spiro likes to stay there. It's one of his most favorite hotels in the world, sort of like a home away from home. You can always leave messages for us there. Well, it looks like the game has ended and my driver is here. Look forward to seeing you then. Cheers!" said Nika, before she headed toward an old shiny Bentley and driver waiting for her.

Even though Kate was obviously thrilled by the idea of the Pagonis yacht party, Steve was even more thrilled. He was ecstatic. Ascot Mews had just officially won. And the team players were now receiving their trophies. Steve smiled as he watched the horses get decorated with roses and the players sprayed with champagne. Then he thought about the Pagonis yacht party again. He had heard that Spiro had gambling aboard his yacht. This interested him immensely. Then he reached over and kissed Kate right on the mouth, forgetting about Samantha entirely.

Kate looked at Steve disheveled and somewhat stunned. She didn't quite expect that kiss from him at that very moment. And it was evident that she was also thinking about the Pagonis yacht party herself. Her only concern now was what she would wear and who else might be there.

On their drive back to their house in the exclusive Belle

Haven area of Greenwich, Steve hummed to songs on the radio. Two large, fierce-looking lion statues from France welcomed them in their driveway. The statues were originally wedding gifts from a top fashion designer in Paris named Pierre LaBlanc.

"Just look at those lions, dear. Don't you think that one resembles me? Grrrrrrrrrrrrr," growled Kate, feeling a little whimsical.

Steve looked over at her and blew her a kiss. He was still thinking about what a great day he had, winning his bets, great sex, and now a yacht party invitation. Then he felt like having sex again but not with Kate. And he knew that if he kept thinking about it, he would have to do something to satisfy his desires. This was not a problem when Kate traveled to her spas. He often stayed at different hotels in Manhattan and used the services of call girls to satisfy himself. He even had affairs with some of the young ladies in his office, seducing them by promising them promotions. And when he tired of them, he would find a way to fire them anyway. Then he would do the same thing again with newer and younger ladies starting out in his department store. It just seemed to him that he never could get enough of what he wanted. He always wanted more.

The Woods home consisted of ten bedrooms, a guest cottage, a large swimming pool, a tennis court, an outdoor covered gazebo, and a small movie theatre. It had its own mooring with a sailboat and water views of Long Island Sound. It was also finely decorated with expensive art from all over the world. Kate entered the house first. Louise, one of the house-keepers, opened the front door for her. Then two neatly groomed

Maltese dogs ran up to Kate, barking and jumping in the air with excitement.

"They don't know when to stop. Do they, Louise?"

"No, Mrs. Woods. They miss you so much when you are not here. Did you enjoy the polo match today?"

"Yes, it was truly a great time, thank you. I'm wondering though, have you heard from the children?"

"Only from their chaperon, Maria. She called on her cell phone and told me that they have reservations to fly back from Colorado on September the first," answered Louise.

"Great, I really hope they are enjoying themselves. Summer goes by so quickly. I'll ring them tonight when I have a chance. Thanks, Louise," said Kate, heading upstairs to her bedroom. Then she decided to take an aromatherapy bath. She wanted to unwind a bit.

Louise and her husband Claude had been the Woods housekeepers for the past several years. They were all pretty contented with the arrangement.

"How's it going, Louise?" Steve asked as he came inside the house.

"Fine, sir," she answered, as her eyes followed him going into his study, closing the door behind him.

The study was one of Steve's favorite rooms in the house. He had a lot of personal and sentimental items throughout the room. Many of his most favorite paintings hung on its walls. He even had an authentic Picasso that hung above a marble fireplace. He had picked out the marble himself during a trip to Italy and had it shipped to Connecticut.

Steve didn't waste any time dialing John Dillard's number in New York. John was a partner at a prestigious investment bank in the city called Buckleven Swaith. The two hundred and fifty grand would come in handy for his future bets. Pocket change for John thought Steve.

"John buddy, you there?"

"Yep, I got the news. I lost the bet. You lucky son of a bitch," answered John.

"Well, maybe you'll have better luck next time. We do have plans to go to Vegas soon right?" asked Steve.

"Yeah, there's always another bet I suppose. No hard feelings. What about the other guys? Did you drench them too?" he grumbled.

"A little." Steve smiled, pleased with himself, calculating his winnings on a piece of paper on his desk.

"That figures. Okay. I'll see you in a couple of days for cocktails and give you a check then," said John, relieved that he didn't bet any more than he did.

"You bet, buddy," Steve replied.

"You don't have to remind me of that," choked John, before hanging up the receiver.

Steve laughed again. Then one of the dogs pushed his way into the study. "Way to go, Chipster buddy," he told the dog as he petted him.

Steve sure loved it when he won bets. He even loved it more than sex. So he again became fixated on the upcoming party on the Pagonis yacht. He wondered what kind of gambling there would be and how well he could do at the party. He spent the rest of the day and night thinking about it. Eventually, he also forgot about sex. He knew he could get into a lot of trouble if Sam's father found out about the affair. It was really risky. And he was even more thrilled thinking about gambling anyway. Even though he had a lot of money, he liked to bet big and usually owed a lot of money back. He didn't want his reputation, his credit, or his legs broken, so he always looked for opportunities to make some more.

$\mathcal{B}$LOOMINGDALE'S

EVER SINCE CHANTEL WAS A TEENAGER GROWING UP IN Southport, Maine, she dreamed of going to New York and making it in the beauty industry. There was nothing she wanted more. She would collect popular beauty magazines, practiced doing make-up on friends from school, and even experimented with herbs and flowers grown in her backyard to create her own perfumes. She had just turned twenty-one, previously working at a small beauty salon in her hometown. She worked there until she saved up just enough money for her travel expenses to New York and to get herself an apartment. She felt like her dream was closer than ever now. And the thought of sacrifice and hard work did not discourage her. All she needed was a beginning and a break so she could get started in the world of beauty.

What Chantel lacked in city sophistication or education, she made up for with common sense and good looks. She was five foot seven, had striking blue-green eyes, strawberry blonde hair, and was blessed with an abundance of overall natural beauty. Her face and complexion didn't require any makeup to look good. Her figure was naturally attractive and sexy. And men admired her far more than she was aware of.

Chantel had come from a rather old-fashioned upbringing in Maine. Her family had some concerns about her leaving their hometown and going to a big city like New York. But they knew they couldn't stop her. It was obvious that she had her own dreams and life to live. So they wished her well and told her how much they loved her and would miss her.

Fortunately, Chantel quickly found an apartment in Manhattan on East Sixty-third Street between First and Second Avenues. She found the apartment listing online just before she left Maine. It was a small one bedroom apartment with a tiny kitchenette. For now, it was all she could afford, and it would have to do. The building itself was an old red brick five- story walk-up with dated finishes. It was kept clean though and had pretty little flower boxes outside some of the windows facing the street. And there was a medium-sized birch tree in front of the building that gave it a little more charm.

The landlord's name was Elaine Mangano. She was a heavyset woman who required two months security rent and the first month of rent in advance. Elaine lived in the building for the past twenty years in an apartment on the first floor. She took care of it as best she could. Her husband was long gone, and she had hired a handyman to help her from time to time. Elaine seemed pleasant and warm. She had told Chantel the most important thing was to stay current with her rent and not to make too much noise in the building. Elaine didn't want to be bothered with noisy tenants making any trouble.

A few days after Chantel arrived in New York, she already had an interview scheduled in Bloomingdale's at the Champs of Paris counter. Champs was one of the most distinguished fragrance, cosmetic, and skin care companies in the world. Chantel knew that this was a great opportunity. She also knew that she needed a job badly. She couldn't afford to pay her rent without one.

Bloomingdale's was only a short walk from Chantel's apartment. Her appointment was at eleven in the morning. When she got there, she navigated her way to the beauty counters along the main floor. The main floor always had a spirited buzz of excitement in the air. Men and women salespeople eagerly lined up to promote the latest perfume creations, offer samples to customers, and hope they would buy some. And since this was Chantel's first time in Bloomingdale's and it was a busy place, she decided to ask someone for assistance. So she went up to one of the salespeople who was giving out samples.

"Excuse me, can you tell me where I can find the Champs of Paris counter?"

"Oh, it's in the middle of the floor next to Christian Dior," answered the woman, quickly turning her attention to potential customers walking around in front of her.

The strong smell of perfumes in the air was noticeable to

Chantel. And she had never seen so many beautiful products in such a colorful and vibrant place before. There was even music playing in the background, and a lot of people looked like they were right out of fashion magazines themselves. People were bustling here and there. Some of the salespeople were even singing out loud. It was more exciting than she imagined. Then she finally found the Champs counter and walked over to one of the ladies standing behind it.

"Good morning. I'm looking for Helena Greer. I have an interview scheduled with her," Chantel told her.

"She's standing right over there. Wait here a moment. I'll get her for you," answered the woman politely.

A few minutes later, Helena greeted Chantel. "Hello. I'm Helena Greer. You're Chantel Du Maurier, right? I've been expecting you. Please follow me inside to my office."

So Chantel followed Helena into a small office hidden away from the sales floor. Helena sat down at a desk and asked Chantel to sit down also.

"I see from your resume that you are from Maine. Why did you decide to relocate to New York? And, why do you want to work for Champs?" Helena asked, watching Chantel's facial expressions closely.

Chantel felt a nervous feeling in her stomach. But she knew this was no time to let nerves get in her way. She knew she had to pursue her dream and show confidence in herself. Then Chantel composed herself and looked at Helena with all the confidence she could radiate, smiled modestly, and said, "It's my lifelong dream to work for such a successful beauty company and to live in New York. Ever since I can remember, it's all I've ever wanted to do. I only hope you give me an opportunity to prove myself to you. I know that Champs has an excellent reputation and I sincerely appreciate the opportunity of working here." Chantel's eyes sparkled as she said this.

Helena couldn't remember the last time that she saw so much sincere enthusiasm and intense desire in a candidate. She wondered if this was too good to be true. But maybe it wasn't, she thought. Helena knew that Chantel didn't have much experience yet in such a large city and with so many sophisticated beauty products and customers. Her resume wasn't that impressive either, and there were many other experienced salespeople competing for the job.

"Did you ever study cosmetology or perfumery, Chantel?" asked Helena.

"Ms. Greer, I haven't been that formally trained, but whatever I lack in formal education, I will make up for with talent and hard work. As you can see from my resume, I've sold various beauty products in my hometown in Maine. Most everyone I helped loved the results they would achieve," Chantel answered.

Helena was becoming further impressed. She admired Chantel's spirit and the fact that she was brave enough to venture to New York at all and all the way from Maine. She thought to herself that perhaps she should at least give her a chance. Then Helena got up from her chair and asked Chantel to wait for her. She excused herself for about ten minutes. When she returned, she told Chantel that she had made her decision and that she decided to hire her.

"You will start as a sales associate and we'll take it from there. I'd also like for you to begin right away, meaning tomorrow morning when the store opens. Is that okay with you?"

"Is it okay? It is the most wonderful thing ever! Thank you so much. You won't be disappointed. I promise you," Chantel told her with a genuine excitement and joy in her voice.

"I hope not. See you tomorrow morning at ten."

"Yes, first thing," Chantel replied.

Finally, thought Chantel to herself, her dreams would begin to come true. Even though everything was new to her, she knew that she would work hard and learn what she needed in order to become successful. She was grateful to have the opportunity to work at Champs and make enough money to support herself.

AFTER CHANTEL LEFT BLOOMINGDALE'S, SHE DECIDED TO TAKE a walk to Central Park. She had never been there before and heard lots about it. She walked to Fifty-ninth Street and Fifth Avenue where she found an entrance to the park. It was across from the renowned Plaza Hotel. The streets surrounding it were also very crowded with horses and buggies decorated with feathers and flowers. There were also lots of people taking photographs. Chantel figured many of them were probably tourists. After she made it into the park, she sat down on one of the park benches and started to watch the people passing by in front of her.

Several minutes later a panhandler walked toward her putting his hands out for money. His clothes looked like they hadn't been washed in months. Chantel didn't know quite what to do. She'd never seen a person in such dirty clothes in all her life. Then a woman sitting next to her yelled out at him, "Get out of here!" He pretended not to hear her and started walking away from them. The woman turned toward Chantel and said, "Damn jerk. Those guys are so full of shit. You would think they would go out and find a job just like everyone else. Some of them really give me the creeps. You never know what they might do. Can you believe it? And all we're trying to do is enjoy a sunny afternoon in the park." It was obvious that she was annoyed.

"I guess he's one of those crazy people New York is known for," said Chantel, turning her head left and right.

"Crazy my foot. Half of them have more faculties than a lot of so- called normal people than I know. I work hard, pay taxes, and expect the city to keep these guys off the streets, or at least help them, so they don't need to live on the streets," she said. Then the woman let out a sigh of relief, pulled out a cigarette from her jacket pocket, and asked Chantel if she had a light.

"Yes, I think I do," answered Chantel, reaching into her purse to pull out a book of matches.

"Thanks."

"You're welcome. You can keep them. I don't smoke. Say, would you mind telling me where you are from? I hope you don't think I'm being nosy. But, you seem to have a Southern accent. Not that I have ever been to the South. But you sound Southern. And, I guess I'm just a little curious. I haven't met too many people from the South," said Chantel.

"Not at all. I'm originally from Atlanta, Georgia. Except now, I live in New York…the Big Apple," she replied.

"Wow, that's interesting and impressive also. This is actually my first time to New York. I just moved here from Southport, Maine," said Chantel smiling.

"Maine, there's a big change. I'm sure it's going to take a while getting used to a big city like this. I bet you come from a small town also where most people are really sweet and kind."

"Yes, it's certainly smaller than New York City. That's for sure," said Chantel, nodding her head up and down to confirm it. "By the way, my name is Chantel Du Maurier. Nice to meet you."

"Same here. My name is Dora Moore. Hey, one word of advice for you. Be careful of some of the guys around here in New York. They can be pretty aggressive sometimes. Just giving you some words of advice since you're new. Hope you don't mind. On another note, are you working yet? Can I be of any help to you? I know it's not easy moving to New York from another place," Dora asked, puffing on her cigarette.

"Thanks. That's okay about men. I understand. It's just advice. As far as a job, I got my first break today. I came here to work in the beauty business and I just got a job at Bloomingdale's at the Champs of Paris counter. They make skin care products, cosmetics, and fragrances. I'm so excited," Chantel told her, looking up at the sky as if she was thanking something beyond it.

"Well Congratulations, Chantel. I love Bloomingdale's and shop there all the time when there are sales. It does get pretty crowded sometimes though, especially when there's a lot of tourists in town," said Dora.

"Come by and say hello sometime. Being here for such a short time, I haven't made any friends yet. Maybe we can get together. If you don't mind me asking, Dora, what do you do? I mean what kind of work are you in?"

Dora looked at her smiling, "Me. I work for an investment banking firm as an administrative assistant. I do secretarial types of tasks. The company's name is called Buckleven Swaith. It's located at Rockefeller Center across the street from St. Patrick's Church. It's in a group of buildings actually. Most people call it Rock Center. Now there's a place that gets mobbed with tourists. In the wintertime, it even has a tree lighting ceremony with a huge Christmas tree display and an outdoor skating rink. It's very festive during the holidays but again very crowded also. Well, hey, I have to get back to work. Just wanted to be in the park for a little bit. Here's my phone number. Give me a call sometime. Or, maybe I'll see you at Bloomingdale's. Even New York can be like a small town when you make friends. See ya," said Dora, handing Chantel a card with her phone numbers on it.

"Thanks, Dora. Take good care. Look forward to seeing you again. Make sure you come by and visit me at Bloomingdale's. But before you go, here's my cell phone number. My apartment phone is still getting connected," said Chantel, handing her a piece of paper with her name and number on it.

THAT EVENING CHANTEL CALLED HER PARENTS AND TOLD THEM the good news about getting the job at Bloomingdale's. They still sounded skeptical though. The thought of Chantel being in such a big city like New York scared them. But they were glad to hear that Chantel had found a job already and had a place to live. They didn't want to sound negative so they wished her the best and told her that they'd be there for her if she needed anything. They also told her to call often because they missed her so much already.

Chantel knew that her parent's finances were limited. So she was happy that she would be making her own money and not relying on them. Her father worked part-time and a lot of his work was seasonal. He mostly did odd jobs in carpentry and farming. Times were sometimes a bit rough and he didn't make a lot of money. She didn't want to ask him for anything. And he had to take care of her mother. Chantel didn't mind struggling as long as she could survive. She felt she already had a lot though. She firmly believed in herself and had ambitious dreams for her future.

CHAPTER 4

THE PAGONIS PARTY

THE PAGONIS PARTY WAS JUST AS MAGNIFICENT AS EVERYONE expected it to be. It was clear that Spiro and Nika were good at entertaining. Mouthwatering delicacies had been flown in from all over the United States. And bottles of Dom Pérignon and Louis Roederer's Cristal were popping open everywhere. A classical pianist performed on the upper deck of the yacht and a harpist on the lower one. In another area, there was also a disc jockey playing popular dance music.

All in all, there were about a hundred and fifty guests. They ate, drank, laughed, sang, danced, and seemed to be having a great time. Some sipped on cognac, smoked cigars, and told stories from their lives. Lots of guests also talked about yachting, given the fact that they were on one. All this took place while the Pagonis yacht sailed around New York City with views of Manhattan and other boroughs in the background.

"There he is," said Steve, when he found Spiro among friends. "Tremendous party, Spiro. I'm so glad that Kate and I were invited. Incredible yacht you have here. I think it's the best one I've ever been on."

Spiro looked at him, clearly pleased to be getting a compliment and said, "Thank you. I find it suits my needs. It's quite comfortable. One has everything they need. And yachting is my true passion, more so than partying. But my wife Nika loves to have parties, so I have to please her. She personally oversees all the party preparations. I'm proud of her. She does such a great job. Some women of her statue do not take the time she does to ensure that everything is just right. But Nika does. She is so lovely. I'm so grateful to have a woman like her." Spiro was getting a little sentimental. Then he cleared his throat, looked up at the starlit sky and smiled.

"Yes, I understand what you mean. She surely is a lovely lady. You're a very fortunate man, Spiro," said Steve.

Spiro looked up at the sky again and laughed. Then he said, "Most of the time I'm fortunate. But tonight I'm not fortunate in everything. I just left our game room where I was playing blackjack, and I lost every time. You see one isn't always lucky in everything. Have you been to the game room yet? You might want to try your luck tonight. You might be luckier than I. Here's a tip for you though, watch out for a man named Max Conners. He's really good. He's been beating everybody in there."

Steve shook his head up and down, pursed his lips, and said, "That sounds like great fun. I think I'll give it a go. Thanks for the tip. And thanks for inviting my wife and I. You and Nika are truly an exceptional host and hostess."

Turning another direction, Spiro commented, "It's a pleasure to see you again. Enjoy." Then he disappeared into the crowd.

Steve headed directly to the game room. While he got himself a drink, he watched some men playing craps and roulette for some time. In particular, he watched Max Connors closely. Then he noticed that in one corner of the room there was a small round table made of black and white marble. It was the most ornate backgammon table he had ever seen. There was no one playing on it, so it was available. Steve thought to himself that maybe this could be his game of choice for the night. He knew that he was an excellent backgammon player. He had played for years ever since he was a young boy in private school. Then he thought that he should approach Max Conners. Max was playing roulette though. So he wandered over to the roulette table, quietly introduced himself to Max, and asked him if he would like a game of backgammon when he was finished with roulette.

Max looked at him and said, "What's in it for me, chap? I never play for fun, only money. Do you not play roulette?"

At the moment, Steve wasn't interested in playing roulette. So he didn't go for the bait. Instead, he said, "Say, Max, if it's backgammon you're afraid of, let me entice you some more. How about three hundred thousand to the winner of two out of three games? Are you game now?"

The otherwise noisy and smoky room suddenly became quieter. Steve loved this kind of attention. The scene was part of the thrill of gambling to him. There were the big stakes, the winners, the losers, and everything in between. One of the men listening to their conversation choked on his cigar. But Max looked intrigued. He had already made at least that at the roulette table and he didn't like someone daring him. He especially didn't like Steve's cockiness. Max had the ability to look right through people like him.

"Okay, chap, you're on. But be prepared to lose. You see, I've been lucky all night and I don't think my luck is going to change," Max told him with a self-assured smile. His smile was so broad that he looked just like the Cheshire Cat from Alice's Adventures in Wonderland.

"Good," said Steve. "Time will tell just how long you'll be lucky. Let's get started and set up the game."

They walked over to the marble table in the corner, and about five other guests brought chairs over so they could watch the game themselves. After all, they were playing for three hundred thousand dollars. And both of them could afford it. But as Max predicted, his luck continued. He kept rolling lots of doubles with his dice. By the second game, it was easy to tell that Steve was getting anxious. He began to sweat and opened his collared shirt to let some air on his chest. By the end of the third game, everyone else who watched was sweating with anticipation also. Max won the two out of three games. Steve had a look of disbelief on his face. He also looked very angry.

He hated losing and didn't expect to lose at backgammon that night.

"Well, I hope you're satisfied, Mr. Woods. Next time you might be a bit more careful when you choose an opponent. Oh, by the way, a check will be fine," Max told him, while the others cautiously looked at them both.

Steve felt humiliated. Losing on the Pagonis yacht embarrassed him greatly. Losing in front of these people, in particular, embarrassed him even more. It was hard for his ego to accept. But he had to pay up. Otherwise, they would call him a fake and possibly no one would ever bet with him again in the future. He couldn't let that happen. So he reached into his jacket pocket and pulled out his checkbook. He wrote a check out to Max Conners for the money and waved it in his face. Then he said ominously, "You were right, Max. You are lucky tonight. But, you know how luck is, it has a way of running out in time." There was bitterness in Steve's voice that everyone listening could detect.

Max paid no attention to the comment, grabbed the check from Steve's hand, and walked out of the room. Steve left the room also. He went upstairs to the bar on the upper deck. Within the next forty minutes, he almost polished off an entire bottle of Remy Martin and started to stagger. He was drunk. When his vision became unbearably impaired, he asked people where Kate was and that he needed her. He wanted to leave. But he also didn't want to tell Kate that he gambled that night. He knew that she would be extremely angry with him. She didn't like him gambling because she knew it always brought the worst out of him. Steve never told her how often he actually did so or how much he spent on it either. He kept his addiction well-guarded from Kate and only told her some things he does.

When they found Kate, and she saw Steve, she knew he'd been drinking a lot. She knew they better leave. The last thing she wanted was to cause a scene on the Pagonis yacht. So she walked up to him and quietly suggested they go. She didn't want to be any more embarrassed than she already was.

"But first, Kate, don't you think we should say goodbye to our host and hostess before we go?" asked Steve, swaying back and forth and barely standing.

She looked at him and answered, "I think they'll understand if we just go. I'll send a thank you note in the mail."

Kate didn't want them to see Steve like this and knew she had to get him off the yacht fast before he would collapse or something like that. She summoned one of the crewmen to drop down a small boat to take them to one of the city moorings.

"Whatever you say, dear," said Steve, shaking his head in exaggerated agreement, losing his balance entirely.

Kate could see that Steve might fall and had another of the crewmen hold him up. After they arrived at the mooring, the crewmen helped carry Steve to the limo they had waiting for them. And when they arrived at their apartment on Central Park South, Kate had to have the doormen help Steve upstairs. Fortunately, they made it home without any more incidents. And within minutes, Steve was fast asleep and snoring on one of the living room sofas. But before he was, he thought about Max and how he might get back at him.

CHAPTER 5

IPRIANI'S

THINGS WERE WORKING OUT WELL FOR CHANTEL AT CHAMPS. IN a very short period of time, she became the top salesperson at the counter and was quickly promoted to a manager of sales. She was making three times more money than when she started and tried to save as much as she could. She only occasionally treated herself to something special or expensive. She liked to buy designer clothes to look more sophisticated and bought these when they were on sale. Her Bloomingdale's discount helped to make them more affordable.

During that time, Chantel and Dora kept in touch and became fairly good friends. They frequently got together to see a movie, try a new restaurant, or go to a museum exhibition.

Chantel liked Dora for her easy-going nature and sense of humor. And Dora liked Chantel for her honesty and warmth. So when Buckleven Swaith was having their annual holiday party for employees near the end of November, Dora invited Chantel. It was being held during the week at the Cipriani's event space on Forty-second Street. Chantel agreed to go.

Holding her cell phone in her hand, Dora teased Chantel over the phone, "You never know who you're going to meet. There are lots of eligible bachelors at Buckleven. I just haven't met the right one myself yet. But I believe it happens when you least expect it. Love can be like a comet. You never know when it's going to fall right on top of you."

Chantel laughed over the receiver and answered, "Oh, sure. Very funny, Dora. But you're right. You never know. I'm not really looking for a relationship right now though. I'm busy enough with work. But a party should be fun. What time am I supposed to meet you there tomorrow?"

"Five o'clock. What's this about work? That's all I hear you talk about. Don't you realize you're not going to be young and gorgeous forever? Mother nature catches up with all of us. And right now, she is being mighty generous with you. Haven't you taken a good look in the mirror at yourself lately? Use what you got and get yourself a good man with a Maserati."

Chantel laughed, "Come on Dora, there's more to life than a man with a Maserati. I'm contented just being myself and working at Champs. I like my life just as it is."

"That's because New York is still new and exciting to you.

But have you thought about being in love? I hear it's a wonderful thing you know."

"Enough already. I'll see you tomorrow." Chantel didn't mind the suggestion though. She knew Dora meant well.

"Yep, see you tomorrow. I'm sure we'll have some fun. The food is always fabulous. Bye."

"Bye," said Chantel, relieved to be off the phone.

THE FOLLOWING DAY CHANTEL HAD THE DAY OFF. SHE TOOK advantage of the free time to shop for groceries, clean her apartment, and pay some bills. At three in the afternoon, she went to the hairdressers to get her hair done. She wanted to look good at the Buckleven party. When the hairdressers were done, she went back home to get dressed. She chose to wear a red silk dress with black patent leather shoes that had a matching purse. She also decided to wear the new Chesterfield coat that she just got on sale at Bloomingdale's. Since five o'clock was rush hour in the city, Chantel decided to take the Lexington Avenue subway down to Forty-second Street.

When she arrived at Cipriani's, Chantel couldn't help but be impressed by its ornate decorations. She thought the place looked unbelievably beautiful. And she felt even more excited because this was the first holiday party she would attend since moving to the city. After going inside to find Dora, she could see the festiveness in people's faces and hear lively holiday music in the background. A gray-haired man approached her and asked if he could be of some help. He was one of the chaperones for the guests entering the party.

Chantel smiled at him and said, "I'm looking for Dora Moore from Buckleven. Do you know where I would find her?"

"Dora Moore," repeated the man. "If I remember correctly she is at table ten towards the right side of the event room." Then he looked down at several pieces of paper, seeming to confirm the information, and nodded his head up and down.

"Thank you. I'll find her," replied Chantel, as she quickly went toward the back of the huge room, dodging the many people in the crowd, and making sure not to get her clothes caught in any chairs or tablecloths on the way. Chantel found Dora near table number ten sipping a cocktail and sampling some of the hors d'oeuvres. Dora was talking with a couple of colleagues from work. Then Chantel walked up to her.

"Well, here I am. Made it," said Chantel smiling.

Dora gave a big welcoming smile back and announced, "Hey everyone, this is my friend Chantel Du Maurier. She's the new friend of mine who I told you all about from Maine."

One of the men in the group, clearly admiring Chantel commented, "We'll let's hope you bring her around more often. Can I help you with your coat?"

"Yes, but please bring me back the coat ticket. Thanks," replied Chantel, finding the attention kind of flattering.

Dora chimed in. "Oh, don't worry. You can trust him. That's Nelson from accounting. He's harmless. By the way, do you see that man over there?" pointed Dora. "That's my boss John

Dillard. What a sourpuss lately. It's a wonder he's here. Don't mind him though if you meet him. Just don't talk about me if you can avoid it. He's very nosy. But if you have to and he wants to know what I think of him, just tell him that I think he's fabulous. We didn't get our bonuses yet." Dora laughed out loud.

"Don't worry. You can count on me," remarked Chantel, smiling while Nelson gave her the coat ticket as promised.

"Thanks, Nelson. We'll see you later on. We're going to get something to eat. Chantel didn't have anything yet, and the buffet is out of this world," said Dora. Nelson nodded at her that he understood. Then Dora looked at Chantel and said, "Well, let's get some food. And, I'd also like to introduce you to some more people. I warn you though. You might find the banker types a little dull. Sometimes they bore the living daylights out of me. Everything is finance, money, and more money and finance."

Chantel looked at her curiously, "I thought you said that they were eligible bachelors?"

"Yes, they are. It's just some of them can be kind of geeky and conservative, or they only think about making money and more money. I kind of prefer guys who like to have more fun and worry less about finance all the time."

Then they walked over toward the food banquet tables. In the center of the tables, there were huge frozen sculptures of dolphins carved out of ice. There was an extraordinary assortment of seafood, oysters, clams, mussels, crab, shrimp, and more. And on the other tables, there were also large platters of assorted seafood salads, roasted turkey, steak, and just about anything one could ever dream of eating. So they made up some plates and headed back to their table to eat. On the way, they bumped into three popular investment bankers from Buckleven. Dora introduced them to Chantel. Their names were Andrew Cummings, Harry Fisher, and Bill Stuart. But an hour later when Dora wanted a partner to dance with, she wondered why none of them had come over to ask her.

"What is it with these men. Just because we're sitting at another table doesn't mean we're on Mars. Maybe they're a little intimidated by all the attractive women at our table. Don't they realize that we need more than food and drinks," said Dora, rolling her eyes at the ceiling.

"Have some patience, Dora," said Chantel, holding her laughter in as much as she could.

"Patience. Here we go again," Dora sighed.

"Dora, who's that sitting over there next to who I believe was Harry Fisher?"

"That's Marco Puccio. He's gorgeous, isn't he? He works at Buckleven as an intern. They say he's very bright. I think I heard him mention once that he's from Southampton, Long Island. But wait. Are you actually asking me about the opposite sex? Have the heavens fallen?" Dora was surprised to hear the question. She wondered if she had heard right.

And just at that moment, Marco got up from the table he was sitting at and headed toward theirs. He looked as if he belonged in a magazine. Marco had a perfect masculine figure, soft light brown hair, and deep blue eyes that had a sparkle to them. They were sexy and mysterious looking. He was wearing a navy pinstripe suit with a burgundy tie that complimented his good looks. He walked straight over to Chantel.

"Excuse me, I understand you met some of my colleagues earlier. They told me that you are a friend of Dora and your name is Chantel Du Maurier. Let me introduce myself. My name is Marco Puccio. I am wondering if you would like to dance?"

Trying not to look too surprised, Chantel answered yes. She was a little uncomfortable because she didn't know how to dance that well. She was also a little shy. But she thought he was very attractive, so she joined him on the dance floor. After a livelier song played, a slower one came on. This gave them a chance to hear each other talk.

Marco asked her, "So tell me, how do you know Dora?"

Chantel blushed a little, "We met when I first arrived in New York from Maine. We met in Central Park. Since then we've become good friends. And she invited me to this party tonight. I have to say, I've never been to such a big party like this before."

Marco looked at her, smiled, and asked, "Do you like it?" He could tell she hadn't lived in Manhattan for a very long time like most of the people he knew.

"Yes, I like it a lot actually. Everyone is so full of life and pretty friendly for a big city. Most people are nice, and there's so much to do and see. It's a fascinating place."

Marco looked at her a little concerned, "But it can also be a tough town too. There's a lot of people out there that I'd hardly consider friendly or nice. Although, I'm glad you feel the way you do. And you seem very nice to me. Do you mind if I call you sometime? I'd like to get your phone number before you leave tonight."

Chantel couldn't believe what was happening. She took a deep breath and answered, "Sure." Then she and Marco danced some more before she went back to the table where she was sitting. Chantel wrote down her number and gave it to Marco. He also gave her a card with his contact information. And for the rest of the night, they didn't take their eyes off of one another. There was already something special they were both feeling inside.

Meanwhile, Dora finally got to dance with Harry Fisher. She looked like she was having a good time also. And when the party was over, Chantel and Dora left together.

"Looks like somebody really likes you, Chantel. I've never seen Marco so interested in anyone before. And you tell me to be patient while you reel in a guy like that," said Dora.

"Doesn't mean you can't still have patience, Dora. I'm sure the right one will come to you someday. You've got a lot to offer. And anyway, I just met Marco this once. I do like him though. But I really don't know much about him yet," replied Chantel.

"You're right, Chantel. You never know what's going to happen and when it's going to happen."

Then they shared a taxi together on their way home.

❧

THE NEXT DAY CHANTEL RECEIVED A PHONE CALL FROM Marco. He wanted to take her out the following Saturday night. She was surprised to hear from him so soon. And she oddly felt like she already had a crush on him. So she accepted the invitation. It was going to be her first date with a guy in Manhattan.

CHAPTER 6

E CIRQUE

CHANTEL WAS A FEW MINUTES EARLY WHEN SHE ARRIVED AT THE bar at Le Cirque. It was where Marco had asked her to meet him for cocktails before they would have dinner. Le Cirque was one of the most distinguished restaurants in the city. Marco wanted their date to be special. Chantel decided to wear a light blue cashmere Furla dress with a white silk scarf. And even though she was never to such a famous restaurant, she looked very elegant and at home there. When Marco arrived, he gave her a long stem white rose. Ironically, it also had a tint of blue color on it.

"How did you know what color I'd be wearing tonight?" Chantel asked him, finding the blue in the rose interesting.

"I kind of cheated. I phoned the headwaiter from the florist down the street and asked him to look for a beautiful blonde woman who'd be at the bar and what she was wearing," said Marco, smiling as he confessed.

"How clever of you. Thank you," said Chantel, feeling flattered.

"You're welcome. So, what would you like to drink?" he asked her, looking extremely polished in a Brooks Brothers suit.

They decided to order two mojitos and shared an appetizer at the bar. Then Marco asked Chantel if she would like to stay at Le Cirque for dinner and later go downtown to a nightclub. He told her that he knew a nightclub inside the Gansevoort Hotel that was very popular in the city. Chantel thought it sounded like a good idea. She hadn't been to any nightclubs in Manhattan yet. And she was only south of Forty-second Street once when she took a tour bus around Manhattan.

After they finished their cocktails at the bar, they were seated for dinner. One of the waiters held a chair out for Chantel as she got ready to sit down. They were seated at a lovely table near a large window in the restaurant. Then a waiter gave them menus and asked them what they would like to drink. They decided to share a bottle of white wine from Italy. Marco knew it was a good one because he had tried it before and figured he'd suggest something he'd already had instead of experimenting with one he hadn't. Since this was their first date, they both felt a little nervous and awkward together. Marco tried to break the ice by asking Chantel what kind of work she was in.

Chantel told him about her job as a sales manager at Champs in Bloomingdale's. She also told him how much she liked the beauty industry and that she wanted to do well in it. Then she told him about the small place she came from in Maine and her family there. Marco found her story interesting. He started asking her many questions that made her feel a little uncomfortable. She didn't know him yet, and he was so inquisitive. But she still found him to be quite charming and attractive.

Eventually, the conversation focused on Marco. Marco told Chantel about his family in Southampton, Long Island. He told her he had a mother named Luna, an older sister named Laura, and a younger sister named Lila. He talked a little about how his mother and father met in Europe during World War II and that they were both Italians.

Then their waiter came over with their wine and took their dinner orders. They decided to have salad, black bass, and red snapper. Marco explained to Chantel that Le Cirque was known for superior quality and presentation. She was curious as to what he meant by that. Then she wondered why he hadn't mentioned anything more about his father.

"Marco, you didn't say whether or not your father was still living," commented Chantel.

"Oh, Dad died over ten years ago from heart disease. My mother was especially devastated by his death. She still isn't over losing him. But he left her plenty of money, so she's financially comfortable. At least I don't have to worry about her in those regards," Marco told her.

"And what about your sister's?" asked Chantel.

"Well, Laura never married and still lives at home with mom. I suppose she never really had a good enough of a reason to live on her own. She works at a florist shop in Southampton just to keep herself busy. And my other sister Lila moved away ever since she went to college. She lives in San Diego with her husband and two children. We also have an aunt who visits us from time to time. She also lives on Long Island."

"They must enjoy your company, Marco. I mean your mother, sister, and aunt. You're the only male."

"Yes, but I don't spend as much time in Southampton as I used to. I've been going to graduate school in California. Over the past few years, I've only spent holidays and summers there. It was only this semester that I decided to spend more time in the city and to get some practical work experience. I'm still working on finishing my master's degree in business at UCLA. And I often stay at my friend's apartment when I'm here in the city. His name is Harry Fisher. I think you met him at the holiday party. He has a very large apartment in the Galleria building on East Fifty-seventh Street. I've been renting out a bedroom from him. So, I don't spend all of my time in Southampton," Marco explained.

"When will you finish your degree?" asked Chantel, feeling a little intimidated by his education. Chantel had never been to college. It wasn't that she felt inferior. It was just that she didn't know what having all that education was like, and many people around her had college degrees from some pretty well-known schools. This made her feel a little self-conscious.

"I have one more semester. I'm looking forward to finishing. I prefer the real business world instead of academia. Well, enough about me, and all that boring stuff. So, would you still like to go dancing after dinner? I think it would fun," he asked, taking one of her hands to hold.

"All right. Sounds good. It'll be my first time to a nightclub in New York," Chantel answered, smiling at him shyly.

"Great. And what would you like for dessert before we go? I suggest the crème brulee or the chocolate souffle. Even better, why don't we get one of each? Is that okay with you?" Marco asked, looking deeply into her eyes and smiling back at her.

"Yes, it's fine with me."

After they finished dinner, they headed downtown to the Gansevoort. Somehow they managed to squeeze through the mob of people waiting in line to get in. Marco knew someone at the door so they didn't have to wait like everyone else. The nightclub had spectacular views of the city and was very crowded. The music was also very loud. They were seated at a table near the penthouse terrace. The table had several candles placed on it for extra light and ambiance.

When one of the waiters came over, Marco ordered a bottle of Perrier-Jouët champagne. Then, for the first time, he leaned over and kissed Chantel on her lips. And even though Chantel was taken aback by his kiss, she had already felt some passion inside for him that she didn't fully understand. She barely knew him, but she was glad she did. There was something about him touching her heart. This was unusual because she normally only thought about work and her career. She realized that she never gave much thought to the possibility of moments like these. She never had any serious relationships with men in the past. So she didn't have anything to compare her intuition or her feelings to. In a way, she felt sort of vulnerable of the unknown.

But Marco looked very comfortable to her. He moved closer to her again, held one of her hands, and asked her, "What are you doing tomorrow? Why don't we spend some more time together?"

She looked at him puzzled. She couldn't believe that he wanted to see her again so soon. Then she remembered that she had the day off so she could see him if she wanted to.

"Why don't we go out for lunch? How about we go to The Loeb Boathouse in Central Park? That's a restaurant. Then maybe we can go ice skating afterwards. I'm wondering if you would enjoy that. I'd like us to do as much as we can together," Marco told her, with an expression on his face that looked like a puppy that needed a home.

The look on his face tugged at her heart. She didn't know what she should say. But she shook her head yes anyway. Then Marco took her onto the dance floor, and they danced to several songs together. When one of the songs was slow, Marco held her closer and kissed her again. He felt a deep feeling for her that he never felt for any woman before. The feeling was instant.

When they finished their champagne, Marco took Chantel home. On the way uptown, he held her again and kissed her some more. He felt his heart and new emotions more than he ever did before. For the very first time, he believed he had an idea of what being in love was like. And he silently wondered to himself if she was the forever woman for him.

THE NEXT DAY MARCO MET CHANTEL AT HER APARTMENT. HE brought her a lovely bouquet of red and white roses tied together with a large red velvet bow. He wore a brown tweed coat with a blue cotton shirt and camel khaki pants. And Chantel decided to wear a beige angora sweater and a white wool skirt that had pleats just above her slender knees. Her blonde hair was brushed back from her face in a playful ponytail. Whether she realized it or not, this showed off her eyes and striking cheekbones.

"Wow, you look remarkable. And, these flowers are for you," Marco told her, giving her the roses.

"Thank you. Come in. I want to put them in some water before we go," she told him.

"Nice place you have here. I see you like seascape pictures."

"Yes, I do. I like them a lot actually. Some of my fondest memories growing up were at the beach in Maine. I always loved watching the sailboats come back from a day of sailing or fishing and the sun setting at the end of the day. Sometimes the colors in the sky would be so amazing with different hues of pinks, oranges, and blue tones of color. How about you? Do you like the ocean?" Chantel asked him.

"Yes, quite a bit. Having grown up in Southampton, my family often went to the beach. Our home there is a short drive to the ocean. I guess we were pretty lucky that it was so close."

"Yes, very lucky," Chantel agreed.

Then Marco reached his arms around her waist and gently pulled her body closer to his. He touched her face and lips with his fingers and kissed her. He suddenly felt very aroused but didn't want to be too forward and make a bad impression on her. So he let her go gently and suggested they leave for the park.

They took a taxi together and got out at Fifth Avenue and East Seventy-second Street where one of the park entrances was located. For a winter day, there were many people walking in the park. During the holidays the city was even more crowded with tourists and visitors posing for photos and selfies. Chantel remembered Dora mentioning it. And there were always families with grandparents taking pictures with their cameras as well. They would often be juggling hot drinks and bags of warm chestnuts in their hands. The smell of chestnuts was always recognizable. And the voices of families and their children could be heard from different directions.

When they arrived at The Loeb Boathouse, they were seated at a table with a perfect view of the lake inside the park. The trees were bare at this time of year. But that gave them a better view of the city buildings in the distance. Marco explained to Chantel that in the warmer weather people came there to rent rowboats and take gondola rides.

"This is really impressive. It's amazing how much nature is in the middle of such a big city like this," commented Chantel, admiring the lake in front of her.

"Yes, it is. That's what makes New York one of the greatest cities in the world. It's diversity of people and places like this. So, let's look at the menu and see what you would like for lunch. How about we order some champagne in the meantime?" asked Marco, while he signaled a waiter to come to their table.

When the waiter arrived, Marco ordered a bottle of Moët Chandon. Then they ordered mixed salads, crabmeat, and grilled octopus for lunch. Chantel had never had octopus before and laughed when Marco ate it. Then he put a small piece of octopus on his fork and asked her to try some. While she tried a piece, she made a funny face that made him laugh as well. And they were both starting to feel a little lightheaded from the champagne. They were also feeling more and more comfortable with each other. Anyone observing them could tell they were having a great time together.

"Chantel, it must be a little strange being in a big city like this coming from a small town as you did. I just want you to know that I'm here for you if you need anything. You're already very special to me. And, I'm wondering if you would like to be my steady girlfriend? I know it's quite quick, but I haven't felt this way about any other woman before. And I don't want anyone else to have a chance of getting you before I do. I guess you could say I'm being a little selfish," Marco told her.

Chantel was stunned. She wasn't used to things moving this quickly. She wasn't used to having a boyfriend either. "But you barely know me," she said.

"Okay, so tell me more about yourself so that I more than barely know you. I already know that you come from Southport, Maine. You want to keep working in the beauty business. And, you're pretty serious about that. Maybe you can tell me more about your family. What are they like?" Marco asked, trying to be a bit clever.

"Well, my father's name is Edward, and my mother's name

is Susan. They are both living. My father works part-time as a carpenter and farmer. And during the warm seasons, my mother helps him with a small farm. I also have a sister who is a few years younger than me. Her name is Claudette. When she isn't babysitting or waitressing, she helps out my father and mother. They all live in Southport, Maine. But my grandfather was originally from Quebec. He was French Canadian. And my grandmother was English and had come from New Brunswick. That is why I have a French name," Chantel explained.

"That's quite interesting. Do you miss Maine much?"

"I often miss my family. But I'm having such a great time in New York and working at Champs. It's all I really ever wanted to do since I could remember. So here I am. I guess I was lucky to get a job that I love right away. It's sort of like a dream to me really."

"I see. Well, since your family is so far away, you'll have to come and visit mine. They're only about fifty minutes outside of the city. I mean perhaps you can meet my mother and sister in Southampton. Would you like that?" Marco asked, hoping to hear yes for an answer.

"Sure. I guess so," answered Chantel, not knowing exactly what she should say.

"But in the meantime, since you like the ocean so much, I was thinking of inviting you away for a weekend. Harry also owns a beach house on the ocean in Montauk, Long Island. It's very nice. I don't think he'll mind if we stay there. Do you think you can get away one of these weekends, say the next one or two? In case you're worried, I promise to be a gentleman. I just want to be with you," Marco told her, trying to sound as sincere as he could.

Chantel felt a little uneasy with the sudden question of going away overnight with him. Yet, she also felt strongly drawn to him. Normally she wouldn't even consider going away with someone she had only known this short a time. But she felt differently about him.

"Can I trust you?" she asked, looking at him with a contemplative expression on her face.

"I just want to spend some time with you alone. It's so nice out there. I know you would like it. We can leave sometime Friday or Saturday and come back on Sunday. It's that simple," Marco told her.

"Well, I can't believe I'm about to say this. But yes, I'll go. No surprises though. Okay?" Chantel answered, much to his liking.

Then they finished their lunch and planned to go to Harry's house in Montauk one of the following weekends. And they walked over to the ice skating rink in the park and skated together for a couple of hours. After that, Marco took Chantel home by taxi. On the way to her apartment, he put his arms around her and kissed her again passionately on the lips. They kissed during the entire ride back to her apartment. Then Marco told her that he would call her the following day.

CHAPTER 7

IANCHI'S

IT WAS SEVEN-THIRTY AT NIGHT WHEN JOHN DILLARD LEFT HIS office. This was early for a workaholic like him. Many nights during the week he didn't leave the office until nine or ten at night. Sometimes Dora would be asked to stay and work late hours with him. This aggravated her at times. But she rationalized it with all the paid overtime. She was glad to make the extra money. Thank God, she thought, when he finally left the office for the evening. She was starving and decided to go out and treat herself to dinner at a quaint little Italian restaurant near the office called Bianchi's. It was a casual place with a large bar where people hung out after work. A lot of the customers knew each other by name, and most were familiar with the bartender Johnny.

Johnny was a friendly guy who had grown up in Little Italy. He spoke both English and Italian and was very popular with the regular customers. When Dora walked in, she got a seat at the bar so she wouldn't be sitting at a table by herself. Johnny quickly took her order consisting of a vodka martini and pasta with broccoli rabe. When she finished eating, she moved down the bar and sat next to two acquaintances of hers named Iris and Kenny. They were regulars.

"Hey Dora, saw you come in. How's it going? Were you working late again tonight?" asked Iris.

"Yep, working late again. Feeling better since I got something to eat though." Dora paused to get Johnny's attention. "Johnny, please give me another martini. These are so good."

"Yes, ma'am. Coming right up. Say, have you ever met Vinnie Marciano?" he asked Dora, while he looked over at Vinnie. "Vinnie, come on over here. I want you to meet one of my favorite customers."

It wasn't uncommon for Johnny to introduce people at the bar. The place was more like a social club. Dora wasn't that surprised by the introduction and just smiled back at Johnny. Then Vinnie walked over and sat down next to her.

"Hello, Dora. Pleased to meet you. Sorry, but I don't remember seeing you in here before," Vinnie commented.

Vinnie had dark brown hair and eyes. He was of Sicilian descent and attractive in a macho kind of way. Yet, even with his macho look, he still had an air of warmth about him. Dora thought he was pretty attractive. And she also started to feel a little self-conscious about how she looked.

"It's been a little while. Been working a lot. And with the holidays, I've been pretty busy. I do come here from time to time though. I like the food, and it's not far from where I work. I don't remember seeing you here either. But it's nice to meet you also," Dora said, taking another sip from her drink with a friendly smile.

Vinnie liked something about Dora instantly. He didn't need a formal list of reasons. When he liked someone, he just did. And that was that. All he had to do was have a good gut feeling about someone. With Dora, he already had one. "You sound like you're from the South. Are you? It's your accent."

"Yes, that's right. I'm originally from Atlanta but have decided to move to the big city. What about you?" Dora asked, curious to what he would say.

"I was born in Brooklyn. But in my teens, my family moved downtown to Little Italy. Have you ever been to Little Italy?"

Twirling the ice in her drink with a straw, Dora answered, "I've only been there once. I haven't spent much time downtown."

"Well, you'll have to go again sometime. I see you like Italian food. The restaurants down there are amazing. So, I gather you are not Italian? What's your background if you don't mind me asking?" Vinnie became more relaxed with their conversation.

"I'm a hundred percent Irish American," Dora answered.

"Nice. I have a lot of Irish friends in New York. There's a lot of history here in the city among the Italians and the Irish. That's for sure."

Then he took a sip of his drink, noticed that hers was getting low, and asked her if she would like another one.

"Okay," answered Dora, pleased by his offer.

"Johnny, would you give us both another please," Vinnie requested.

After they finished two more drinks together, Vinnie invited Dora to another place nearby called The Monkey Bar for some after dinner drinks and desserts. Feeling both adventurous and curious, Dora decided to go. She had heard of the place before but was never there.

"Take care, Johnny," said Vinnie, as he waved goodbye at the exit door. Dora waved goodbye at Johnny also.

"Have fun. Don't do anything I'd probably do," Johnny said to them with a big smile on his face, suggesting that he was glad that they had hit it off. He liked that. It made him feel good to bring people together.

The Monkey Bar was a dressier place than Bianchi's and had a lively piano player. When they arrived, they quickly got a table near the piano and began requesting some songs. Then they ordered two glasses of Sambucca and an assortment of miniature desserts to share.

"Vinnie, I'm curious. What do you do for a living?" Dora sensed that he wasn't quite the Wall Street type.

"Me, well, I made a lot of money here and there. I'd admit some in gambling. I've been in several different kinds of businesses. Some did well, and some didn't. That's all part of the game. I still have my interests in a couple of places, mostly health clubs. You could say I'm sort of an entrepreneur. I also provide some food supply services," Vinnie answered trying to sound sophisticated, adjusting his shirt collar at the same time. "What about you, Dora? You look like you're doing all right." Then he picked up his glass and took a slow sip of Sambucca waiting to hear her response.

Dora rolled her eyes at him and chuckled. She thought he was charming in a fun and different way. "I work at an investment firm called Buckleven Swaith as an admin. I help keep the executives there organized. But sometimes I feel like I don't get treated with the respect I deserve. Sometimes people can treat you like some brainless little girl. Or, they look at you like you're a piece of meat. They wouldn't treat their wives, their girlfriends, or their sisters that way. Sometimes I think they treat other people that way if they can get away with it. All I'm trying to do is make an honest living. I'm hoping to find something better eventually. For now, it pays the bills. The money's not bad. And fortunately, I still manage to have a good time on my own outside of work. Well, that's all about me for now," she added, slurring her words a little, sounding a little irritated. It was clear that she wasn't completely happy doing what she was doing.

Vinnie patted Dora on her shoulder to comfort her. "Somehow that doesn't surprise me. You seem like a tenacious person though. I mean that as a compliment. But, I have to be honest with you. You're so very attractive. If you worked for me, I'm not sure if I'd be able to get any work done. I'd love it though. But I sure would treat you right and with respect. Only an idiot would treat a beautiful woman like you without respect," Vinnie said, smiling at her affectionately.

Dora smiled back. Then she thought to herself how long it had been since she had made it with a guy. Vinnie was turning her on. She was attracted to his carefree spirit, spunk, and the overall way he carried himself.

"You'd love it, would you?" Dora responded in a flirtatious manner.

"Maybe one day you'll get a chance to put me to the test. Do you have a boyfriend? I gather you're not married. You're not wearing a ring. Are you okay with a guy from Brooklyn and Little Italy? Just checking."

"Nothing serious," said Dora, feeling aroused from the thought of him asking her about her availability. "There's nothing wrong with Brooklyn or Little Italy either. Very popular, I understand." Dora continued to flirt with him.

Vinnie chimed in, leaned over, and asked, "May I have a kiss for the guy from Brooklyn? Or, do I have to steal one from you?"

Dora blushed and let Vinnie kiss her on the lips. She couldn't believe that she was making out in public with a guy she just met. But the way he kissed her made her feel very sensuous all over her body. For that reason, she imagined that he would be good in bed.

Catching his breath for a moment, Vinnie told her, "You're quite a woman. If I'd known you longer, I might invite you to my place." Then he looked closely in her eyes and hoped for a positive response.

Dora knew what he was getting at. After some more Sambucca together, she looked at him and said, "Well, maybe you might not invite me yet. But, I'd like to invite you to mine. It's not that far from here." Dora couldn't believe what she just said to him.

Vinnie couldn't believe what he just heard. "I'm not sure what to say? You aren't thinking of taking advantage of me, are you?" His eyes rolled up at the ceiling as if something spectacular had happened.

"Guess you're just going to have to find out for yourself, Vinnie."

At that point, Vinnie wasn't going to miss the cue. He paid the check and got ready to go. He knew when a good thing was coming to him.

It took them about fifteen minutes to get to Dora's apartment. It was a one bedroom in a doorman building just off of Second Avenue and Fifty-second Street. Dora had decorated the living room in pale colors, mostly pinks, beiges, and blues. Her bedroom was painted in a soft periwinkle that looked very Nantucket. It was furnished simply but with taste. She didn't like a lot of clutter. And a few mirrors were hung on the walls, making the rooms look bigger.

"Nice place you have, Dora. Guess I'll sit here on the sofa." Vinnie sat down and stretched his arms out in the air.

"Thank you. Can I get you a drink? I have wine, scotch, vodka, and a little Sambucca of course. What's your pleasure?" she asked him, as she put her arms around his chest and shoulders, obviously getting much friendlier.

While she waited for his answer, Dora started to pour a little Sambucca in a glass. She was feeling good and didn't care if she was drinking a bit too much. She was having too much fun with him.

"Some more Sambucca would be great. Not good to mix too much," Vinnie said, as he observed the living room in greater detail. "You have a nice touch for decorating, Dora."

"Thanks, Vinnie. My sister is a decorator in Atlanta. I learned a few things from her. Here you are," she said, as she gave him his drink. "I'm wondering, do you like Sinatra? He's one of my favorites. I'm kind of nostalgic about his songs. Guess you would find that a little strange for a Southerner, I suppose." She laughed out loud.

Vinnie smiled and also laughed at the way Dora sounded.

"I love Sinatra, especially his early recordings."

"I just had a feeling you might. After all, you are Italian."

Dora turned on the stereo in her living room, found a Sinatra CD, and turned it on to play. Then she sat down on the sofa next to Vinnie while they listened to music.

"Somehow, I'm not surprised you invited me over, Dora."

"Why is that?" she asked, looking at him curiously.

"Because you appear to be a woman who is very independent and strong-willed, a woman with a mind of her own. You seem like a person who does things in her own ways. Whatever people think at work really doesn't matter. You're also incredibly sexy. Do you realize just how sexy you are?" Vinnie said to her with a more intense look on his face.

"Well, listen here Vinnie, you're no slouch either. And I bet you do lots of things in your own ways also," she said to him, moving closer to him on the sofa.

Then they both started making out. It became clear to them that they wanted each other very badly. There was no turning back now. Dora became so aroused that she couldn't help herself any longer. She took one of Vinnie's hands and led him into her bedroom. She slowly undressed in front of him while he watched her in awe. The only thing she left on was a transparent bra and panties. Then he started undressing himself, got on the bed with her, and took off her bra and panties. He kissed every bare part of her body. This drove Dora even crazier.

"Who needs dessert when they have something like you?" he whispered in her ear. "If I knew this earlier, I would have skipped dessert."

Dora sighed with pleasure as Vinnie's tongue put her into a complete state of ecstasy.

"Don't stop, Vinnie. It feels too good. You're wonderful… incredible," she cried out, wanting him so much between her legs.

Vinnie didn't intend to stop. He became as hard as a rock. And after some more foreplay, he gently spread her legs apart and got on top of her. Dora moaned louder with pleasure. Then Vinnie lifted up her legs around his shoulders to get inside of her even deeper. They continued to make love for the next few hours. Neither of them had had such great sex in a really long time.

~

THE NEXT MORNING, AFTER THEY SHOWERED TOGETHER, THEY went out for a quick breakfast at a nearby coffee shop. They also made sure they could reach each other by phone. Vinnie told her how much he wanted to see her again. And Dora told Vinnie that she felt the same way. They were hot for each other.

Even though Dora was pretty exhausted from the night before, she went straight to the office from the coffee shop. She still couldn't believe that she went to bed with someone she'd just met. But she didn't care either. She thought that sex felt so natural with him. And she hadn't been with a man in a while. Vinnie made her feel like a desirable woman again. He felt great inside of her. She even had several orgasms. This made every molecule of her body tingle inside. She felt that there couldn't be anything wrong with that. He was absolutely tantalizing to her.

CHAPTER 8

EWELS

THE WOODS DEPARTMENT STORE WASN'T DOING VERY WELL THIS holiday season. Sales had been consistently declining for several years now. Steve's marketing and sales team kept reassuring him that things were going to pick up. But that was hardly the case. The store kept losing more and more money and remained in financial trouble. Steve ignored many of the accounting statements given to him and blamed the economy for the downfall. He also denied that he could be any part of the problem. But the truth was that he often took money from the store's business accounts to fund his gambling indulgencies. Part of the reason for this was to keep Kate from finding out how much money he spent on gambling. His own accounting team suspected something was going on but kept quiet about it. They didn't want to jeopardize losing their jobs. And it wasn't their business that was sinking.

Steve's office was located on the top floor of the Woods store. It had unobstructed views of Fifty-seventh Street and Fifth Avenue. This used to be his father's office. Malcolm had bought the building just before he opened the store. Steve kept it very much the same as his father had left it. And he loved it there. It made him feel powerful and important. Steve also relished in the fact that he was the boss. There was no one he had to answer to. Everyone catered to him. He loved the undivided and compliant attention that people gave him. Yet he never cared about the genuine interests of his employees. No one on his management team even knew that he was also secretly refinancing the building to spend more money on his personal gambling habits.

The people that Steve did care about the most were his children. Mark was his favorite. He believed Mark would be the child to carry on his legacy. Steve kept this to himself. In truth, he cared more about his son than he did about his own wife, Kate. If he had to choose between the two, he would choose Mark.

Steve's private secretary Rita had worked for him since he took over for Malcolm. She was very loyal to him, never revealing any suspicious or questionable behaviors. In return, Steve rewarded her handsomely in salary increases and generous yearly bonuses. She was a single mother from Queens, so the money made her very happy.

"Rita, would you get Kate on the phone please?" Steve asked her, holding down the intercom button from his office.

"Yes sir, Mr. Woods." Rita got Kate on the phone immediately. She was at their home in Greenwich. "Line one, Mr. Woods."

"Darling, how are you? Just wondering, what would you like Santa to bring you this Christmas? What's your pleasure? Any ideas?" Steve asked Kate.

Kate loved jewelry. She would usually make a recommendation of some kind to help him in the process of finding a gift. This was the one time of the year when he really splurged on her.

"Well, to be quite honest, there is an unbelievably astonishing necklace I saw in Harry Winston's window recently. I'll give you a hint. It is green and white. If there were anything I would wish for, it would be that. There's nothing else to compare it to," Kate answered.

Steve knew Kate well. He was sure one of the reasons she wanted this necklace was because she either didn't want a friend of hers to get it. Or, she just wanted to show it off to some of her wealthy friends. That was one characteristic they shared. Kate was also competitive around other people, especially New York's elite. She was also used to getting what she wanted and didn't expect no for an answer.

"How much is it, darling?" Steve asked, hoping it wouldn't be too astronomical.

"It's just over a million. But I know it's worth every cent," Kate casually replied over the phone.

"Over a million, Kate. Oh, is that all?" he replied a bit sarcastically.

"Well, you did ask. And since Woods is doing so well, I'm sure it's not an issue. Right? Didn't you tell me that the store is making more money than ever?" Kate inquired.

Steve had told her that because he didn't want her to know the truth. He knew he would have to get the necklace for her or she would find it very suspicious. He feared that she might start questioning him about what was really going on at Woods or elsewhere. So he convinced himself that he could make up the money by gambling soon again. He already had a trip planned to go out to Las Vegas.

"We'll see what Santa can do. But for now, how about we all go out to dinner in the city tonight? Why don't you bring Mark and Julia with you? How about Petrossian? I'm in the mood for a little caviar. Does that sound good to you?" Steve asked her.

Steve liked to go to Petrossian during the holidays because his father used to take him there since he was a young boy. It had become a family tradition that they did together at least once a year, and usually during the holidays.

"That would be terrific. I'll get Claude to drive us into the city. We'll meet you at the apartment by seven tonight. See you later my love."

Steve hung up the receiver and asked Rita to make the dinner reservation for Petrossian's. Then he asked her to get the manager of Harry Winston's on the phone. He knew he had to cough up the money for the necklace. When the manager got on the phone, Steve explained what he was interested in and that he wanted an immediate appointment to view the necklace. He told him that he would be there in an hour.

When Steve arrived at Harry Winston's, he was taken into a private room where he viewed the emerald and diamond necklace. He figured he might as well get it over with. Otherwise, there might be a risk that someone else might buy it. This would not go over well with Kate. It was indeed over a million dollars, much more than he would have liked to spend. But he felt stuck. So he made payment and delivery arrangements with the sales manager. Steve was going to have the necklace delivered to Kate at their home in Greenwich just in time for Christmas.

"Mr. Woods, I'm certain your wife will be most delighted. If there is anything else we can do for you, please do not hesitate to ask," the manager told Steve as he was leaving the store.

"Wouldn't your wife be delighted too? You ass. When was the last time you spent over a million dollars on your wife for Christmas? You moron." Steve yelled at him, giving him a dirty look.

"Absolutely, sir. I'm sure she will. I mean would be delighted."

"I thought so. Now make sure you get it to my wife on time before I change my mind," Steve said bitterly, slamming one of the entrance doors behind him.

～

WHEN STEVE ARRIVED AT THEIR APARTMENT LATER THAT DAY, Kate, Mark, and Julia were already waiting for him. He poured himself a drink while everyone got ready to go out to Petrossian. Kate also loved going there. It had some of the finest caviar in the world and was especially festive during the holidays. It was always decorated beautifully with exquisite floral arrangements and holiday lights.

During dinner, Kate asked Mark and Julia what they wanted for Christmas. As usual, they wanted some of the latest electronic games and toys. But they also said they wanted to go to Walt Disney World in Florida for a weekend. Kate told them that she would have to discuss that further with their father and that they'd get back to them on that.

After dinner, they all went back to their apartment together. And after they watched a movie, Kate asked Mark and Julia to go to bed. Then she joined Steve in their bedroom. She put on a pair of white satin pajamas, curled up next to him, told him how much she loved him, and that she enjoyed their family dinner together.

Steve smiled at her also and said, "I love you too, darling."

Then, with an expansive view of Central Park in front of them, they decided to make love to each other and fell asleep in each other's arms. It wasn't until the next morning that Steve began to think again about the cost of Kate's necklace and his plans to go to Las Vegas.

CHAPTER 9

SHARING SECRETS

"DORA, I'M SO GLAD YOU COULD MAKE IT FOR DINNER tonight," Chantel told her, as she placed two plates of home-made chicken curry shrimp with rice and vegetables on her small dining table. "Would you like a glass of wine to go with that?"

"Yes, thanks. That would be great. Everything looks so delicious. It smells better than a restaurant in here. There's nothing like a home-cooked meal. It looks like you sure know how to cook. Reminds me a little of the shrimp dishes I had growing up in the South. Wow, this is really good. But Chantel, I have something I want to tell you about, something that is even spicier than these shrimp. I mean you wouldn't believe what I did."

"What did you do, Dora?" Chantel asked, sensing the excitement in Dora's voice.

"Well, I had the most incredible sex with a complete stranger that I met after work at Bianchi's restaurant last night. You know, the one close to where I work. I'm not sure what got into me. I broke all of my own rules. I just found him to be so drop dead charismatic. He was so charming, so funny, and so gorgeous. I hope you don't think I'm a tramp or something like that. But I just had to tell you. I had to tell somebody." Dora took a sip of wine and tried to regain her composure.

"No. I don't think you're a tramp, Dora. Yet, I am a little shocked. I never would have thought you would ever do anything like that. I guess there's always an exception." Chantel giggled and stuffed a large green olive inside of her mouth.

"Normally, that would be the case. But he made me feel so much like a woman. He was so sexy and made me laugh so much. And he had an incredible body. Please don't tell anybody," Dora said, batting her eyes at the ceiling.

"Of course not. You're my closest friend. What's his name? Where does he come from?" asked Chantel, becoming very curious.

"His name is Vinnie. I know it's a real Italian name. And like I explained before, I met him at Bianchi's. He told me he is from Brooklyn and Little Italy. I can't believe I met someone in there. I've been going to Bianchi's for a while and this never happened to me before. Maybe it's just lust or the fact that I wasn't with a guy in such a long time. But he really turned me on. I just couldn't resist him. And, we're planning on seeing each other again very soon."

It was obvious to Chantel that Dora was really captivated by Vinnie.

"Hey look, I can't judge you. If he made you happy, he made you happy. That's the most important thing. Yes, you might be taking a chance or a risk. But who am I to say. If it makes you feel good, go for it. But I have something to tell you too. That's the reason I wanted you to come over tonight. It's about Marco Puccio. I want you to keep it to yourself also and not to tell anyone in your office. Can you keep a secret?" Chantel asked her.

"Sure. This sounds interesting. What is it?" asked Dora, sounding giddy.

"Well, we also had a great time together the last time we went out in the city. I didn't expect to feel this way. But I already feel like I know him much longer than I do. It feels like it's more than just passion or lust with him. Something feels so special between us. It's like I've known him forever. He's the kind of guy I've always dreamt about but wasn't really sure existed. Like, am I crazy or something? I can't even believe I'm saying all of this to you."

"Well, don't feel bad. Look what happened to me last night," Dora said laughing.

"That's not all, Dora. We're planning on going to Montauk for a weekend together. Marco told me that Harry Fisher has a house out there and that we can use it as a place to stay. Marco says it's beautiful and that he'll be on his best behavior. Hope he's being truthful about that one. But, I thought, why not? I've never been out to the Hamptons. And, I really like him a lot," said Chantel, sort of defending her decision to go.

"That just figures. So many women are after him at work, but you're the one he's going out with. Don't worry. I won't say a word. I can keep a secret. I only hope that Harry can. He can be such a tease sometimes. But I'll keep an eye on him. It's nice of Harry to let you both use his place. When are you going?" Dora asked, genuinely happy for Chantel.

"This coming weekend on Friday. We're going after I finish work and pick up my travel bags. We were going to go the following week, but Harry would have been there. So we're going sooner rather than later," Chantel explained.

"That sounds very romantic. I mean the two of you at a beach house alone together."

"Yes, I know. But I hope I'm not making a mistake."

"Hey, you never know, he could be your forever love. Wouldn't that be something? And I'm the one who brought you two together. Don't forget that." Dora felt kind of proud of herself.

Chantel blushed a little. "True, life is funny that way. Sometimes, it can be serendipitous. So, I'm kind of just going with it. At least you've known him for a while. He seems like a decent guy, right?"

"Yes, he does. And if you need me for any reason, just give me a call. I'll go out there and rescue you myself," Dora told her.

Just then Chantel's telephone rang. It was her sister

Claudette. Claudette told Chantel all about the holiday festivities back home in Maine and how much everybody missed her. Chantel wasn't going to be with them over the holidays because she was very busy at Champs. A few minutes later, Dora heard the phone being turned off. Chantel was a little teary-eyed. She really missed her family as much as they missed her.

"Dora, it's just that this is the busiest time of the year at Bloomingdale's. And, I just got started to build my career. I want a different life for myself. I'm not sure if they really understand. I do love them very much though."

"Don't be ridiculous. They know you love them. Now cheer up. Hey, there's someone knocking at your door."

Chantel opened the door to her apartment and saw Mrs. Mangano holding a brown parcel in her arms. "This is for you, Chantel. The carrier just dropped it off in the hallway. I didn't want it to get lost or stolen so I thought I'd bring it to you myself," she said quickly, giving the parcel to Chantel.

"Thank you, Mrs. Mangano. That was so kind of you."

"You're welcome, Chantel. Have a good night."

Chantel grabbed a pair of scissors and opened the package. It had a note inside of it from Marco. It said, *Dear Chantel, A little something to keep you warm on our trip. Love, Marco.* Then Chantel tossed away the pile of tissue paper inside and saw the most beautiful nightgown she had ever seen. It was made out of the softest pink silk. It also had tiny pearls and lace sewn into the fabric. Underneath, there was a matching robe that was made out of a heavier fabric. Dora looked at Chantel with her eyes widening.

"Wow. This is elegant," said Chantel, holding the nightgown set up against her body.

"Sure is, Chantel. Don't forget your slippers, princess," joked Dora.

"But, it's time for me to go. It's getting late, and I really should get some rest. We can talk more about this tomorrow. Thanks for the delicious dinner. I really enjoyed it."

"I understand, Dora. Thanks for coming over and sharing with me." Chantel was glad to have had the company. Then Chantel unlocked her apartment door, and Dora left for the night.

CHAPTER 10

*M*ONTAUK

It was around three o'clock in the afternoon when Marco arrived at Chantel's apartment to pick her up for their trip to the Hamptons. He had left work early so they could see a bit of Montauk before it got dark. And he had already made reservations at the renowned Gurney's Inn for dinner. Gurney's was located near Harry's house on the ocean. Marco also called one of the housekeepers at the house earlier in the week to pick up some wine and food for their visit. After he rang Chantel's bell, he leaned up next to the town car he came in and waited for her.

Chantel was both excited and nervous. She wasn't used to going away with someone she only knew for a short time. But she wanted to be with Marco and the thought of the experience to go somewhere new with him felt special to her. Her face was cheerful and rosy, and her eyes sparkled when she saw him.

"Come on, Chantel. Our pilot is waiting for us at the East Thirty-fourth Street heliport," Marco told her, taking her small suitcase in one hand while kissing her quickly on the cheek.

"Heliport? Did you say heliport?" she asked.

"Yes, we're going to take a helicopter to Montauk. I also have a jeep rental waiting for us. The terrain is a bit hilly out there. So a jeep will be fun to ride around in. Weather conditions look good, so I don't expect we'll have any trouble taking off or landing," Marco told her smiling. "By the way, you look fabulous. But I hope you're okay with all of this. I just wanted to surprise you."

"Well, you sure are surprising me." She laughed. "I was never in a helicopter before," Chantel told him, feeling a little queasy in her stomach at the thought of the idea.

"Don't worry, Chantel. We'll be there in no time. This way we'll get there before sunset. The airport isn't far from Harry's house. And I already have dinner reservations made for us. It's kind of quiet out there this time of the year though. It's much more crowded with people from the city during the summertime. But there are also many people that like to stay there all year round. They like the solitude during the winter months. You'll find it's a lot different than city life here in Manhattan. Coming from Maine, I'm sure you can appreciate it. And this will also be the first time I'll be sleeping overnight at Harry's place myself. So the experience will be as new to you as it will be for me. I also know the area very well, so we'll be fine."

When they arrived at the heliport, they were quickly shuttled into a small blue and red helicopter. Their driver helped them with their bags. And a pilot named Joe Bailey greeted them warmly.

"Nice to see you again, Mr. Puccio. It's been a while."

"Great seeing you, Joe. By the way, this is Chantel Du Maurier. She's my companion for the weekend. I'm hoping she's going to fall in love with Montauk," replied Marco.

"I'm sure she will, sir. You know it quite well. You're a great person to show her around out there."

"I hope so," said Marco.

Joe had been a pilot for many years. When he got tired of working for the large airlines, he started doing private charters. He was a jolly Irishman who liked to tell jokes about good people being naughty. There wasn't anyone who didn't like him or his sense of humor. He was always considered good company on their trips.

When they left the island of Manhattan, Marco pointed out and identified many of New York's bridges and other interesting parts of the city. And when they got further out above Long Island, Chantel commented on the long stretches of beach along the ocean that she could see. She remarked on the many homes that were lined up along the beach in some areas and other places that she thought looked rather uninhabited.

"We'll be arriving at the airport soon," Marco mentioned to her, holding one of her hands tightly. "Then we'll pick up the jeep and go to Harry's house on Star Road. It's a couple of minutes from Gurney's. We'll have dinner there tonight. I think you'll enjoy that."

When they landed at the airport, Joe helped them off with their bags and wished them both a great time. Then they found the red jeep that Marco had arranged to be waiting for them and headed to Star Road. As Marco said earlier, the roads were hilly. On the way, at higher elevations, Chantel could see the Atlantic Ocean below them. And other than the dwarf alpine spruces, the trees and vegetation along the side of the roads were bare of greenery and covered with a light dusting of snow. Some of the homes also looked empty, as if their owners hadn't been in them for some time.

"Chantel, can you read the sign up ahead there? Does it say Star Road? I think we're almost there," said Marco, adjusting his sunglasses.

"Looks like it from here," she replied.

"Please don't be nervous, Chantel. I'll take good care of you like I said I would. Ah, it looks like we made it, number seventy-seven. What do you think so far?" asked Marco, pulling into the gravel driveway.

"Wow, it's much larger than I expected. And the location on the ocean is as unbelievable as you said it would be. It sort of reminds me of some of the places back home in Maine along the ocean," she told him.

"Well, let's go in and make ourselves at home," said Marco, lifting their luggage out the jeep, and searching his coat pockets for the keys to the house. On his way to the entrance door, he stumbled a bit and dropped one of the bags. "You see how clumsy I am around an attractive woman. And you think you have something to be nervous about?" Then he picked up the bag and shook his head. "Just goes to show you."

When they got inside, they took off their jackets. They also found a note left from one of the housekeepers that the heat was taken care of and there was food and wine in the kitchen for them to enjoy.

Harry's home was decorated handsomely with thick crown moldings and wainscot paneling throughout. There was large floor to ceiling windows with open views of the ocean waves pounding on the surf. There was also a polished stone fireplace that stood between the windows. It didn't look like it was used for a while. And there were also mirrored glass tables, antiques, and artwork that looked like they belonged in the Museum of Modern Art in Manhattan. White area rugs covered the floors, giving a crisp contrast to the stained wood below. The sky outside was beginning to change colors. And the sun was setting with evening soon to come.

"Look at that sunset. What a phenomenal place this is, Marco."

"Yes, it is. But you are even more phenomenal." Marco put his arms around her waist and kissed her gently on the lips. "Why don't we see what's in the kitchen? Would you like a glass of wine? Then soon, we can go to Gurney's for dinner," Marco inquired.

"Sounds like a good plan," Chantel said, as she followed him into the kitchen.

They found a couple of bottles of wine on a granite kitchen

counter and a couple of bottles of champagne in the fridge. They decided on the champagne. Then Marco opened a small jar of caviar and a box of water crackers to go with it. He thought it would be a good time to try some before they would leave for dinner. After finding a tray to put everything on, and a place to sit down in the living room, they sat down together and toasted each other. And after a while, they decided to take a quick tour of the house.

There were four tastefully decorated bedrooms upstairs. The one Chantel liked the most was the largest. It had a very open loft-like space. And she thought the pale blue colors of the room were pleasing and very soothing to the eyes. The colors of the room were also transformed by the light coming in from the skylights on the ceiling above and the glass doors below. And simple paintings were hung on the walls. The minimalist decorations contrasted well with the antique brass lanterns that were placed throughout the room.

After they toured the upstairs, Chantel decided that the room she liked the most would be the one she would sleep in. Marco didn't mind. He was just delighted to be with her alone in such an intimate setting together and away from the bustle of the city.

THE DINING ROOM AT GURNEY'S WAS ABOUT HALF FULL WHEN they arrived. That wasn't unusual around the holidays and during the winter months. In the middle of the restaurant, there was a beautifully decorated holiday tree that had velvet ribbons strung all around it. There were also festive lights everywhere, and candles lit on every table. The strong smells of cinnamon and spice were present in the air and were only tapered by the arrival of sumptuously smelling dishes from the kitchen. A three-piece band was also playing music on a small dance floor in the background.

After the maître d' seated them, Marco ordered a bottle of vintage Dom Pérignon. Then they looked at the menus together. After they ordered their food, Chantel commented on the many stars she could see outside the windows in the sky. She also looked closely at the rough and wild waves that pounded the shore. It was an amazing place to her.

During dinner Marco talked about his plans after graduate school and that he would like to move back to New York. And Chantel talked about her career aspirations in the beauty industry and her job at Champs. Marco admired her ambition. He was impressed with her confidence and belief in herself. Yet, he also recognized her modesty. He admired this about her also. Most of the women he had met in his life were so different from her. He felt that she had a special warmth that many of the women he met before lacked. And he decided to bring her a special gift to make the memory of their time together even more memorable.

Reaching into one of his jacket pockets, Marco told her, "I brought something for you. I hope that you will really like it." Then he took out a small red box with a white ribbon tied around it and gave it to her.

Chantel looked at him perplexed. "I wasn't expecting a gift,

Marco. You really shouldn't be doing all of this. I'm simply happy to be here with you. I really am."

"Come on, please open it. I spent a lot of time picking it out for you. It is from a store called Cartier."

Chantel opened the box. A gold necklace and charm were inside. The charm was a small golden box with little diamonds and a bow on top. She looked at Marco like he was crazy or something. "I can't believe you did this," she said, with a surprised expression on her face.

"I'm happy to. The box opens also. Take a look inside," he told her.

Chantel opened the charm box and saw two tiny gold birds kissing one another inside. She thought of how unusual it was, laughed, and said, "Actually, I really love it. I've never seen anything quite like it. Thank you, Marco." Chantel was extremely touched. No one had ever given her anything like it before.

Then Marco got closer to her and kissed her. "They're supposed to be two doves kissing each other," he whispered in her ear.

"I see that. It's certainly different. Do you mind if I wear it now?"

"Not at all. I'd love you to wear it now," he answered. "That means a lot to me."

While they dined, Marco thought about finishing his last semester at school and coming back to be with Chantel indefinitely. He thought to himself that he'd only be gone a couple of months and that she could wait for him, especially if they kept in touch on Skype or Facetime. He had begun to realize that he had fallen for her. He wasn't sure earlier, but he sensed it even more now. And he thought that maybe she would be willing to be with him forever and perhaps marry him. There were two things he felt he needed to find out. Was she feeling the same feelings? And, would she even consider marrying him one day? These thoughts made him nervous inside. He had never really known what it was like to be in love or to love someone else romantically. Just discovering what falling in love was like was enough for him. He was feeling emotions that he never felt before. It made his heart open up and feel a joy he had never experienced before.

Then Marco asked her if she would like to dance. And after they danced to a few slow songs and settled the bill, they drove back to Harry's house. On the way, they sang a couple of holiday songs together, exaggerating some of the lyrics. Chantel laughed so hard that she almost cried. She also felt joy in her heart being with him. She felt a new wonder of life, the future, and happiness.

When they got to Harry's, they decided to play charades and some modern-day trivia games. Marco won most of the charades. And Chantel won most of the trivia questions. Then they went upstairs to see where they would each sleep. Chantel reminded Marco that she wanted to sleep in the blue bedroom they'd seen earlier. Then she changed into the nightgown that Marco had given to Mrs. Mangano to give to her and jumped into bed. Marco wasn't sure what to do next. He didn't want to make her feel uncomfortable. So he put on a pair of flannel pajamas and asked her if it would be all right if he could just watch her fall asleep. She told him that was okay. Then they kissed each other again and fell asleep under the stars that they could see through the skylights in the ceiling.

~

THE NEXT MORNING CHANTEL WOKE UP ALONE IN THE BEDROOM. She heard sounds coming from downstairs and smelled coffee brewing. Then she jumped out of bed, took a quick shower, put on some clothes, and went downstairs. Marco was seated at a table in the kitchen wearing a lime green Ralph Lauren sweater, faded blue jeans, and a pair of brown leather Gucci loafers.

When Marco saw Chantel, he got up to kiss her, and said enthusiastically, "Breakfast is ready. We have strawberries, blueberries, blackberries, pancakes, and syrup. If you also want cream, there's some in the fridge."

Chantel was impressed with his culinary skills. "I cannot believe that you know how to cook? It looks delicious though, and I'm starving. So, don't mind if I just dig in. I'll also make whipped cream so we can put some on the berries. And since you worked so hard this morning, I'd like to make dinner for you and me tonight. Would that be okay?" she asked him smiling.

"Are you sure? I was planning on taking you out tonight," he said, kissing her on the neck.

"Yes, I'm pretty sure. There's a lot to work with in this kitchen. I'd like to make us dinner. We can also stop at a market if we need anything. I'd love to make something for you." She smiled back at him.

After they finished their breakfast, they put on their winter jackets, hats, and gloves to venture out together for some sight-seeing. Marco wanted to take a drive to the tip of Montauk where the Montauk Lighthouse was. It was situated on top of some very scenic hilly land that also had beautiful views of the ocean. But when they got there, the wind was so vigorous that it was too cold for them to walk around. So they stayed inside the jeep with the heat on and looked out at the waves crashing against the nearby cliffs. And they spent the rest of the time kissing each other.

When they were ready to leave, they drove to the village of Montauk. On the way, Marco pointed out some of the horse stables that he visited as a child. He told Chantel that he used to ride a horse named Pumpkin, and that was his favorite horse when he was a child. When they got to the village, they decided to go into some of the antique and art stores that were open. So they parked the jeep, walked around the village holding hands, and bought a couple of souvenirs. Chantel found a lighthouse that had a place for a bulb inside of it that lit up its miniature windows, a silk scarf, and a pair of seashell candlesticks. And Marco found a funny looking hat that had a silly photo of rein-deers on it. Then they walked around some more until they were hungry and decided it was time to have lunch.

Marco suggested that they go to a restaurant named Harvest on Fort Pond. It was a charming restaurant that was popular with locals and visitors alike. It was also near a market where they could pick up some more things for dinner if Chantel still wanted to cook.

"It's so quaint out here, Marco. Thanks so much for showing me the lighthouse and sharing some of the memories you've had here."

"It was really my father who loved it here. He and I would drive out together when I was growing up to go to Ditch Plains Beach and horseback riding. At Ditch Plains, I used to go surfing. Some of the best memories of my life were here with him in the summertime."

"I can tell you miss him a lot, Marco."

"Yes, I do miss him a lot. Life at home in Southampton was never the same without him. I never bonded with my mother the way I did with my father. For some reason, she always seemed a bit distant to me. I'm not really sure why. It's just a feeling that something was missing compared to my experience with my father. Who knows? Maybe it was because he was a male that we bonded more? I'm not really sure."

"I'm sure she loves you very much, Marco. Maybe it's that she doesn't know how to show it or something like that."

"I just sensed something missing," Marco added.

After lunch, they picked up a few more groceries and drove back to Harry's house. The temperatures were starting to drop, so they decided to put some wood inside the fireplace and start a fire to warm them up. Then they sat together on one of the sofas and watched the fire grow. Harry telephoned in the meantime to ask how they were doing. He reminded Marco that they had a meeting on Monday morning at work for some important business they were doing together. He also told them not to worry about locking up the house when they leave. A housekeeper would meet them there before they would head back to the city.

When evening came, Chantel decided to start working on their meal for dinner. She prepared arugula salad, shrimp with linguine, swordfish, and strawberry mousse for dessert. When everything was ready, Marco opened a bottle of champagne and put it in an ice bucket. Then he put on some soft jazz music for them to listen to. Chantel also found some candles and lit them for ambiance.

"Everything is ready, Marco. Are you hungry yet?" she asked him, hoping that he would find her cooking utterly delicious. Her cooking experience was still somewhat limited. But she learned a few things from her mom back home in Maine and trying different recipes in magazines. She remembered that Dora complimented her cooking. So she hoped it would please Marco as well.

"Yes, I'm ready. I'm looking forward to tasting everything. Wow, it looks and smells delicious. Are you sure you didn't go to school to be a chef? But before I sit down, let me pour some more champagne and put more wood in the fireplace."

During dinner, Chantel asked him about the charm he gave to her. Marco told her that when he was a child, there was a neighbor who lived nearby who had some rather elaborate birdhouses. One of them housed two doves and that had become his favorite. He said his neighbor would tell him fantastic stories about the doves, how unique they were, and all the things they represented. His neighbor also told him that the doves were a symbol of peace, love, and eternity. Chantel thought the story was a little peculiar but charming in its own way. She couldn't believe that Marco was so sentimental about such things. But she admired him even more because of it.

After dinner, they laid down in front of the fireplace. Marco arranged a comforter and some pillows for them to lay on together. In the meantime, the fire became robust since they ate. They both admired it and appreciated its warmth. Then they held each other, looked into each other's eyes, and started kissing. Everything, all at once, felt completely perfect between them. They felt utterly aligned together as if they had been together for years.

Chantel decided to put on her nightgown and robe. She excused herself and told Marco that she'd be right back. When she returned, he just stared at her, thinking about how precious she looked. Inside of his heart, he felt like he was in a dream. It was a dream of love becoming true. For once, he thought he knew what love was like for a woman. Knowing this made him very happy inside. Then Chantel laid down next to him again and looked into his eyes intensely. He gently pulled her closer until there was no room left between them. He kissed her with a passion that he felt in every vein of his body. And he began outlining the curves of her body with his hands.

"Are you okay, Chantel? I'd like to go further. I want you so much. But I understand if it's too soon for you. I can wait. I don't mind," he told her, trying to contain his emotions and passion. He didn't want to risk upsetting her.

"Yes, I'm okay. But I feel it strongly too. Let's stay here and just let it happen. It's really comfortable next to the fireplace together," she told him, as she began to pull off his sweater and take off her robe.

Within a few minutes, they were both completely undressed, within each other's arms, and feeling every contour of each other's bodies. There was no feeling in the world that they could compare their experience to. They realized what they never knew about love before. For the first time in their lives, they felt complete and pure joy. It was the joy of being in love. They also watched the flames in the fire that danced beside them. It was as if the flames were joyful too. And after they were entirely acquainted with each other's bodies, Marco and Chantel made love for the very first time. They spent the next few hours making love and simply discovering one another. They gently held each other in each other's arms until they slept. As they became totally at ease and at peace with one another. And the glowing embers of the fire next to them kept them warm throughout the night.

THE NEXT MORNING THEY MET ONE OF HARRY'S HOUSEKEEPERS before they left for the airport back to the city. Joe Bailey was waiting for them when they arrived. During their trip, Marco asked Chantel if she would like to go to a party in Southampton the following weekend at his mother's house. He told her that his mother was throwing a holiday party and thought it would be a nice time for Chantel to meet her. He really wanted Chantel to see where he grew up.

"Sure, I'd love to go. It would be nice to see your home and meet your family," Chantel answered, hugging him.

"Great. I'll tell her you'll be coming. I can't wait," Marco replied, sounding pleased.

Then they held and kissed each other all the way back to the city.

CHAPTER 11

AS VEGAS

MEANWHILE THAT SAME WEEKEND, STEVE AND JOHN TOOK AN airplane to Las Vegas to do some serious gambling. They had an understanding between them, never to tell their wives how they did at the gambling tables. There was also an understanding to never tell of any promiscuity with other women. They knew that if either of their wives ever found out that they were cheated on, they'd likely end up in divorce court. This code of secrecy kept them safe. And there was a strong male bond of trust between them.

They rented a large penthouse suite together in the exclusive Mirage Hotel on Las Vegas Boulevard. It was everything they expected it to be. Both of them had their own private bedrooms and bathrooms. The living room was very spacious and had a bar designed by the famous Frank Lloyd Wright. The rooms were sleek and modern looking, mostly colored in silver and grey tones. And the views they had of Las Vegas were exceptional.

Steve took a few minutes in his bedroom to phone Kate.

"Yes, honey. Of course, I'll go easy. Give the children my love. See you in a few days. John is fine. Yes, I'll tell him you said to look after me. Bye, darling." Steve hung up the receiver feeling relieved. He also felt a greater sense of freedom.

John was waiting for him downstairs at a restaurant named Bartel's. He'd already ordered a scotch and soda when Steve walked in to join him. He suspected from the look on Steve's face that he had been on the telephone with Kate.

"How is she?" asked John.

"Worried as usual. I wonder if someone leaked out what happened on Spiro's yacht? Some asshole took me for a lot of money in a lousy backgammon match. The son of a bitch was lucky that I didn't throw him in the East River to drown." Steve's face flushed red with anger.

"Shit happens, Steve. Sometimes you take risks with the wrong people too." John was trying to be a little more realistic about it.

"He's just a fucking asshole. I don't know what the hell he was doing there in the first place. Seemed like he was some kind of a hustler or something like that to me."

John leaned over his drink and stirred the ice in it with his right finger. "What's gone is gone. Let's change the subject. I want to have some fun tonight and pick up where we left off last night. Don't you?" John knew that Steve was a sore loser. He thought the incident was par the course if one gambled and took risks.

"Yeah, yeah, yeah. Last night, I didn't score so well. Maybe I'll have more luck tonight. My wife just got me to spend a bleeding fortune on another fucking necklace from Harry Winston's. I bet she just wants to show it off to her society friends. Like she needs another one. You wouldn't believe the price tag. It's over a fucking million. Anyway, let's eat. I came out here to have a good time and win some money. I could use it."

After dinner, a limousine picked them up in front of the Mirage and took them over to Caesars casino. It was only a short ride away, but they liked to go in style. Caesars was regarded as a carpet joint. There was usually a lot of action between the high rollers who went there to compete. Sometimes the competition got mighty fierce. Egos would inflame. The casino loved it though. The more money people wagered, the more money the casino made.

John was a craps man. Steve favored both blackjack and roulette. The vibe in the place made them both feel lucky again. That was not the case by the time they left. John did okay. He managed to win some money. But Steve lost two million at the roulette table. At first, he was doing fairly okay. But when he spotted Max Conners at another roulette table again in the room, things changed quickly. Steve went over to his table and wanted to beat his winnings and failed. Steve became so emotionally high strung at the sight of Max that he went wild at the roulette table where he was playing. John warned him to take it easy, but Steve wouldn't listen. It was the largest loss Steve ever had in one night of gambling. It really hurt.

Somehow John finally managed to get Steve out of Caesars and back into the limousine waiting outside for them.

Pissed off, John said, "What the hell were you doing in there? You just lost two million dollars. You went totally berserk at the table. Come on now and calm down. What's going on with you?"

John knew Steve loved to gamble, but he'd never seen him lose so much control of himself. He would have guessed that Steve was on drugs or something. But he knew Steve wasn't into that sort of thing. In all the years he'd known him, he never saw him so much as take a puff from a marijuana cigarette.

"That bastard. I'll get that son of a bitch if it's the last thing I ever do!" Steve shouted while he grabbed a bottle of Hennessy cognac from the bar in the limo.

"Who? Who the hell are you talking about? The dealer? Who, dammit?" asked John confused.

"Conners. Max Conners was there. The guy I told you about. I can't believe it. He was there tonight playing roulette."

"What? So that explains you throwing around money like that and losing your mind. Why didn't you tell me he was there? You completely lost it. You ought to take it easy out there, no matter what."

Steve didn't answer. Instead, he poured a mouthful of cognac down his throat. In a matter of minutes, half the bottle was empty.

"Cut that out. You want to kill yourself or something? You shouldn't have let him get to you. But if I know you, he'll get his one day." John was trying to change Steve's frame of mind. He'd never seen him so angry with anyone before.

"I'll find a way. And when I do, I'm going to give it to him right in the balls," Steve shouted out loud.

Then the limousine pulled up in front of the Mirage.

"That's it, Steve. Easy now. You'll get even with him one day. Just be patient. Good dice and opportunity come to those who wait. You'll get your turn buddy. You'll see," said John, trying to appease him some more.

Steve smiled at him for the first time since they left Caesars.

"Come on. Let's go upstairs. I've got a surprise coming for you. We've got two babes scheduled for eleven. What do you say, buddy?" John patted Steve on his back.

"You're right. His day will come. Maybe I should do a little investigation work on him." Steve paused. "So I have a surprise coming. I could use a little cheering up tonight."

The booze was taking effect on Steve. So he decided to let the gambling episode go for the rest of the night. What else could he do, he thought to himself. He knew he wanted to get even with Max winning his money on Spiro's yacht. And running into him tonight and losing all that money made him even more determined. But, he had the sense that he would have to give the situation some more thought and careful planning.

When they got back to their suite, John made a quick phone call. Then he turned to Steve. "They'll be here as scheduled."

"At least I have something to look forward to tonight. Thanks to you. Let's make it a good one. I sure as hell need it," said Steve, opening another bottle of Hennessy cognac.

Twenty minutes later, two prostitutes arrived at their suite. Steve asked them to take off their clothes and do a dance routine in front of them. The women obliged and were eager to please. They even danced on the living room coffee table, bounced their huge breasts in the air, and spread their legs wide open in front of them to entice them into having sex. Then Steve and John each took one of the women into their bedrooms. And for the rest of the night, the repetitive sounds of sexual pleasures echoed in the air. But before they were finished, they switched women and had sex with both of them until they were too sore and couldn't get hard anymore.

THE NEXT DAY, STEVE AND JOHN FLEW BACK TO NEW YORK. They arrived in Manhattan in the afternoon. John was dropped off first at his apartment on East Fifty-eighth Street. Steve went straight to his office. Both were relieved that they survived Las Vegas and didn't say much to each other on the ride from the airport.

Since it was a Monday, Steve's assistant Rita was working. She followed him into his office, handing him a handful of messages. Kate had already called there twice. She left a message that she would be at their home in Greenwich and that she was planning on having dinner with him there that night. A couple of executives who worked for Steve had been looking for him also. But the message that interested him the most was from Spiro Pagonis. He knew Spiro would likely have some information on Max Conners. So, he decided to phone him right away. When Spiro's secretary answered the phone, she asked him to hold on a minute and transferred the call.

"Mr. Woods, Mr. Pagonis is now on the line. Go ahead please."

"How are you, Spiro? I have a message that you called my office in New York." Steve heard his voice echo over the telephone.

"Yes, I called to ask if you would be interested in being a sponsor for a large fund-raising project I'm involved with. Myself, along with some of my colleagues, are putting together a special yacht race to benefit children with disabilities in the United States. So far, we have several top corporations and private companies involved. And knowing you are a person who appreciates yachting, I thought you might be interested. The race will take place next summer off the coast of Newport, Rhode Island. Would you like to participate?" asked Spiro, sounding cheerful and upbeat over the phone.

Steve was surprised by the question. He hadn't any idea that Spiro was involved in charitable events like these. Things of this sort didn't really interest Steve. But he wanted to make a good impression on Spiro, so he told him that he'd be a sponsor. Then Steve made his move and asked about Max.

"By the way Spiro, can you tell me anything about Max Conners? If you remember, I met him at your yacht party. I was wondering what you might know of him?" Steve asked, tapping a pen impatiently on his desk.

"Why yes. He's from California originally. I believe he owns a few hotels and some commercial property in Los Angeles and San Francisco. But he's also well-known for his success at gambling. I'm particularly impressed with his skills at chess and roulette. He's quite good actually."

Steve found out exactly what he hoped to, another game that Max plays. It would give him an additional alternative.

"That's interesting, Spiro," replied Steve, trying to sound matter of fact about his questioning.

Then Spiro got a call from Zurich and told Steve he had to go.

"Good speaking with you. Thank you for your support. I'll be in touch with your office concerning the sponsoring details. Goodbye."

"My pleasure, Spiro. Goodbye."

Steve thought to himself that he couldn't care less about the noble cause of the fund-raiser. He pledged to be a sponsor because he figured Spiro might be of help to him in the future. He simply wanted to get cozier with Spiro and keep in his good graces. The yacht fund-raiser was just the perfect opportunity to do that.

∾

STEVE'S RIDE BACK TO GREENWICH WAS SMOOTH AND WITHOUT much traffic. His driver had picked him up earlier at the office around six-thirty that evening. By seven-fifteen, he was home. Kate looked happy to see him. And Mark and Julia were also home. It would be their first family dinner together since they went to Petrossian's. Dinner was already on the dining room table. Yet, none of this diminished Steve's thoughts and feelings of hatred and revenge for Max Conners.

During dinner, Steve thought again about his conversation with Spiro. He thought there had to be some way to get Max to the betting table again and get him for good. He thought there had to be some way to get even. Now he knew that Max plays chess. So he wondered about finding a chess master of the game and perhaps putting the two together.

Kate sat down and thought about Steve's trip to Las Vegas. She could tell by looking at him that it was hardly terrific. She simply could tell. His face showed signs of anxiety. That told her he must have lost a lot of money. If he had done well, there would surely be a bigger smile on his face. Instead, he looked pretty somber to her.

Later that evening, after Mark and Julia went upstairs to bed, Kate decided to ask Steve about his trip. She never liked to talk about gambling in front of their children. They had no idea that their father had a gambling addiction.

"Darling, how did you make out in Vegas?" she asked.

Steve would never divulge his losses. He answered, "Fairly well, dear. Fairly well." Then he looked down at his wristwatch and said, "Sorry, I'm really tired. It's been a long day. I'm going to retire to the bedroom. I'll tell you more tomorrow."

Kate knew she was getting the brush off. She knew he wanted to go to bed in order to avoid answering any more questions. This sort of evasiveness was not unusual when he lost.

CHAPTER 12

SOUTHAMPTON, NY

THE FOLLOWING DAYS THAT PASSED WITHOUT SEEING CHANTEL felt like a lifetime to Marco. He was on his way to spend the night in Southampton at his mother's house. He was feeling happier and more alive than he'd ever felt in his life. And he thought to himself that tonight would be a good night to tell his mother about Chantel. Marco planned on proposing to her that coming weekend, right after his mother's holiday party.

Marco wasn't sure exactly how he was going to tell his mother about Chantel. He'd never spoke to her about a girlfriend before, let alone bring one home that he intended to marry. But since his feelings were so strong, he really wanted to tell her about Chantel. He wanted to share the excitement and joy that he felt in his heart.

When Marco arrived, Luna watched him come in and got up from the dining room table in the kitchen. Since her husband died, Marco always sat at the head of the table. Marco didn't know that his sister Laura was jealous of this seating arrangement. But Laura tended to be jealous of just about anything. Laura also felt that Marco got more attention from her parents in the past because he was a male. Marco was completely unaware of her jealousy. He was not the jealous type or competitive among his sisters. Laura didn't see things that way though. She carried a chip on her shoulder ever since her father didn't go to her college graduation and her mother didn't care.

One thing Luna loved to do was to cook for her family. She only used outside help when she entertained or needed the house cleaned. Sometimes she would do a little gardening herself. Gardening was the only hobby she had. She was not interested in many things outside her life at home and her children. She didn't have any particular interest in music, the arts, or reading books for that matter. Conversations with her were usually limited to specific topics. They often revolved around her deceased husband who died several years earlier. There was no joy in her personality. She didn't seem to care much about happiness or the happiness of others. Her children were used to her being that way. They simply accepted her the way she was.

"Hi Mom, how are you doing tonight?" Marco asked after he came into the house.

"Fine, dear. And you? How was work today? Are you still enjoying your job at Buckleven?" she asked him while he hung up his coat.

Marco grew used to questions regarding work. Work was the most important topic of conversation with his mother. Work came before anything. Saving money came second. And the importance of enjoying life or the fruits of one's labor treated as trivial. Work and frugality were the only things that mattered to Luna. Frugality was worshiped and esteemed like a false god. Everything else in life was discussed more or less on a superficial level. Luna was not concerned about the other needs of her children outside of work or making money. So their opinions on anything else were usually regarded as insignificant. Because of this, Luna's children were hesitant to open up to her. But Marco felt too strongly about Chantel and needed to tell his mother about his plans.

"Yes, I am. Things are going very well at Buckleven. I've also made a couple of good friends since I've been there. Ah, your dinner smells great. Chicken scallopini is one of my favorites. How about we have a glass of wine with that? Did you have any yet?" Marco asked her.

"No, I haven't. But let's eat in the formal dining room tonight. It's been a while since we've eaten in there. Laura already had her dinner. So, it'll just be the two of us."

Luna loved to have Marco to herself. In a way, she also regarded him as a surrogate husband. Marco was not aware that his mother viewed him this way. He was completely oblivious to how she really felt inside. He simply assumed that all mothers were sort of possessive and somewhat like her. In the meantime, Luna put their food on the table while Marco poured some wine into their glasses. Then they both sat down to eat together.

Marco looked at his mother with a big broad smile on his face, grinning from ear to ear, and said, "There's something important I want to tell you about, Mom. Something that might surprise you a lot."

Luna looked at him with a strange curiousness in her face.

"It's nothing bad, Mom. I want to tell you about a young lady that I met in New York City recently. We've been spending a lot of time together. And, I'm in love with her."

Marco figured that it would be best to tell her right out. He thought that certainly, she would understand what love was like. Surely, she was in love at least once in her own life with his father.

"And, I'm planning on proposing to her. I want to marry her after I finish my degree next semester."

But Luna was shocked and stunned. She had heard enough. She wondered how her son could be telling her something like this.

"What are you saying? You're in love? Who is this person?" she asked inquisitively, trying to keep her composure.

"Her name is Chantel Du Maurier. And again, I met her recently at a holiday party for Buckleven. She's simply wonderful. And I've been spending as much time with her as I can before I go back to school," he told her.

Luna braced herself with this answer, and asked some more questions, "You met her recently, did you? Where does she come from? What does she do? How can you possibly want to marry someone that you barely know?"

Marco smiled at her to try to make her feel more at ease.

"She is originally from a small town in Maine. She works at Bloomingdale's in the city. And I feel like I've known her much longer than I actually do. I'll admit. I'm in love."

"Come on. How do you know you really love her? Again, you barely know her. You can't know someone well enough to propose to them that quickly. You don't want to make a mistake, do you? Marriage is a serious thing."

Marco felt like he was being treated like a child being scolded for doing something wrong. Then he thought that she was probably just being a protective mother.

"I understand your concerns. But, I've been spending a lot of time with her. She's everything I want in a woman. She's funny and very easy to talk to. That's part of what I love about her the most. And I feel like I'm ready to settle down. I've only got one more semester at business school. Then I want to come back to New York, work at Buckleven or another investment firm, and marry Chantel."

"Do you have any idea what her family is like?" Luna asked.

"A modest one. They are not wealthy or anything. However, Chantel is very ambitious and is doing very well at her job at Bloomingdale's."

For a few moments, Luna was silent. She wasn't sure what else to say yet. She figured it was no use talking to him about his future plans. Instead, she figured that it might be a better idea to talk with Chantel herself. Remembering that she was having a holiday party on the weekend, she suggested to Marco to bring Chantel. Luna thought that perhaps she could handle the situation on her own. But Marco was being misled and thought it was a good sign that his mother had invited Chantel. He didn't have to ask her if it was okay to bring Chantel himself. Although, he had no idea what the real reason was and why his mother wanted Chantel to come to the party.

A modest family wasn't what Luna wanted to hear from her son's mouth. She wanted her son to marry someone who came from a family with a lot of money. She didn't want to tell him that though. She figured that Marco would probably bring Chantel to the party that weekend. So she planned to take advantage of the opportunity and to take care of the matter herself.

"Well, I'm looking forward to meeting Chantel. Make sure you bring her to the party. Now let's change the subject and finish our dinner. Then we can relax," Luna told him, already scheming in her mind what she would do to Chantel when she meets her.

"Great, Mother. I'm looking forward to introducing her to you."

Yet Marco would never imagine what would take place next.

CHAPTER 13

HREATS

BY THE WEEKEND, LUNA HAD HER HOME EXQUISITELY decorated for the holiday party. She had the landscapers decorate a stately, forty-foot Douglas fir tree with lights in front of her house. She also had them set up a large sled with decorative reindeer's next to it. And they also put lights on the other trees near the house and on the house itself. This made her home look very festive as if it was out of a holiday storybook.

Inside the house, Luna had a traditional Christmas tree decorated. It had lavish white and gold ornaments that she collected over the years. It was about nine feet high and placed in the entryway. There was also a large table display with different gingerbread houses and holiday novelties.

Thirty-five guests in all had been invited to the party. They were mostly people Luna had met while her husband was still alive. As they arrived, they complimented her on how lovely everything looked. Then they went inside to mingle at the party while servers offered them drinks and appetizers.

Luna even hired a pianist to play holiday songs for the night. That was unusual for her because she never listened to music on her own. And she and her daughter Laura spared no expense on new dresses to wear for the occasion. This was the only time Luna wasn't frugal. She found a stunning gold gown at Saks Fifth Avenue. And Laura found a lovely green velvet dress at Neiman Marcus. Laura looked quite pretty too. If it weren't for the extra twenty pounds she had recently gained, she would have been one of the most attractive women at the party.

Marco and Chantel hadn't arrived yet. They were still on their way from Manhattan. Marco had driven into the city to pick Chantel up and bring her to Southampton. He was dressed in a navy wool blazer, red corduroy pants, and shoes from Brooks Brothers. And Chantel had bought herself a new white satin dress made by Dior to wear for the occasion. She wanted to make a good impression on Marco's family. She looked heavenly in it.

It was about eight o'clock when they arrived at the house. By then, there were multiple cars parked in rows all around the driveway. After Marco parked his car, he and Chantel walked toward the house.

"We're finally here," he said cheerfully. "Come on. I'll show you around."

Just at that moment, Chantel looked up at the sky and saw a shooting star. "Did you just see that? I think I just saw a shooting star above that tree over there. That's incredible."

"What? Above the tree?"

"Yes, a shooting star," she answered.

"I've heard they're supposed to be good luck you know. Did you know that?" Marco asked her.

"I'm not sure about that. But it was wonderful to see one. I haven't seen one in years."

Chantel looked up again at the sky while Marco tugged her arm to follow him. Once inside the house, Marco led her to the main living room where he saw his mother talking to one of the guests at the party.

"Hey, there's my mother. Let's go and say hello to her. She's the one in the golden dress. And there's my sister Laura over there next to the bar station."

As they tried to make their way over to Luna, a petite woman server came over to them and asked them if they would like some champagne. She was holding up a tray of full glasses. They each took one and kept heading toward Luna.

Chantel looked around the room and thought the antiques and paintings she saw were beautiful and resembled pieces that she had recently seen at the Metropolitan Museum. She had never been in a home so ornately decorated before. It was nothing like the home in Maine where she grew up. And when she thought of Maine, she thought of her family and how much she missed them. Then Luna saw the two of them and went over to greet them.

Marco made the first move. "Mom, I'd like you to meet Chantel Du Maurier. This is the young lady I told you about. And Chantel, this is my mother, Luna."

Luna extended her hand to shake Chantel's. "Ah, yes, Chantel. I've heard good things about you. Welcome," said Luna coyly.

"Pleased to meet you, Mrs. Puccio. You have a very lovely home. It's so beautifully decorated for the holidays."

"Thank you. Please, call me Luna. You don't need to be so formal with me. So why don't the two of you go and eat something. I'll catch up with you two later on. I've got a few things to attend to at the moment," Luna told them, sizing Chantel up from head to toe.

"So what do you think?" Marco asked Chantel.

"I don't know. We didn't get to talk much."

"You will. I'm sure she'll love you as much as I do. Now let's get something to eat while all this food is being served. At Christmas, my mother goes all out."

Sure enough, there were tempting foods to try. There were smoked salmon rolls, shrimp, oysters, lobster tails, crab cakes, crab legs, and an assortment of roasted vegetables and salads. And there was an assortment of sweets such as cakes, cookies, chocolates, and fruits. There were also several liquors to accompany them after dinner.

The sound of piano music and people singing filled the house. Some people even sang opera songs while others were enjoying their cigars. By then, Chantel had already met many of the guests. She found them to be friendly, became more relaxed, and started to have a good time. A little later in the evening, Luna came up to Chantel and asked to have a word with her alone. Chantel followed her into what looked like a study. The room had mahogany wood bookcases and paneling. It was dark and kind of dreary looking compared to the rest of the house. Luna asked her to sit down at what looked like an old card table.

"Chantel, I want to have a talk with you. I understand that my son is quite smitten by you. So, let me get to the point. The problem is that he has informed me that he intends to propose to you. And I know that you are not the kind of woman for my son. He comes from a different world than you do. He should be with someone who comes from the same. You will never fit in our family and circle of friends. I'm asking you to stop seeing him and to let him go. Or else, I will do everything in my power to make both of your lives miserable." Luna told her this with no compassion or remorse. "I will disinherit him from my estate and never see him again. I lost my husband. And, I'm not going to lose my son to a gold digger like you."

Chantel was shocked. No one had ever spoken to her so cruelly before. She felt like she was in the middle of a nightmare and the experience was surreal. But she knew it was real. Then she looked at Luna with fear and disgust. She had never met such a nasty and mean person in her life. And she never wanted to see this woman ever again for the rest of her life. This was Luna. She couldn't believe that she was such a cruel person. Chantel was speechless.

"Well, I guess you have nothing to say. Remember what I

told you. He will lose everything if he marries you. If you really love him, let him go. Or else," warned Luna leaving the room.

Chantel felt like throwing up. But she wouldn't allow herself to do so. She didn't want to draw any more attention to herself, not even with Marco being there. She felt that being around a woman like Luna would be a miserable future anyway. She wondered how Marco could be so kind with a mother that was so mean. She also thought that it would not be good for Marco either to get disinherited from a future estate. She thought that perhaps she should give him up. Luna seemed like a curse to her.

Chantel went back inside to the party and found Marco as quickly as she could. He was discussing economics with one of the guests. She walked up to him, tapped him on the shoulders, and asked him if they could go right away. She told him that she was not feeling well and wanted to go home. He offered her some medicine to make her feel better. But she told him that she didn't want any. So they got their coats, said goodbye to Marco's family, and left.

"You know, you were the prettiest woman there tonight," Marco told Chantel on their way back to Manhattan.

"Thanks, Marco."

"When we get to your apartment, do you mind if I stay with you for a little while? I miss you so much. I just want to be with you a little longer tonight."

Chantel didn't know what to say to him. She was experiencing a whole range of difficult emotions. Her heart felt like it was being shredded into a thousand pieces. But she didn't want to turn him away completely that night.

When they arrived on the East Side, Marco parked his car and went upstairs with Chantel to her apartment. Chantel began feeling worse. The horrid words she heard from Luna's mouth were repeating in her head. She started feeling even more sick to her stomach and nauseated.

"Chantel, are you okay? I've never seen you like this," asked Marco.

"I'm not sure exactly. I'm just not the same," Chantel answered.

"Well, I've got something to help make you feel a whole lot better." Then Marco kissed her and said, "I want you to know that I love you very much. I meant it when I told you that. I know things might be moving a little quickly for us, but I'm certain that my love is genuine and will just get stronger for you."

Marco took out a little red jewelry box from his pocket. It was also from Cartier. He looked deep into her eyes and let out a deep breath, almost as if he was blowing out candles on a birthday cake.

"Chantel, as you know I'll be going back to school soon to finish my degree. I only have one more semester. But I don't want to lose you. You are the love of my life. I just know it. So I want to ask you a very important question that has to do with the rest of our lives. It has to do with the fact that we fell in love. Yes, in love. I now know the most beautiful and joyful experience in the world is falling in love. I cannot find all the right words to describe what this feels like for me. I can only tell you that I cannot lose you. I'm asking that you wait for me."

Marco kneeled down on the floor and opened the box he was holding in his hand. There was a round diamond on a white gold band inside. At that very moment, Chantel felt the happiest and the saddest she had ever felt in her life.

"Chantel, I would like to marry you when I finish my degree. But in the meantime, I would like us to become engaged to each other. I would like us to promise one another that we will marry then. Will you become my fiancé and marry me?" he asked her, taking the ring outside of the box to give to her.

But Chantel didn't want to say yes. She looked at him and said, "Marco, I'm not sure this will work out. You know, I was thinking, maybe we both need more time. I can't promise you this right now. I'm so sorry. I just can't. I really need to think about this some more." Then she started to cry.

"What are you saying? What has happened? You told me that you love me just as much as I love you, Chantel. What about our weekend at Harry's together? What has changed since then?"

"Again, I'm sorry, Marco. I need more time to think things over. I can't promise you right now. So please keep the ring until I sort this out."

Chantel felt like she wanted to die that very moment. She thought of how horrid his mother was and that she didn't want Luna destroying their lives. She knew she loved Marco more than anyone or anything in the world. But she had to think things over. She didn't want their lives ruined. She thought to herself that perhaps she should let him go for his own sake, even though he wouldn't know why or understand the reason.

Then Marco had tears in his eyes and asked her again, "What do you mean by all of this? I really love you. And, I know that you really love me. I've never loved anyone else like you. Please, think this over. Think it over again."

"Marco, I need some time by myself. I don't want to hurt you. I just feel that I need some distance. Please understand and forgive me."

But Marco didn't know what was going on, and he cried. Then he reached for some tissues in one of his pockets to wipe his tears away.

"I want you to know that you will always remain in my heart. I just can't promise you that I will marry you, Marco," she continued.

"But," he said clearing his throat.

She interrupted him and said, "I can't promise this right now."

Then she went into her bedroom and brought out the necklace and charm that he'd given to her in Montauk. She asked him to take it back for now. She knew it was expensive, and she knew it would only remind her of him.

But Marco insisted that Chantel keep the necklace and charm. He told her that if she changes her mind to let him know. He also reminded her that he'd only be in the city a little longer until he goes back to school. Then she opened the door to her apartment, and Marco left.

Marco was very confused and needed to clear his head. So

he decided to take a walk around Sutton Place. When he got there, he found a bench to sit on at a little park that looked out onto the East River. He sat there and wondered what had gone wrong. It never occurred to him that his own mother might be responsible. He figured it had to be something else. He stayed there for a long time looking out at the shadows in the river. Then he decided to go to Harry's apartment to get some sleep.

ROMOTION

GLANCING AT THE TIME, CHANTEL TOLD ONE OF THE SALES girls at the Champs counter that she had to leave for a meeting at corporate offices. She asked her to keep an eye on things while she was gone. Chantel was to report to the human resources department and meet with Priscilla Brooks, one of the Champs human resources executives. She was told to be there by three o'clock in the afternoon. Chantel wasn't exactly sure why she was asked to go. She hoped, however, that upper management had recognized some of her hard work and dedication. Chantel knew that ever since she started at Champs that she'd been quickly raising sales for them at Bloomingdale's. The Champs counter in Manhattan had quickly become the most profitable one in the country. Chantel was beginning to stand out. A lot of people around her noticed her drive and talent and either admired or envied her.

Earlier that morning, Chantel took great care in getting dressed and chose to wear a tan linen suit with a tailored white blouse. She wore her hair conservatively, pulled up into a French bun, and applied her makeup professionally. This preparation gave her a look of youth, promise, beauty, and health, all to make a flawless impression.

Champs corporate offices were only a short walk away on Park Avenue and Fifty-ninth Street. The walk to the building only took about ten minutes. When she arrived there, she saw a receptionist sitting at a desk on the telephone answering a mountain of calls. The buttons on her phone were flashing continuously. It was easy to tell that she was frustrated from the volume. When she caught up with the calls, she lowered the phone from her ear and looked over at Chantel. She also admired Chantel's suit and wished she had one like it herself.

"Can I help you?" she asked.

"Yes, my name is Chantel Du Maurier. I have an appointment with Priscilla Brooks. Can you please tell her that I am here?" answered Chantel with poise and confidence.

"Is she expecting you?"

"Yes, she is."

Then the receptionist pushed an intercom button on her phone. "Mrs. Brooks. Miss Du Maurier is here to see you." She paused. "Yes, I'll tell her. Please have a seat. Mrs. Brooks will be with you in a few minutes."

It wasn't for seven more minutes until Priscilla Brooks

appeared from a doorway behind the receptionist desk. She signaled Chantel with her hands to follow her. The touch of gray in her hair and the noticeable lines on her face made her look about sixty. She was actually ten years older than that, but years of diligent skin care had paid off for her. She was also wearing a suit. But hers looked custom made. It was dark navy and much more traditional than Chantel's. She was also very attractive. One would imagine that she was quite popular in her day.

"Miss Du Maurier, please have a seat," she said, after shaking Chantel's hand and brushing her skirt off beside her.

Chantel sat down across from her desk and looked at her anxiously.

"I am very pleased that you could make it today. I guess you are wondering why I have asked you to come in. Well, I have very good news for you. Whether you know this or not, in a very short time, you are the most outstanding retail sales manager we've had at Champs in a long time. Naturally, we are thrilled with your performance. And given this performance, the executives at Champs would like to offer you another promotion into our sales and marketing groups here at corporate offices. We think we can better utilize your talent here. And our company would provide any necessary training you might need. You would also have opportunities to get involved with product development. We create and design new products here as well. So, what are your feelings about what I have just told you? If you need more time to think any of it over, that's fine also," said Mrs. Brooks.

Then Mrs. Brooks lifted a silver pitcher sitting on her desk and poured a glass of water, watching Chantel's facial expressions carefully.

Overwhelmed by the good news, Chantel just sat there quietly for a few moments to collect her thoughts. Then, she looked at Mrs. Brooks, with a sigh of relief, and answered, "I would love to have this opportunity. It's exactly what I've been hoping for. And I love working for Champs."

Mrs. Brooks sat deeper into her chair, relieved to hear a positive response. "Wonderful. We would like you to begin on Monday. And please, take the weekend off. This is your last day at Bloomingdale's. Does that work for you?"

Chantel replied, "Yes, it works perfectly."

"Good. And of course, you will be getting a considerable raise along with this promotion. We were thinking in the range of. " Silently Mrs. Brooks wrote a figure on a piece of paper and passed it to Chantel. "Is this acceptable to you?"

Stunned by the number, Chantel replied, "Yes. Yes it is."

"Very good. We want you to be happy." She paused. "The person you will be reporting to directly is Gordon Miles. He is director of sales, marketing, and product development. Gordon is very eager for you to get started. He is traveling today, so he could not join us. On Monday, you should go straight to his office at nine in the morning. Security will show you where it is. I wish you the best of luck."

"Thank you. Thank you very much. I will continue to work hard here at Champs," replied Chantel, both dazed and excited, thinking how proud her parents would be if they knew.

After they shook hands, Chantel left Mrs. Brooks office and

walked to the elevators. When she got outside the building, she had to pinch herself. She thought about all of her dreams and the career possibilities at Champs in her future. The promotion made her feel very happy inside. Her spirit felt so high that she wondered if she would ever come back down to earth. She was overjoyed that this part of her life was going so well. She also felt that no one could take that away from her, especially Luna.

CHAPTER 15

A NIGHTMARE

AFTER HER MEETING WITH MRS. BROOKS, CHANTEL RETURNED to Bloomingdale's to tell her co-workers about her promotion. She explained to the salespeople that she would be working at corporate offices from now on and that she would miss all of them very much. They weren't that surprised, congratulated her, and wished her the best.

It was the same day when Steve Woods walked into Bloomingdale's. He had a chauffeured limo drop him off. Kate had taken a trip to Europe to visit some friends and suggested that it might be a good time for him to stop by some of his New York competitors. She left the children in Greenwich and had Maria looking after them. Steve thought it was a good idea also. So he decided to go to Bloomingdale's to look at what the store was selling and its competitiveness. When he arrived there, he observed the merchandise he saw and compared it to what he had available at Woods. He did this at least once or twice a year. He came straight over from his office wearing one of his expensive Dunhill suits with an Armani tie. He also wore glasses so as not to be so recognizable.

As Steve passed through the main floor, he immediately noticed Chantel. He was also instantly attracted to her. She didn't have her Champs frock on any longer. He admired her from afar and followed her with his eyes as she walked around the Champs counter. He admired her beautiful face and slim and sexy body. He wanted to meet her and decided to think of an excuse to go over to her. Then he thought he'd pretend that he was there to buy perfume for his mother. In reality, his mother was no longer living. He figured it would give him a reason to approach her. And since Kate was away, he thought he'd take advantage of his freedom. He didn't wear his wedding band that day. He wanted to pretend that he was available. After he watched Chantel for a while, he started to feel sexually aroused and lusted after her. He reckoned he would give her a try. Then he walked over to Chantel at the Champs counter.

"Excuse me, I'm wondering if you work here or not? I'm looking for a perfume for my mother. And, I'm hoping for something new and different. Can you help me, please?" Steve asked her, trying to appear as honest and as personable as he could. He wanted to make a good first impression.

Chantel looked at him with the usual politeness and warmth

that she always gave customers. "Yes I do. I can help you. What kind of fragrance does she like?"

"Something sweet and maybe a little woodsy," answered Steve, thinking of how clever he was since his last name was Woods.

After searching through a collection of perfume bottles on the counter, Chantel picked up a bottle called First Forest. Then she sprayed a sample on a paper swatch for him to smell.

"Maybe she would like this one. It has extracts of sandalwood and citrus in it and is quite refreshing. We also have some others which she might like as well," replied Chantel.

"Actually, this is perfect. I'm sure she'll be very pleased. Could you give me the largest bottle you have?" he requested, thinking of what to say next.

"Certainly. Would you like it gift wrapped?"

"Yes, that would be terrific. I'd really appreciate it," he told her, thinking that she was even more attractive up close.

Chantel wrapped the perfume on the counter in front of him. She thought he looked somewhat intriguing and felt oddly attracted to him for some reason she didn't fully comprehend. There was something about him that made her feel drawn. But she didn't know exactly what it was. She thought that he looked very sophisticated and had an air of worldliness about him.

Steve wanted to keep the conversation going, so he asked her, "Have you worked at Bloomingdale's for long?"

"Not very long," Chantel answered.

"Do you like it here?" he asked.

"Yes, but actually, it's my last day here at the counter."

"I see. You are going to work somewhere else I gather. It's too bad for Champs. I'm sure it's a loss for them," Steve commented.

"Actually, I'm not leaving Champs. I've just been promoted to our corporate offices."

Steve found this interesting and asked, "Here in Manhattan?"

"Yes, as a matter of fact. At the Park Avenue and Fifty-ninth Street headquarters to be exact," replied Chantel.

"They have very good taste. Then you'll still be in this neighborhood. It's a great one to work in. I have a store myself not far from here on Fifty-seventh Street. I know the location well."

Becoming more curious, Chantel asked, "What kind of store? What kind of merchandise do you sell?"

"Oh, it's a department store like this called Woods. I'm Steve Woods. What is your name by the way?"

"I'm Chantel Du Maurier. It must be great having a store like that in Manhattan. So why would you be shopping in here?"

"Good question, Chantel. Well, I like to check out the competition once in a while. And, I've always been a fan of Bloomingdale's myself. We also don't carry exactly the same merchandise all the time," he reasoned aloud. Then he paused to catch his breath and get his thoughts together to plan his next move. "So are you doing anything special to celebrate your promotion?"

"Not yet. It happened so suddenly. I haven't had time to plan anything special yet," she answered, putting the perfume inside a bag on the counter.

"Well, guess what? I'm also celebrating. Maybe we can celebrate together. I don't mean to be forward. But, would you like to have dinner with me tonight?"

Surprised and flattered from the invitation, Chantel asked, "What are you celebrating?" She looked at him curiously, waiting for a response.

"My horses won today. It's a hobby of mine. I bet on a few different horses, and they all won. I'm really excited about that." He turned his head to one side, trying to look impressive and pleased with himself. Then he made a funny expression on his face and smiled back at Chantel making her laugh.

Chantel was not in the habit of going out with male customers. But she felt attracted to him. She was moved by his intense blue eyes, dark eyebrows, and distinguished looks. She thought that there was something charismatic about him. Yet, he was older than most of the men she normally would find attractive or go out with. She wondered to herself how old he might be, but decided not to care. She was just too excited from her promotion. Then she thought that it would be nice to have someone to celebrate with. And since he owned a department store, Chantel figured she might even learn something more about merchandise and the retail business.

"There's a restaurant I'm planning on going to anyway to celebrate," Steve added.

"Okay, let's celebrate together, Steve. But I want you to

know that I don't usually go out with customers. I mean clients. This will be a first."

"I understand. What time do you finish work? I was planning on heading up there soon. It's a jazz and supper club I know on York Avenue and Seventy-sixth Street called Bells. They have live entertainment there. It's mostly jazz music of course."

"Actually, I was planning on leaving in a few minutes."

"Good, we can have cocktails at the bar and stay there for dinner if we like. I also happen to have a car waiting outside on Third Avenue and Sixtieth Street. How about I give you a couple of minutes to yourself and wait for you outside?" Steve asked her.

"All right. I'll meet you there soon."

Chantel wondered if it was wise or not to accept the invitation. But she did want to celebrate her promotion. She thought the opportunity of celebrating with Steve seemed like it might be fun. She also felt incredibly good inside from her good news.

Then Chantel spent the next few minutes organizing the Champs counter for the very last time. She knew a new chapter in her life was beginning. She also knew that she would miss working at Bloomingdale's. But for now, life offered her new and probably better challenges and opportunities. These were challenges and opportunities that she had dreamed of and wanted so much. Before she left, there was only one salesperson left besides her who stopped to wish her good luck and to say goodbye. Then she took one more look at the Champs counter, checked her makeup, and headed outside to meet Steve.

When she got outside, she saw him standing near a large black limo next to another man. And when Steve saw her, he waved at her to come over.

"Chantel, Here I am. Are you ready to go?"

"Yes. I'm ready. Is this your limo?"

"It is. And this is Ben, our driver for tonight. Hope you don't mind. I don't like to drive myself. And I'm not too fond of taxies either."

"No, not at all," Chantel said.

Chantel wasn't overly impressed by the limo. After all, she knew Marco had used them also from time to time. She tried not to let things like that impress her too much. She did think it was convenient though. She also thought that it was kind of glamorous riding around in one. It was sort of a novelty to her. Steve's limo was a stretch. So it was very long. It reminded her of some of the ones she had seen in movies. This one had a full bar inside of it and an assortment of different snacks. There was also a tinted electric glass window between them and Ben the driver.

When Chantel and Steve arrived at Bells, a bouncer spotted them right away and opened the limo's door for them. Then he spun around quickly to open the entrance door to the club. Bells was very well-known. It had an excellent reputation for music. Many celebrities frequently went there and were often seen.

When they got inside, they sat down at the bar. It was very crowded already with people coming in from after work. They soon decided to stay for dinner. Steve asked the manager if they could eventually get a table in the dining room. There was a new jazz ensemble playing that evening. Steve was not familiar with them. But he wanted a nice table, so he gave the manager a hundred dollar bill because he didn't have a reservation. This made the manager quite content. He thanked Steve and told him he could have a table whenever they were ready. But Steve told him that he wanted to wait a little while at the bar. Then one of the bartenders came over to them and asked them what they would like to drink. Steve thought they should order champagne. He knew most women loved champagne. And they were supposed to be celebrating that night.

"Is champagne okay with you, Chantel?" Steve wanted to check with her before ordering a bottle.

"Yes, it's fine with me."

"Well then, we'll have a bottle of the Louis Roederer," said Steve to the bartender.

"Very well, sir. It'll just be a moment."

The bartender quickly disappeared and soon returned with a large silver bucket of ice and a cold bottle of champagne. He opened it for them and poured some into each of their glasses. Steve raised his glass in front of Chantel.

"Congratulations on your promotion."

Then Chantel raised her glass toward his, and said, "And congratulations to you on your winnings today."

Steve loved to hear that. He only occasionally told his wife Kate anything about betting. Kate hated to hear about such things but tolerated what she did know. So Steve was getting a kick out of being congratulated for the idea of it.

"Thank you. You know somehow Chantel I have the feeling

you don't originally come from New York. Am I right?" Steve asked.

Having met so many people from all over the place, Steve had a pretty good intuition as to what her answer might be. But, he just couldn't place where she came from exactly.

"I'm from Maine actually. I'm from a town named Southport. It's located along the Atlantic coast," Chantel told him.

"I've never heard of Southport up in Maine. But I bet it's very quaint. Most of Maine is quite nice. It's much quieter there than it is in Manhattan though."

Steve imagined to himself that she probably wasn't very worldly. In his mind, women from small towns were more vulnerable than those from big cities. He figured that she couldn't be too clever if she came from some smaller place up in Maine. Then he glanced at her blouse and her breasts, pretending to be looking at the bubbles in his glass of champagne. He felt lust for her again and wondered how he could get her into bed.

"So how do you like it here in New York so far?" asked Steve.

"It's quite a bit different. But I really love it here," Chantel told him.

"So what are you going to be doing in your new job?"

"Well, I will continue to work with beauty products and probably get more involved in product development. I really like perfumes. I'd also like to create something of my own one day."

Steve almost choked on the cashew he was chewing on. He

thought to himself, don't they all have such ambitions? He wasn't taking her seriously and couldn't care less about her dreams or future. He thought again about how he would get her into bed later that night. But he wanted to seduce her, so he pretended to care about what she was saying.

"I wish you nothing but the best of future success, Chantel. I'm sure you'll do spectacularly. I can tell you're bright and have a lot of talent. That's probably why you were promoted," he told her, trying to flatter her, make her feel good, and gain her trust.

"So, tell me, what's it like owning a store in Manhattan? That must be really incredible. But I'm sure it can be very demanding as well. Where is it located exactly on Fifty-seventh Street?" Chantel asked him.

"It's between Fifth and Sixth Avenues."

"That's a great area," commented Chantel. She was becoming more taken by him.

Steve wanted to change the subject. The last thing he wanted to do was talk about work. But before he did, he asked one of the waiters to move them to their table for dinner and ordered more champagne. The jazz ensemble had just started their performance. After they were seated and ordered their entrees, Steve wanted to get a little more personal.

"I'm just wondering, Chantel, do you have a boyfriend? You're such an attractive woman," he asked her.

Chantel looked down at the tablecloth and twirled one of her forks in the air. For a moment, she felt sad because the question reminded her of Marco.

"I did for a while. But it didn't work out," she told him.

Chantel thought this was a good time to ask him if he had a girlfriend also. She hoped that he would tell her no.

"What about you, Steve? Do you have a girlfriend? Someone steady?" Chantel asked him.

"Well, to be honest with you, I'm in the middle of a rather nasty divorce. My wife fell in love with another man and decided to leave me. Right now, she's in Europe with him living it up. The only correspondence I have with her are from her attorneys. It's really sad," Steve told Chantel, hoping to get her to feel sympathetic towards him.

"I understand. Sounds like a real difficult time for you."

Chantel believed what he told her and began to feel a little sorry for him. His situation reminded her a bit of her own heart being at a loss with her first love Marco.

"Yes, but we're celebrating tonight remember. It's not too bad. She's been gone a while now. I'm just waiting for my attorney to finish up our divorce agreements. Our property and everything else hasn't been worked out yet. We still have to divide our real estate and other assets. But this should all be finalized in the near future. I just want to get on with my life, like being with you tonight for example."

There was no way for Chantel to know that Steve was being deceitful and lying through his teeth. Steve just wanted to give the impression that he would be entirely divorced and single soon.

Chantel was curious and asked, "Where are your homes?"

"One is in Manhattan and one is in Greenwich, Connecticut.

I spend most of my time here in Manhattan though. It's not too far from my store. It's on Central Park South facing Central Park," he answered.

Chantel nodded at Steve and acknowledged his answers. Then they ate their dinners and sipped on some more champagne. Chantel also thought a little more about Marco again. Even though she was attracted to Steve and felt sorry for him, she realized that she still loved Marco. And even though she tried so hard to bury her feelings for Marco, it was still a struggle to do so. But as the music played on in the dining room, Chantel and Steve became more relaxed. Steve took one of her hands and kissed it tenderly with his lips. It wasn't long after that before he asked her if she would like to visit his apartment after dinner. He told her about the views of Central Park that he would like to show to her. Chantel was curious and agreed to go for a little while.

When they got outside, Ben was still waiting for them. Steve asked him to take them to his apartment. When they arrived at the building, a doorman ran to one of the limo doors to open it for them. Steve usually didn't bring women to his apartment. But tonight he made an exception because Kate really was in Europe and would never catch him. He also thought that it would be more thrilling to bring Chantel there. And Steve knew the doormen would lose their jobs if they ever told his wife Kate that he brought a woman to their apartment. Steve was very friendly with the management company of the building and knew all the top executives there. So, if any of the doormen told Kate about it, it would be serious trouble for them.

When they got upstairs to the apartment, Steve took Chantel into the main living room that did indeed have stunning views of the park. The apartment itself was extremely luxurious. It was a duplex and as large as some houses. It was filled with antiques and gold finishes, incredible paintings, and exquisite furniture. Chantel was spellbound. She had never seen an apartment like it, not even on television. Then Steve went to get them after dinner drinks. He brought back some liquor that he knew was quite strong. Then he put the glasses down on a marble coffee table and asked her to join him.

"This is an extraordinary apartment, Steve," Chantel remarked.

Steve put one arm around her shoulder and held up her drink with the other. He put the glass to her lips.

"Thank you. It's relaxing looking out at the park, isn't it? You can even see some stars tonight if you look closely," he said, stroking her hair.

"Yes, I see some. It's really beautiful. You're so lucky to have a place like this. But tell me a little more about yourself?"

Steve took a deep breath. He wasn't focusing on talking about himself at the moment. But he had to keep the conversation going to make her feel more comfortable and to maintain her trust.

"Well, I like sailing a lot. Sometimes I sail up to Rhode Island with some friends of mine. I also like to play golf and tennis."

"Oh, yes, you probably mean Newport, Rhode Island. I have heard of it. It is well-known for yacht racing and sailing, isn't it?

And I understand there are a lot of old mansions there as well. I'd like to go there myself one day," Chantel told him.

"That's right. Newport is the place for sailing. One of my friends has a very large yacht up there that I've sailed on quite a bit, especially in the summer and on weekends. There's a picture of me on the yacht over there," said Steve, pointing to a photograph displayed on a table nearby.

Steve could tell that Chantel was beginning to feel a bit dizzy and intoxicated. So he decided it was a good time to coax her into one of the bedrooms upstairs. He asked her if she would like to see the rest of the apartment. He planned on making his move and just wanted a place to take her. He also brought up their glasses so they could have some more to drink. Then he brought her to a sofa in a sitting area that was part of a large bedroom. It was the master bedroom that he and Kate shared. Steve asked her to sit next to him on the sofa and started to kiss her.

"How are you feeling, sweety?"

Chantel started to feel really drunk. She wasn't used to drinking as much as she did with him and wondered if something was wrong with her last drink. She started to feel completely out of balance and hoped the feeling would pass. "I'm a little dizzy."

But the room started to get quite blurry to Chantel. So Steve suggested that she lay down on the bed. After they laid down together, Steve started kissing her again. But this time he was getting more aggressive. Then he started to unbutton her blouse, unhook her bra, and touch her breasts with his hands.

"Steve, what are you doing? Don't do that. Come on. Stop. I didn't come here for that," she told him, slurring her words, trying to roll away from him.

Steve didn't pay any attention to what she was saying and continued to take off her blouse and bra. Chantel was too intoxicated to push him away. Then he pulled off her skirt, took off her pantyhose, and pulled down her panties until she was completely naked. Then he undressed himself as quickly as he could and touched every part of her body with his hands and tongue. He played with her entire body some more and spread her legs apart in front of him. He also played with himself. And when he felt he was hard enough, he got on top of her and forced himself inside of her.

"Stop, Steve. No. No. No. Please don't do this to me!" Chantel yelled out, trying to push him off of her. But she didn't have the strength and coordination to do so.

"I know what you want, Chantel. That's what you're really here for, isn't it. I know you want it as much as I do. I'm going to give you what you want, baby," he told her, ignoring what she said completely.

"No. Don't!" she yelled out again.

But Chantel still couldn't push him away. She felt like the entire room was spinning all around her. Chantel groaned and moaned in pain. But Steve still ignored her. He just kept forcing himself inside of her as deep and as hard as he could.

"Come on. I know you want this. I know you do. That's why you are moaning so much. You don't want me to stop. You want more, don't you? I know you women always say no when you mean yes," he said to her as he continued to push even deeper and harder inside of her.

The only thing that Chantel felt now was the pain of him thrusting himself inside of her over and over, harder and harder, hurting her inside. He didn't stop until he came. But once wasn't enough for him. He continued to force her to have sex with him for several more hours until he was too tired to have sex anymore. Then he finally stopped and left her alone on the bed.

Chantel was in shock. She realized what had just happened to her. But she couldn't yet find the strength to move. She started shivering and cried. Then she fell asleep. When she woke up in the morning, she remembered everything from the night before. And she felt awful and filthy. She felt like dying from the nightmare of what Steve did to her. She went into the bathroom and vomited. And when she came out, she noticed a note on one of the dressers beside the bed. It said that Ben the driver would be available in front of the building to take her anywhere she wanted to go in the city. Then she got dressed, fixed her hair, and left. When she got outside, she saw Ben and got inside the limo. She didn't want anyone seeing her. So she asked him to take her home to her apartment.

After Chantel entered her apartment, she looked at herself in a mirror and began to cry. Then she took a shower and thought about what had happened to her. She wished it had only been a bad dream. But she knew what happened was real. She realized she was raped. This ugly reality began to haunt her now. She thought about how stupid she was to go to Steve's apartment. Then she went into her bedroom, laid down on her bed, and cried for the rest of the day and night. She wondered what she should do about it. She wasn't sure yet. It was too shocking, too painful, and too horrifying. She wondered how Steve could have done this to her. And if that wasn't enough, she also felt the physical pain and soreness between her legs where he had pene-trated inside of her for hours.

CHAPTER 16

Hope

MARCO LET SOME TIME PASS BEFORE APPROACHING DORA AT work. He had tried to get in touch with Chantel ever since he last saw her, but he couldn't get through to her. He walked over to her apartment building several times to see if she was home. But each time he went, there was no answer. He began to figure out that she was completely avoiding seeing him. But he still didn't know why. He couldn't comprehend what he had done wrong and why she didn't want to see him anymore. He just didn't understand.

Dora was sitting at her desk working on a letter when Marco approached her. He figured he would try to find out any information he could get from her. It was late in the afternoon, and many people had already left the office.

"Dora, how have you been?" asked Marco, looking rather lost.

Startled for a moment, Dora glanced up at Marco and regained her composure. She was embarrassed because she knew that Chantel no longer wanted to see Marco and that he wanted to marry her. She felt very sorry for him.

"I'm okay, Marco. I've just been busy with a lot of work. John's been keeping me out of trouble working late on a couple of deals. That's the nature of the business though."

"Yes, I know what you mean. But I came to see you to talk about a personal matter. Would you have some time after work today? I would like to talk to you about Chantel. I know the two of you are best friends." Marco looked at Dora with both hope and sadness in his eyes.

Dora could tell that he was upset and couldn't say no to him.

"Sure Marco. Actually, I should be finished soon. Where would you like to talk?" Dora asked, with a compassionate tone of voice.

"Would Bianchi's be okay? We can get a table near the bar. How about we meet there in half an hour?" Marco asked her.

"Sure. That's fine with me. I'll see you there, Marco. Don't worry," Dora said, as she smiled at him, fussing with some papers on her desk, putting them under a heavy glass paperweight that she'd recently bought at The Museum of Modern Art gift shop nearby.

Marco felt a little relieved. At least he'd be able to share his feelings with someone who knew him and Chantel both, someone who might be able to give him some answers. He didn't want to talk about it with Harry yet. He hadn't told Harry that he had proposed to Chantel. Marco didn't want to tell him that Chantel wasn't talking to him anymore. He felt the situation was too confusing at the moment.

On his way to Bianchi's, Marco passed the Rockefeller Center skating rink. He had remembered a time when he and Chantel went there together. He remembered them holding each other in their arms, watching the skaters, and laughing at their falls. But now his happiness was at a loss. He felt cheated by life somehow. He wondered why he was losing the first woman he ever loved.

When Marco got to Bianchi's, he found a small table where he and Dora could talk. A few minutes later, a waiter came up to him to ask him what he would like to order. He decided to get a vodka martini on the rocks. Marco concluded this was no time for a glass of wine. He needed something a little stronger to help him settle his emotions and his mind. When the waiter arrived with his drink, he quickly took a big gulp and put the glass down in front of him. It wasn't long before Dora arrived. When she saw him, she walked over to the table he was seated at and joined him.

"Well, here I am, Marco. Made it. Today is actually a good day to meet. Sometimes, I'm not sure when I'm going to get out of the office. John didn't want me to stay too late today," Dora said, as she pulled her chair into place and rubbed her eyes, looking a little stressed and tired. "Sure is cold out there. We might get snow later tonight."

"I hope not. It makes driving to Southampton much more

difficult. Anyhow, thanks for coming. I really appreciate it. I haven't talked to anyone about this. I mean my situation with Chantel. I'm pretty puzzled by it," said Marco.

The same waiter came over to their table and asked Dora what she would like to drink.

"I'll have a glass of the house chardonnay. I'm also starving, so I think I'll order some sliders with that. I skipped lunch this afternoon," Dora told the waiter, pointing at the menu in front of her.

"Coming right up," said the waiter, acknowledging her requests.

Then Marco ordered another drink for himself. He didn't feel like eating. He was too upset to think about food for the moment. Then he began inquiring about Chantel with a look of desperation.

"Dora, have you spoken to Chantel lately? I've been trying to reach her by telephone. I have even walked over to her apartment a few times. I know that she's avoiding me. Ever since I told her that I wanted to marry her, I haven't been able to get in touch with her. The last time I saw her, it seemed like there was someone else, as if another person was the reason she could not marry me. I'm hoping this isn't true. Do you know if there is someone else? I don't really know. I just don't understand. I thought she was in love with me. I felt her love. But now, I don't know anymore. It's bewildering, to say the least," Marco said to her, explaining his thoughts.

Then their waiter interrupted them when he delivered their drinks and Dora's sliders.

"I know it's difficult, Marco. But for some reason, she just can't bear to see you anymore. I thought she loved you also. And, I don't feel like she is purposely intending to hurt you. I feel like there's something we don't know about her. Like, there's something she is hiding from us. I wish I could help you, but I just don't know what to do or say," Dora answered, while taking a bite of one of the burgers on her plate.

Marco sipped on his drink and asked the waiter for another. He was distraught. Dora could tell he was holding back his tears.

"What about another guy? Do you think one exists?"

"I don't really know, Marco. Truthfully, I've never seen her with another guy. That's the strange part in all of this. That's the part that doesn't make any sense. I can't figure out why she's doing this. I wish I understood myself. You two were really getting close, just like soul mates. I could sense it. And she never said anything bad about you to me. It's all so strange."

Marco took a deep breath and asked her, "Would you mind getting a message to her from me? I'd really appreciate it. Especially since she no longer works at Bloomingdale's, I have no way to run into her myself."

"Of course, Marco. What do you want me to say?" asked Dora.

"Tell her that I've been trying to reach her. I know she already knows that though. Tell her that I still love her very much. Tell her that I'll always be there for her. She knows that I'm going back to UCLA to finish my degree. But if there is a chance at all for her and I, please tell her to contact me there.

Here's my address and a local number in California where she can reach me. I'll be leaving Buckleven in only a few days." Marco again held back his tears. He didn't want to cry in front of Dora or in a public restaurant.

Dora could see what Marco was going through. Her heart had been broken once too. She also thought that there had to be a really odd reason why Chantel didn't want to see him anymore.

"I'll do what I can, Marco. But I can't promise you that she will contact you. That's up to her. But I will tell her what you want me to. By the way, I'll miss you at the office. I wish you all the luck in the world."

Marco looked at Dora with gratitude in his eyes. "Thanks. Before I forget, will you give this to her also? It's a Christmas present. Tell her that no matter what, I would like her to have this," said Marco, shuffling through his suit jacket.

Then Marco put a small gift box on the table, wondering if it would be the last present he would ever get to give Chantel.

"I would like you to give this to her on Christmas Eve if possible."

Dora was so moved by Marco's sentimentality that she felt like crying herself.

"You can count on me, Marco. You're so good and kind. One of the best guys I've ever met. I hope you don't mind me saying this, but I think it would be a terrible mistake for her to let you go."

"Let's hope not, Dora. I will try to hold on to hope for a while."

"That's what love is all about, Marco."

Then they talked a little longer about Buckleven, the city, and went their separate ways.

~

MARCO DECIDED TO GO TO SOUTHAMPTON FOR THE NIGHT. As usual, his mother Luna had dinner waiting for him on the dining room table. Marco told her he wasn't hungry. Then he went into his bedroom and closed the door behind him.

Luna knew what was wrong. She was pleased that she wouldn't hear any more talk about Chantel. This made her feel good. She felt like she had won over Chantel and was untouched by her son's unhappiness. She convinced herself that there would be another woman out there for him. It would be someone who she would approve of and someone with financial means.

CHAPTER 17

EARLS

It was Christmas Eve, and Chantel and Dora decided to go to a favorite neighborhood restaurant called Pearls. Dora had originally introduced Chantel to the place. It was walking distance to Chantel's apartment. They liked it there because there were always regular customers they knew at the bar. And since neither of them was going to see their families during the holidays, they decided to go there for dinner.

Dora noticed that Chantel was in good spirits. But she wondered if Chantel thought about Marco much. Dora had already given Marco's messages to her and wondered if she followed up. If Chantel was lovesick, she was hiding it well.

"Guess what? I've got a couple of surprises for you," said

Dora, pulling out a present from a shopping bag. "Thought you'd open these now before we get too toasted."

Even though Chantel brought a gift for Dora, she was very touched that Dora had brought one also. Dora was the only person she was celebrating Christmas with, so it meant a lot to her. Other than that, she sent some gifts to her family in Maine. She also got a small Christmas tree for her apartment. And she put the cards she received from her family around it.

"For me, thank you, Dora. I don't know what I would do without a friend like you. Cheers," said Chantel, toasting Dora with her glass of wine.

"Cheers, Chantel. Merry Christmas," Dora said hugging her.

Chantel opened her gift. It was a silk scarf from Hérmes.

"This is beautiful. You don't know how many times I've looked at Hérmes scarves in the stores. I have always wanted one. Thank you. You're the best. But, I have something for you too."

Then Chantel gave Dora a gift box wrapped in shiny gold paper with a Bloomingdale's sticker on it. Dora tore into it, eager to see what was inside.

"Only you would give me a red crystal ice bucket with tongs. It's very nice and has my initials engraved on it also. Now all I need is a butler and a maid to serve me something with it," remarked Dora, laughing out loud.

Dora wasn't the least bit shy to hold it up and admire it.

"Thank you, Chantel. But I have something else to tell you about. And I have something else to give you. Do you remember what I told you about Marco? Do you remember that he told me to tell you that he would always be there for you?"

"Yes, why?" Chantel looked curious, taking another sip from her drink.

"Well, he also gave me something to give to you. And he wanted me to give it to you on Christmas Eve. I promised him that I would. That's why I didn't tell you about it any sooner. I felt so sorry for him. I couldn't disappoint him either. And, I wanted to keep my word."

"You're kidding?" replied Chantel, with mixed emotions on her face.

"No. I'm not kidding, Chantel. I have it in my bag. So, here it is. See for yourself," said Dora, putting another gift on the table in front of Chantel.

"Well, thank goodness, he doesn't hate me completely. I pretty much told him it was over between us," Chantel said, lifting the present into her hand.

"Hate you. He loves you, Chantel. I know he does. I bet it's not too late for you two. I mean if you would reconsider," Dora said, emphasizing the word reconsider.

Dora was still confused as to why Chantel broke it off with Marco.

"I'm afraid it is. But since you went to all this trouble, I'll open it anyway."

It was another box from Cartier. When Chantel opened it, she found a solid gold watch inside. She was amazed that he would send such a gift again.

Dora looked at it and gasped. "Oh my God, it's gorgeous! Put it on, Chantel."

Now feeling sad, Chantel put the watch on and began to cry. Dora held her for a moment and wiped away her tears with a tissue she had in her purse.

"Don't cry, Chantel. He just doesn't want you to forget about him. I have a feeling that he will always love you. I just know it. I could see it on his face when I met with him. I think he wanted you to have something special for Christmas and to think of him."

"I understand. But for now, I rather not talk about Marco. Let's enjoy our Christmas dinner together. I need to get my mind off of him right now," said Chantel, putting the watch away.

"Sure, Chantel. I get it. I don't want to put any pressure on you. Well, on another note, guess who is meeting us here tonight? Now don't get nervous. It isn't Marco."

"Who is it?" asked Chantel.

Looking mischievous, Dora answered, "Vinnie. Do you remember Vinnie? He was the guy I met at Bianchi's. He's coming here tonight with some friends."

"You're kidding me?" Chantel smiled, no longer teary-eyed.

"Nope, I'm not kidding. In the meantime, let's have our dinner. They won't be here for a little while yet anyway."

The timing was perfect. Chantel and Dora had just finished their dinner when Vinnie arrived with some of his friends. They pulled over a table next to them and ordered some drinks. At the same time, a disc jockey started to play dance music for everyone.

"Hey Dora, how are you doing, beautiful? Merry Christmas," said Vinnie cheerfully, kissing Dora on the cheek.

"Good Vinnie. Merry Christmas. By the way, I'd like you to meet my friend Chantel Du Maurier. Do you remember? She's the one from Maine."

"Oh yes, I certainly do remember, Dora. It's very nice to meet you, Chantel. Merry Christmas. And how are you doing tonight?" asked Vinnie.

"Better now. Thanks. It's nice to meet you also, Vinnie. Merry Christmas," Chantel told him, impressed by his good looks. Chantel could also tell that Vinnie was a humorous person who liked to have fun. This was just what they needed right now.

Then Vinnie introduced them to his friends Bobby and Joey. Bobby and Joey were from the Fulton Fish Market downtown and were also cheerful. They started telling jokes about strange fish deliveries in the middle of the night and people who looked and smelled like fish. This made Chantel and Dora laugh a lot. And this was also what they loved about New Yorkers. They could be so unique and funny at times.

But the evening would not have been complete unless they all danced together. So they took turns on a small dance floor next to the bar. The music in the background was mostly oldies and holiday music. But they were fun to dance to. And everyone seemed pleased with the disc jockey's selections.

Being with such a fun group of people helped Chantel keep

her mind off of Marco. It was her first Christmas in Manhattan, and she didn't want to feel bad, no matter how difficult that was. She wanted to enjoy herself and to have a good time with Dora. So she had a few more drinks and enjoyed the company. That was also one of the reasons she didn't want to tell Dora about what happened with Steve Woods yet.

A couple of hours later, after they were all partied out, Dora and Vinnie walked Chantel home. When Chantel returned to her apartment, she began to think about her family in Maine again. She planned to phone them in the morning to wish them a Merry Christmas. Then she thought about her job at Champs. She wanted to keep succeeding in her work. She loved what she was doing also. Her career success and dreams were things she felt she was in control of. She felt this was one area of her life that no one else could manipulate.

Then Chantel thought about what Steve Woods did to her and became angry inside. She still hadn't decided what she was going to do about him. Sometimes she thought of going to the police. She wondered whether that would be the best thing to do or not. In the meantime, her intuition told her that Steve would get his someday. Somehow, she just knew this and felt it would only be a matter of time.

CHAPTER 18

RUTH

CHANTEL'S NEW POSITION AT CHAMPS CORPORATE OFFICES WAS working out well. She had only been there for several weeks and was already admired for her work. Even Gordon Miles seemed to be pleased with her so far. This aspect of her life continued to be very promising.

Dora was expected at Chantel's apartment for dinner that evening at about eight o'clock. Dora had wanted to go out, but Chantel insisted that she come over to her apartment instead. Chantel told her that she had something very personal to talk to her about. Dora hoped it would be good news, like Marco getting back into Chantel's life.

It was about ten past eight when Chantel heard her doorbell ring. Dora had arrived. Chantel could hear her breath huffing and puffing in the hallway from climbing the stairs. Then Chantel opened the door for her.

"I've got to get into shape. I'm tired of my butt dragging like this," said Dora, flopping herself down on Chantel's sofa. "Sitting at the office all the time makes me out of shape. And I never get to the gym because I'm working all the time. I know it's no excuse, but it's hard for me. I'm just too tired at the end of the day. John keeps me busy from the time he gets into the office until the time he leaves. And the others are always asking me to do things for them too."

Chantel nodded at her, and told her, "I understand what you mean. I try to do some exercises myself in the morning before I go to the office. Otherwise, I just get caught up in my day and forget everything else. Well anyhow, you did make it up the stairs. Bravo. And you look terrific anyway."

Chantel looked at Dora thinking of how she was the only person who she could trust and confide in. She loved Dora for that and was grateful that they were friends. Whatever she was going to tell her wouldn't matter somehow. No matter what, they would still be friends. This gave her some comfort and courage.

"So what's for dinner tonight, Chantel? Here I am talking about exercising, and right away I'm talking about food."

Chantel laughed.

"That's okay, Dora. I made a light dinner for us tonight. I have salad, fish, veggies, and cauliflower mashed potatoes. A classic meal for two."

"Sounds excellent, healthy, and good. Can we eat soon

though? I'm really starving. I didn't eat much earlier today," Dora told her.

"Sure. But while I get this on the table, I'm curious, how is everything going with your friend Vinnie? Have you been seeing him lately?" asked Chantel, hoping there would be good news in someone's love life.

Dora blushed.

"I must confess. I saw him again quite recently. He's so much fun, Chantel. I'm not sure if he's marriage material, but I do have a good time with him. He makes me laugh so much. I really enjoy his company, not to mention his you know what."

Chantel laughed again.

"Oh, he told me this crazy story about some friend of his who was driving his Mercedes to a church uptown to meet his wife for a wedding. In the meantime, he get's drunk and lost on the way. He's dumb enough to ask a policeman directing traffic for directions. Then the policeman, who knows the guy is drunk, arrests him and puts him in jail. His wife had to bail him out," Dora said, shaking her head in disbelief.

"You're kidding me? Maybe it was a godsend? Maybe he needed to learn a lesson before he hurt himself, or someone else for that matter. I'd hate to have been his wife. Wow."

"Yea, maybe you're right. You never know. I'm glad it wasn't me though," said Dora.

"Well anyway, dinner's ready. Come and eat. Don't worry about your body so much. Just start exercising in the morning before you go to work like I do. Then you'll feel better about food," said Chantel, trying to be encouraging.

"Thanks, I'll try. At least I'm still a size eight and can still get into my favorite Guess jeans. I'm happy about that."

Then they sat down at the table and started to eat.

"And then Vinnie told me another story about a customer at Bianchi's one night. Some woman went into the bathroom near closing time. And by the time she came out, the restaurant was closed and locked. She didn't have a cell phone with her and couldn't find the phone in the restaurant, so she spent the entire night locked in there. And in the morning, one of the workers came in and found her sitting at a table eating something. Then she had the nerve to ask the worker what he was looking at as if she's supposed to be there in the first place. Isn't that something?" said Dora, rolling her eyes up at the ceiling.

"Funny, very funny. I like the part when she asked the worker what he was looking at. I would have liked to have seen his face when she told him that," commented Chantel, hoping that would never happen to her, and temporarily distracted from what was weighing heavily on her mind.

Then after dinner, they sat down on Chantel's sofa to be more comfortable.

"So tell me, Chantel, what did you want to talk about? Are you ready to tell me now?"

"Yes, but would you mind if I make some tea first?"

"Sure. I'll have some too. I'll tell you something though. The guys where I come from would sure be chasing you. The way you cook is really excellent," said Dora, complimenting her.

"Too bad I'm not in Atlanta," Chantel said with a distressed look on her face.

"Did I touch a nerve? You're not thinking of going back to Maine are you?" asked Dora, a little puzzled.

"No, that's not it. At least, I hope I'm not."

Then Chantel finished making them tea and put the cups on the coffee table in front of them. Her face looked unhappy when she sat down. She wasn't sure about the best way to tell Dora about her situation. Then she took a deep breath to collect herself.

"There's no easy way to tell you what I'm about to tell you or anyone else for that matter. But you'll find out sooner or later. So here it is. I'm pregnant, Dora."

"Oh, my God! You're joking me right?" asked Dora, shocked from the news.

"I wish I was, Dora." Chantel's eyes welled up with tears.

"What? Who's the father? Is it Marco's? Or is the baby someone else's?"

Chantel looked down at the floor and frowned.

"Well, on the night of my last day at Bloomingdale's, I met this man before I left the store. I should say he was really an evil person. But I didn't know it. I was just so excited about my promotion when he came over to the counter to buy some perfume. We started talking. Then he asked me out to celebrate my promotion. He told me he was celebrating something also. So I went out with him, and we had dinner together."

Dora gave Chantel a look that she was prepared to hear the rest of what happened.

"We were drinking a lot of champagne. And I became a little intoxicated. Then I went over to his apartment. And I think he might have put something in one of my drinks. The next thing I remember, I was in one of his bedrooms. He took off my clothes. I told him to stop, but he wouldn't. I was really dizzy. I didn't have the coordination or strength to throw him off of me. He wouldn't stop until he had sex with me. He forced himself inside of me for what seemed like hours."

Chantel broke down and started to cry uncontrollably. She clenched her hands into fists. She felt so ashamed and angry.

"He raped you? Oh my God, Chantel. This is atrocious. How horrible! I wish you told me about this right away."

"And in the morning, he was gone. He left me in his apartment with a note that his driver would take me back home. He hasn't tried to contact me since. And I haven't tried to contact him either. I didn't even go to the police. I just didn't know what I should do."

"Do you know who he is, Chantel?" asked Dora.

"He told me his name was Steve Woods. He told me that he owns the Woods department store here in the city. He had a driver who called him that also. And the waiters in the restaurant we went to together addressed him that way too."

Dora's face turned red with anger and repulsion. She was boiling inside and wanted to kill him.

"This is unbelievable. That bastard! I'd like to cut his balls off. In fact, I'd like to cut his penis off along with his balls. So, tell me, what are you going to do? Does he know you're pregnant?" asked Dora.

"Dora, I only found out yesterday. Before that, I took a test that I got from the drug store, and it was positive. Then I went to a gynecologist to find out if it was accurate. The timing makes it certain that the unborn child is his. The child is his," Chantel repeated and continued to cry.

"Do you want to keep this baby?" Dora put her arms around Chantel and hugged her to comfort her. Chantel cried in her arms.

"I don't think I want to get an abortion, Dora. I just can't do that, even though I'm afraid. At least, I'm making better money now. I could probably pay someone to help me take care of the child. I just don't know what they will think of this at work. I mean me being pregnant with no husband. They just recently promoted me. Great."

Dora was outraged by the whole situation.

"Look, Chantel, I've heard of Steve Woods and his store. He's a rich man. In fact, his store has a long history in Manhattan. It's appalling what he did to you. But even though it's a difficult thing to do, I'd let him know you're pregnant and that it's his baby. So he better do something for you or else. I know you must hate him for what he did. I'm not sure why you didn't go to the police. But you should tell him about the baby and that he better help you. Yet, I bet he's the kind of person who will deny it though. I bet he'll also deny that he raped you. He wouldn't want this in the newspapers. And he'd probably buy peoples words left and right. But I'd still pay him a visit as soon as possible. Maybe you can try his office tomorrow morning before you go to work. He might be at his office then. You should also decide if you are going to press rape and sexual assault charges against him. This whole thing would definitely end up in the papers though. Be prepared for that."

Dora started crying herself. She just couldn't believe what Steve did to Chantel. She just couldn't believe something like this happened to her. But she knew Chantel wouldn't lie to her. She also knew that Chantel would have to decide for herself what she was going to do about it. And she thought that all of this couldn't be good for the little baby growing inside Chantel now.

"What if he denies it? You're right. What if he doesn't want to help? Even the mere thought of seeing him again is horrid to me. But you're probably right. I should go, and I should tell him that I'm pregnant and that he is the father. I'm just not sure if I want to press charges yet. I need to think about that. As you said, the whole thing might end up in the papers. It's not that I want to let him get away with it. It's more what I'd be put through and how it might affect my career. That bastard!"

Dora put one of her hands on Chantel's stomach. "Don't worry, Chantel. I understand. We'll figure something out. I want you to know that I still love you no matter what. And I'll love your child. You're my best friend. Be strong, please. Please be strong," Dora told her, hugging her tightly.

Chantel thought about work again and all the dreams and plans she had for herself. "What am I going to tell them at work, Dora?"

"Try to keep it as much a secret as you can. You're thin. Sometimes even a baby can be concealed. You wouldn't be the first woman who would do it. Pretend you're gaining weight and wear loose clothing. Others have done it in the past. And so can you. Chin up now." Dora lifted Chantel's chin up with her hand.

"Thank you, Dora. I love you. I don't know what I would do without a good friend like you."

Then they held each other a while longer weeping together.

"I love you too. Now, let's cheer up. We'll just have to cope with it. We'll make it okay. And I'm here whenever you need me."

"Thanks, Dora. Thanks."

Chantel rubbed her eyes with a tissue trying to dry up all of her tears.

"Think nothing of it. If this kid looks anything like you, he or she might be a movie star or a model or something like that. It'll be all right. I just know it. It'll turn out all right."

CHAPTER 19

ENIALS

THE NEXT MORNING CHANTEL GOT UP EARLIER TO PREPARE
herself to go to see Steve Woods. She didn't sleep very well the
night before. Everything seemed so confusing and unreal. She
thought a lot about what Dora had told her. And she knew it
wasn't going to be easy emotionally to see him again. But she
felt that she had to tell him about the baby. She had to find out
what his reaction to her would be. After all, it was his child also,
regardless of the fact that he raped her.

Chantel put on a navy blue suit with a pair of black shoes.
And since it was raining that morning, she put on a warm winter
raincoat and took an umbrella with her. After she left her apartment, she walked to Fifty-seventh Street. The Woods store was
not open to the public yet. So she decided to have a tea across

the street at a small coffee shop. She looked at the Woods store from there and noticed how large it was. It was in its own seven-story building that took up a good part of the block. It was also evident to her that the store was very expensive and felt a bit intimidating to her.

Chantel waited until the store was open at ten. Then she crossed the street and walked over to one of the entrances. This time there were doormen opening the doors for patrons. There were also security guards scattered throughout. Customers were already at the counters to purchase merchandise. And employees were running about and neatening up the displays. She thought to herself how it reminded her of Bloomingdale's.

Then Chantel approached one of the security guards.

"Excuse me, do you know where I can find Mr. Steve Woods? I understand his office is somewhere in the building," Chantel asked him.

The security guard looked Chantel over quickly with some approval showing on his face. "Mr. Woods. He'd be in executive offices on the seventh floor. You'll need to take the elevator in the back of the store to get there. His receptionist can help you," he told her, trying to give the impression of being both authoritative and polite at the same time.

"Thank you," she answered, proceeding to the back of the main floor, glancing at all the people in the store. Then she thought to herself that it was no wonder that Steve Woods had such a luxurious apartment.

Chantel didn't know much about Steve and how he spared no expense on anything that had to do with making him or his image look good. He was always remodeling and renovating the appearance of the store beyond its budget. His own accountants had often warned him of spending too much money. But Steve did what he wanted because he controlled the store. He didn't listen much to the advice of others, even his own trusted advisors.

When Chantel arrived at the elevator, a man asked her what floor she needed. Chantel told him that she needed the seventh floor. Then she thought about what she had gotten herself into. She even thought about Marco. She thought about how much she needed him now. But then she thought of how Marco might look down upon her for letting this happen in the first place. And when she got to the seventh floor, she cleared her mind and stepped into the entrance of the executive offices suite. A heavyset receptionist was sitting behind a pair of motion-sensored glass doors and a black lacquer desk. The doors opened automatically as Chantel walked inside.

"Can I help you?" the receptionist asked calmly.

"Yes, I'm here to see Steve Woods," answered Chantel.

"Do you have an appointment with him?"

"No, I do not. But if you tell him I am here, he will know who I am," Chantel told her.

Then the receptionist pointed to an additional set of glass doors further inside. There was another woman sitting at a large mahogany desk wearing small-rimmed glasses on the bridge of her nose. She looked like a seasoned librarian. Then she glanced at Chantel with a curious expression on her face.

"And how may I help you, young lady?" she asked.

The thought of seeing Steve Woods was now starting to upset Chantel's stomach. She was beginning to feel sick.

"I'm here to see and speak with Steve Woods. I understand this is where his office is located," answered Chantel.

"Do you have an appointment?" inquired the woman.

"No, I don't. As I told the receptionist, he will know who I am if you tell him I am here," said Chantel firmly.

"What is your name?"

"My name is Chantel Du Maurier," Chantel answered, with an acute feeling of distress.

"Have a seat please, Ms. Du Maurier. I'll see if Mr. Woods is available. He doesn't usually see anyone without an appointment."

Chantel sat down on a large black leather sofa across from the woman's desk. It had a large table in front of it with several fashion magazines and newspapers.

Steve was in his office when the woman communicated by intercom with him.

"Mr. Woods, there is a young lady here who is requesting to see you. Her name is Chantel Du Maurier," she told him.

Steve didn't like this. But he thought it would be wise to find out why Chantel was there and what she wanted. He wasn't sure if she was going to create a scene or not. So he told the woman, who was his private secretary Rita, that he would see her and to send Chantel into his office.

As soon as Chantel walked in, she felt a cold chill. Steve was seated in a large leather chair behind a desk. She thought to herself that he didn't look at all like the same person she'd met.

She thought that he looked even worse and even more horrid and evil. It was as if a mask was removed from his face. His eyes were emotionless and darker than she remembered. And his overall facial expression gave her an overwhelming and disturbing feeling. She was disgusted that he had raped her and that she was carrying his baby in her body.

"Have a seat, Chantel," he told her.

Chantel sat down and was grateful for the fact that there were windows behind him that she could look out on. Looking at him directly was painful and scary. And she also noticed that the views up there were quite panoramic, just like his apartment facing the park.

"So tell me, Chantel. What can I do for you?" he asked her with an unenthusiastic tone of voice.

"Well, I have something important to tell you. Since you raped me, I found out that I'm pregnant. And I'm certain the child is yours. I checked the timing with a gynecologist."

"Raped you? You have to be kidding me. You seemed to enjoy every minute of our night together. But it was only one night. Do you expect me to believe that you became pregnant from one night of intercourse with me?" he said, sternly mocking her with no remorse whatsoever.

"Yes, I do. You know what you did to me, you son of a bitch. I'm thinking about going to the police and pressing charges against you. Maybe I can put you in jail for a long, long time," she told him.

"Okay, calm down. Tell me what you want from me. You obviously came here for a reason."

"Look, I am here to let you know that your child is inside of me. I am also here to ask if you will help me financially provide for this child. I will have to take care of him or her. I think you have some responsibility here and should help me. It might not do me much good if you are in jail though. Now would it? I will need to pay someone to help me take care of the child while I go out to work. And I only have a limited amount of financial resources. I think you should take some of the responsibility. But don't worry. I will only accept help from you until I don't require it anymore," said Chantel, appalled by him.

Steve looked at her with a vicious gaze. Chantel could tell that he didn't seem to have an ounce of compassion or empathy for her or the unborn baby.

"What? What makes you think that you can just walk in here off the street and make demands on me, let alone tell me you are pregnant with my child? What makes you think that you can ask me for money too? What do you think I am, Planned Parenthood? This is no goodwill charity here, Chantel. You are gravely mistaken. You are deluding yourself. Forget you ever met me. As far as I'm concerned, I never saw you in my life. I'm sure everyone I know will back me up on that. Now please, get out of my office. I have work to do. And I can't help you," he said to her maliciously.

Chantel just sat for a moment and looked into his eyes stunned. She couldn't believe that he would continue to be this cunning and cruel. She began to hate him even more than she already did. And she swore to herself that one day he would get his. She would never forgive him. She would never forget. She figured that he would probably buy his way out of the situation. Then she looked into his eyes one last time and spat at him.

"I will always hate you, Steve. And so will your child. One day you'll regret what you did to me. One day you'll regret what you did to your child. I know you will. You bastard. You fucking bastard," she told him.

Steve felt her words resonate in the room. But he decided to ignore them. It was as if he changed the remote switch on a television. He simply was going to dismiss what she told him. He didn't want to care. He was accustomed to walking all over people, especially women.

Chantel got into the elevator and left the store as fast as she could. She ran up to the corner of Fifth Avenue and again felt like throwing up. But she felt like crying more than anything else. She couldn't believe what a monster Steve was. She thought no decent human being would ever behave like that. She thought that only a demon would act that way. And since she was now too upset to go to her office, she decided to go home and work from there instead. She had a computer in her apartment that she knew she could use if she felt up to it later on. At the very least, she could check for important messages.

But before she went home, Chantel thought about her favorite church, St. Vincent Ferrer. It was located on Lexington Avenue and Sixty-sixth Street. She just had a feeling it would be a good idea to go there. She really loved that particular church. She always felt close to God and peaceful there. So she decided to stop there before she went home, with the hope of feeling somewhat better.

While Chantel was there, she began to pray and thought about her sister up in Maine. She thought that maybe her sister Claudette could help her with her child somehow. She thought that perhaps she could also help Claudette in return.

Thinking of what might be possible made Chantel feel more optimistic. Then she prayed some more to God for help with her new challenges. She believed her prayers would somehow be answered. She always had a strong faith in God.

CHAPTER 20

RYSTAL ARRIVES

APPROXIMATELY NINE MONTHS LATER, CHANTEL'S BABY daughter Crystal was born. She was seven pounds, four ounces, and healthy. Chantel was only in labor for a few hours before her delivery. As with most mothers, she experienced the feeling of loving someone instantly. Crystal gave her a feeling of joy that was incomparable to anything she'd ever felt inside before. It was also a different kind of love than she had for Marco.

Chantel already had plans in place for Crystal. Crystal was going to stay with her sister, Claudette, and her husband Brian, up in Maine. Chantel knew that they would take good care of Crystal and provide a solid family environment. This was something that Chantel felt she couldn't yet give to Crystal. And fortunately, Claudette and Brian were delighted to help. They already had a two-year-old son named Chris of their own. In exchange, Chantel would send them money to help them out with their expenses and to provide for her daughter. She knew that Crystal would be well taken care of and be among loving and caring family. This gave her a great feeling of peace inside. So shortly after the birth, Chantel brought Crystal to them on a small airplane. They flew together from Westchester County Airport to one near the town of Southport, Maine.

Claudette and Brian greeted Chantel and Crystal when they got off the plane. Then they drove together to Claudette and Brian's home on the outskirts of town. It was a modest two-story home painted with white and green trim. It also had a charming old-fashioned porch with rockers for people to sit on and pass the time. The fall weather had already set in, so the flowers around the house were somewhat faded except for the mums that were more recently planted. Mums always lasted longer than the annuals that were planted over the summer.

When they arrived at the house and went inside, Chantel was delighted to find her mother Susan, her father Edward, and little Chris waiting for them. Her parents didn't know too much about Chantel's pregnancy until the last four weeks. So they were still quite surprised by the news. But they were also happy. Grand-children were very important to them. And they imagined that it would be hard for Chantel to remain in New York City and take care of Crystal all by herself. They thought that bringing Crystal to Claudette and Brian's was a very good idea. They would also help out with the children as much as they could.

"Hi, Mom. Hi, Dad," said Chantel, after she walked into the

living room at Claudette's house. Chantel was holding Crystal in a big pink and blue blanket with clouds painted on it.

"Oh my gosh, Chantel, she's so beautiful," said Susan, taking in the precious moment of seeing her granddaughter for the first time.

"Yes, she's very beautiful," echoed Edward.

"We've missed you so much, Chantel. Look over here. Claudette has prepared a nice bassinet for Crystal. But let us hold her first," Susan told Chantel, stretching her arms out to hold Crystal.

Susan held Crystal in her arms and kissed her tiny forehead. Then she passed her to Edward to hold in his arms. It was a very tender moment for all of them. Then Chantel realized that Chris disappeared. He was no longer in the room.

"Where is Chris? Where did he go?" asked Chantel.

"He went into his room. He probably wants to show you his rock collection. He paints them and turns them into artwork. He's very proud of his collection and insists that you see it right away," Claudette told Chantel.

"I see. Well, which way should I go? But first, let me get some presents in my bag that I brought for him," said Chantel, reaching into her luggage to retrieve two wrapped gifts.

"It's through the doorway over there. The one with the dinosaur picture on it," answered Brian.

"Thank you."

Chantel went into Chris's room. He was sitting at a small play table that was a good size for his age. He was dressed in a green cape and had a gold plastic crown on his head. He looked up at Chantel and smiled at her when she entered the room.

"Hello, Chris. It's your Aunt Chantel. Wow, you look like royalty with your cape and crown. Who are you?"

"I'm King Camelot. I am ruler over the forest of rocks. Look here. You can see some of them. They are magical," Chris told her.

"Very nice, King Camelot. They look very magical indeed. Can I touch one?"

"Yes, but please be careful. They should never get broken, or else bad luck will come," he warned her.

Chantel picked up one of the rocks that Chris had painted red and green and held it up to the light in the room.

"I see what you mean. This feels very magical to me. Can it help to make wishes come true?" she asked him, smiling at him tenderly.

"Of course, but you must believe it can. Then the wish or wishes will come true. And remember to keep the wishes secret to yourself," Chris told her, making that a requirement of having them come true.

Chantel pretended to make a wish and put the rock back down onto the table. Then she took the two gifts that she brought for him and gave them to him. "I have something for you also, Chris. I mean, King Camelot."

Chris blushed when he accepted the presents. Then he started to open them. Chantel had given him a sweatshirt with the Manhattan skyline on it and a lego set of the Empire State building.

"Hope these are to your satisfaction," Chantel told him.

Chris smiled and gave her a look of approval. Then he thanked her, and they joined the others in the living room. Chris took a real long look at Crystal who was now in the bassinet playing with a rattle. He reached out and touched one of her tiny little hands.

"Is this my new little sister?"

"Not exactly, dear. Crystal's really your cousin. But she is going to live with us. So she'll be like a little sister to you," explained Claudette.

"That's awesome. Like a little sister! Yea! My wish has come true! You see, Aunt Chantel. That was one of my wishes," Chris told her.

Chantel smiled at him. She was relieved that Chris was so happy to have Crystal there. She could tell that Chris would be a good brother to her.

Then, for the rest of the day, they caught up on what was happening in everyone's life. Chantel told them about her promotions at Champs and how much she liked it there. They were all genuinely happy for her. They had more confidence that things would continue to go well for her at Champs. She was beginning to make more money and was still pursuing the dreams she always wanted for herself. They didn't want her to feel bad or guilty about becoming pregnant and having a baby. And even though they all missed her a lot, they still respected her ambition and the career part of her life.

Later in the evening after dinner, Chantel surprised them all with some more presents. She had brought perfumes for her mother and sister. And she brought cashmere scarves for her father and brother-in-law. They opened them up in the living room while a wood fire burned in their fireplace. Then they ate some strawberry rhubarb pie that Claudette had made for them earlier that day.

The next morning, Chantel asked Claudette if she could speak to her alone. She wanted to get some things off her chest before she went back to Manhattan. She was truly happy that Crystal was there, but she did have some concerns about the future. So they made time to sit on another small porch in back of the house with views of the river nearby.

"Claudette, I'm really grateful for what you are doing for us. I want you to know that. And I will be helping you all out a lot. But I'm a little concerned about the future. What if one day I want to take Crystal away to live with me? I don't know how you would feel about that then. I just don't want you getting hurt or to feel resentful in any way. You just never know. I'm still young, and well, when I'm doing better," said Chantel, with a worried look on her face.

"You mean, how will I feel when the time comes? I think that's what you mean, isn't it?" asked Claudette.

Chantel looked at her emphatically. "Yes, I'm concerned about that one day," Chantel answered.

"Don't be, Chantel. I understand. I'm really happy to help you out right now. It also gives Chris some company. And Mom and Dad are ecstatic. Until you're ready, they will worry less about Crystal if she's here. We'll just deal with it when the time comes. Until then, don't worry. We all love you and understand," Claudette told her.

Chantel felt like a huge weight was lifted off her mind and shoulders. "I love you, Claudette. Thank you so much."

"I love you too. We all love you. So again, don't worry. It's going to be okay."

Chantel also thanked God in silence. Having a sister like this taking care of Crystal was like having a miracle happen. She would never forget the love that Claudette had inside of her to give. Chantel would never forget this showing of love.

Two days later, Chantel boarded another small plane back to Westchester County Airport. During her flight, she reviewed some papers Gordon Miles had given her before she went to Maine. He was setting something new up in product development. There were plans for several new scent and fragrance products that he wanted her to work on immediately. After reviewing the papers, she thought about Crystal again, how much she already missed her, and how much she wanted her daughter to have a wonderful life.

CHAPTER 21

THE WALDORF PARTY

IT WAS FOUR AND A HALF YEARS LATER, AND A LOT HAPPENED AT Champs throughout those years. North America had become an even larger marketplace for Champs, and the company was doing better than ever competing in international markets. At only forty-seven years old, Gordon Miles had become President of the Americas division. Much of his success was due to his innovativeness and risk-taking strategies in marketing and product development. Gordon also had a knack for recognizing target markets and how to sell to them. He worked long hours and didn't have the constraints of a wife and family. And even though a lot of women found him attractive and would have wanted him, he didn't appear to be that interested in them.

Chantel thought it was probably because he preferred men. And that was okay with her. He was also a workaholic and completely into his career. This was a quality that he also admired and recognized in Chantel. She was very similar to him in many ways and was continuously proving herself in their business decisions and goals. Chantel also helped to develop a new fragrance line that made soaring profits for the company. Millions of more dollars were being made throughout the world because of it. The product line was called Golden Doves. Chantel was very involved in its creation. Each Dove fragrance had its own individual scent. Then Gordon decided to promote her again. She was now the executive director of scents and fragrances for the entire United States. And she was always heavily involved with new product creations, designs, marketing, and sales.

Chantel's current office was very different from the first one she had when she started at Champs. She now had a corner office with extensive views of Park Avenue. And since her most recent promotion, she bought herself an apartment in a doorman building on Central Park West and Seventy-second Street. Her new apartment was across the street from the historic Dakota building and had water views of the lake in Central Park. Since she was making so much money at Champs now, Chantel decided to bring Crystal to live with her in New York. Crystal had been with her for a few months now. And Chantel also hired a live-in nanny to help take care of Crystal and enrolled her in a private school within walking distance of their apartment.

Crystal's nanny's name was Margaret O'Reilly. She was

originally from Ireland and had been a nanny in New York for almost twenty years. She was a warm and pleasant woman whom they both felt very comfortable with. Margaret had a nice sense of humor and often told jokes that she remembered as a child growing up in Ireland. It sounded like she had a happy childhood, full of fun and adventure.

Claudette had been very good to Crystal. And Chantel was very grateful for what she did for them. In return, Chantel rewarded her financially. She was so generous to Claudette that she bought her a new and larger home near her previous one.

Chantel was still in her office when she heard the phone ring. She was busy reviewing some product lines up for consideration. Her secretary had already left for the night. So she decided to answer the phone herself. It was Dora.

"Are you still coming to the party? I haven't heard from you all day."

Chantel glanced at her full appointment book laying open on her desk. "Sorry, I totally forgot about tonight."

"How could you forget? It's not often that I'm invited to a party at the Waldorf. John insisted that I bring a friend. And, I've been planning on bringing you for a month now. As you know, we haven't been to a party like this in a long time," Dora told her, sounding impatient over the receiver.

"Yes, I know. Sorry. I've been trying to make up for lost time with Crystal. I've also been really busy at work. Maybe, if you worked with me and not for John, I'd be better organized and have more time for fun."

Chantel was planning on asking Dora if she'd consider working at Champs with her anyway. Then she got an idea.

"If I go to this party with you, will you come and work with me at Champs? I'll make sure you make double than what you're making now. I already know of a position that you would probably like a lot. I have a hunch that you'd do very well and be very helpful to me at the same time," said Chantel, encouragingly.

Dora thought that the offer was quite clever and generous of Chantel. She trusted her and knew that she meant well.

"Are you absolutely sure of this, Chantel? I don't want business to get in the way of our friendship. Yet, it does sound like a fabulous offer. I'll admit that. And the cost of living in Manhattan isn't getting any cheaper."

Then Chantel looked out one of her office windows. She could tell it was getting late. She would soon have to leave in order to make the party. She also needed time to go home first to change into an evening gown.

"I should have asked you a long time ago, but I was afraid to. To be honest, we really could use someone like you to work in our group at Champs. And most of the time, you'd be working closely with me anyway," Chantel explained to her.

"All right, Chantel. You have a deal," answered Dora, thinking to herself it might all work out nicely.

Dora was ready for a change anyhow after all those years at Buckleven Swaith. She was pretty bored with her job being much the same during that time. And every year her annual salary bonuses got smaller and smaller. Only the very top-level employees were immune to such pay deficits such as small raises and meager bonuses. The situation was always blamed on Wall Street and how the company was doing year to year. In reality though, many people at Buckleven were making millions of dollars, and for some, more and more every year. Then Dora also remembered many of the stories Chantel had told her about work. She was always quite intrigued by them.

So even though Chantel really didn't feel like going to the party, she figured a deal was a deal. She really wanted Dora to come and work with her at Champs. She knew she had to go.

"Great. I'll meet you in the lobby at the Waldorf at seven-thirty. I have to go home to change first," Chantel told her.

"Okay, I'll see you then," answered Dora, with her Southern accent coming through.

Chantel packed up her briefcase and took a taxi to her apartment on the West Side. Margaret was in the kitchen preparing dinner when Chantel got there. Chantel explained to her that she was dining out and not to set a place for her. Then she went into her bedroom to find an evening gown to wear. She chose a Valentino black and gold strapless dress. She was waiting for a special occasion to wear it and decided that this was it. When she was ready, she went downstairs and had the doorman get her a taxi to take her over to the Waldorf. Dora was already waiting in the lobby when she arrived. She also looked terrific in a beautiful deep red evening gown made of silk taffeta. Dora had spotted her after she came up the stairs from the entrance on

Park Avenue. They quickly kissed each other hello and were careful not to get lipstick marks on each other's faces.

"Hey, you look great. Follow me. The elevators we need to take are down this way," said Dora, eyeing Chantel over from head to toe.

"Thanks. You don't look so bad yourself lady in red. But I'm wondering, what's the occasion? A bon voyage party for John, maybe? Only joking," said Chantel, smiling cleverly at Dora.

"Very amusing, Chantel. No, it's a fund-raiser celebration of some kind. One of John's wealthiest clients from Greece is throwing it. I hear he is very fond of the Waldorf, so that's why he's having it here. Very old money and a lot of it."

"That sounds intriguing. A Greek. I wonder what this celebration will be like?" Chantel hadn't met many Greek people in her life.

"Who knows? I'm more interested in having some fun and the food being served. I bet it will be out of this world," predicted Dora.

Chantel laughed. She thought it was amusing how Dora emphasized food all the time. "You and food. Forget about the food, Dora. Maybe you're going to meet a charming man tonight. A man that might sweep you off your feet," said Chantel, teasing her.

Dora looked at her like she was crazy and shrugged her shoulders. "Look who's talking, Ms. career woman."

After they got out of the elevator, they checked their coats in the checkroom. Then they freshened up their make-up one last time in the ladies room before they went into the party.

There were many tables in the ballroom and about ten people at each table. But the hosting table was larger. And there was also a band playing lively music for people to dance to. Chantel and Dora were seated at table number nine. Among them, at their table, was a Count from Russia with a much younger woman than himself, a member of the Van Courtlandt family and his escort, a Kennedy and his wife, and two wealthy unmarried brothers from Cyprus. This was lucky for Chantel and Dora because they would now have single dancing partners. It would otherwise be uncomfortable dancing with some other woman's man, even under the best of circumstances. So Chantel and Dora were glad they were there.

The two brothers from Cyprus were also pleased that they had two single ladies at their table. They quickly introduced themselves as Charles and Benedict Milos. And since they were not seated directly next to Chantel and Dora, they kindly asked everyone at the table if they wouldn't mind rearranging the seating arrangements. They knew it would be much easier to talk to them if they were seated closer. They thought this would be better than raising their voices across the table. None of the other guests seemed to mind the request and politely changed their seats to accommodate them.

Charles was the older of the two brothers and sat next to Chantel. He had light brown hair, a thick mustache, and bright green eyes. He looked to be around fifty years old, while his brother Benedict looked about ten years younger. Benedict's manner was also less rigid than Charles. He also had light brown hair, but he didn't have a mustache, and his eyes were a combination of blue and gray, depending on how the lights in the room reflected upon them.

Chantel was still much younger than either one of them. And if there would be a beauty competition in the ballroom, Chantel would probably win it with Dora coming in second place.

Chantel questioned Charles about what he did back in Cyprus. He didn't live in the United States and was just visiting. He explained to her that his family had been in the newspaper business for many generations and that he also enjoyed it. Chantel found him pleasant to talk with. He seemed very worldly and spoke different languages to the other guests at the table. She thought that was quite impressive.

Dora was also enjoying Benedict's company. They were smiling at each other and laughing quite a bit.

Then, all of sudden, the lights in the ballroom were dimmed. This made the entire room seem more elegant and romantic. The band was playing some Greek music. This was the first time either Chantel or Dora had ever heard it played live. Then the band started playing other songs from the thirties, forties, and fifties. Later in the evening, when the band played Greek music again, some of the guests broke plates at the end of the songs. Charles explained to them that it was a Greek custom and not to worry about it. He told them that many people think it is good luck.

"Ah, there's our host," Charles pointed out.

"Where?" asked Chantel, curious to see who their host was and what he looked like.

"Spiro Pagonis. He's over there wearing a white rose on his lapel. Do you see him yet?" asked Charles.

"You mean the person seated in the middle of the table over there?" asked Chantel, wanting to be sure she knew who the host was of such an extravagant and lively party. She was having a great time meeting many interesting people from all over the world. She didn't want to embarrass herself if she accidentally met him and didn't know who he was. In the meantime, Dora was also having lots of fun. Neither of them felt unwelcome or out of place.

The food served throughout the evening exceeded everyone's expectations. Everything was specially prepared and made to satisfy the palates and eyes of guests as much as possible. Spiro had flown in chefs directly from Paris just for the event.

By the time dessert was served, many of the guests were already dancing gracefully on the dance floor. And silver sparkles of light illuminated across the room reflecting off of jewelry and other ornaments the women were wearing. Spiro started to make social rounds to the tables of guests. He also thanked many people for being part of his fund-raiser. John Dillard was one of them. When Spiro made it to table nine where Chantel was seated, he spent a long time talking with Charles. Halfway through his conversation, Spiro noticed Chantel and made eye contact with her. He also asked Charles who she was and to be introduced. Spiro felt a rare and immediate attraction towards her. He thought Chantel was uniquely striking. He also thought that she had an air of femininity and innocence. And even though she was much younger than him,

Spiro was intrigued by her beauty. He quickly learned that Dora, who happened to be invited by John from Buckleven, had invited Chantel to the party. So he decided to take the initiative and asked Chantel if she would like to dance. Chantel agreed and politely excused herself. Everyone at the table was rather proud of this. Somehow, this was considered a social compliment to all of them at the table. Then Spiro led Chantel out onto the dance floor and gently put his arms around her waist.

"I hope you are enjoying our event tonight, Chantel," Spiro said, looking into her eyes.

"It's very interesting. Perhaps, the most interesting event I have ever been to in New York. It is certainly the most remarkable," Chantel told him.

"What makes it so interesting?" Spiro asked her with curiosity.

"The people. There are so many people here from all over the world that actually lives in those places, different countries I mean. It's interesting hearing about their experiences and their stories."

"Have you ever traveled outside of the United States? I can tell you are American. I mean you were born here," Spiro said with some certainty.

"So far, the only country was Paris, France. I thought it was very different from the United States but so beautiful. The architecture of the old buildings there is heavenly. I especially admire the churches and the art museums. But I was only there twice on business in recent years. Other than that, I've only been back to Maine where I come from originally," Chantel told him.

"On business in Paris. If you don't mind me asking, what kind of business are you in?"

"Oh, I work for Champs of Paris. It's a French company that has a large American and international presence. I work at the Americas headquarters here in New York," she explained to him.

"I see. You are in the cosmetic, skin care, and perfumery business. Doesn't Champs make the Golden Doves fragrance collection? It's quite lovely," Spiro commented.

"Yes, it does. I helped create it."

"You helped to create it. Well then, Champs is certainly fortunate to have you. We are fans of the collection. I only wish that one of my companies would develop such a product line," Spiro told her.

Chantel looked at him confused and wondered what he meant by that exactly. She also wondered what a Greek man was doing in the perfume business at all. It just seemed a bit unusual to her.

"What about you, Spiro? What do you do exactly?" Chantel asked him.

"I have many different kinds of companies. For example, I am involved with shipping, building and raw materials, and commodities. I also have a small perfume company in Lucerne, Switzerland. So we have something in common already, don't we?"

"Yes, it sounds like we do. But I'm not sure how you have time for all of those different companies. It must be overwhelmingly difficult for you," Chantel responded.

Spiro smiled at her and stroked her face gently with his right hand. He was thinking of how young, pretty, and lovely she was. He hadn't felt that attracted to a woman in a very long time. In fact, he couldn't remember the last time he was this interested in a woman at all. "Yes, at times. But I have a lot of people working for me and helping me to run these companies. Without them, it would be impossible."

Spiro knew he soon had to get back to his other guests. But he wanted to see her again. "Let's forget about business, for now, Chantel. I will have to get back to many of my guests before they leave for the evening. Before I do, I am wondering if you would give me the pleasure of your company tomorrow evening? I'm staying here at the Waldorf. It's kind of a home away from home when I'm not in Europe. Is there a way I can get in touch with you tomorrow at Champs? I'd like to see you again before I sail back to the Mediterranean. In fact, we could have dinner on my yacht tomorrow evening if you would prefer that instead of a restaurant on land. I have a great chef on board who can make you anything you would like," Spiro said quickly.

Chantel was kind of mystified by Spiro and the sudden invitation. She also realized that it had been quite some time since she went out with a man. She was never quite the same ever since her encounter with Steve Woods. But some years had passed already, and she felt that she couldn't keep distrusting men for the rest of her life. So she decided to say yes and gave him a card with her phone number on it where she could be reached at Champs. They agreed that he would call her to reconfirm and plan the menu together. This seemed a bit unusual to Chantel, but she decided to go along with it.

Then Chantel went back to her dinner table and rejoined the others. Dora was sitting between Charles and Benedict. They were telling Dora about the times their family visited Buckingham Palace when they were growing up. They told Dora that they were mainly invited because their family also had a newspaper published in England that was very popular with the royal family. Chantel laughed as she watched Dora's reactions to the stories. They told stories about many famous people in history and the paintings of them that filled the walls of the palace. For another hour Chantel and Dora listened to them until the guests started to leave. Then they said it was time for them to go also. Charles and Benedict gave them each their social calling cards and told them to give them a call if they ever visit England or Cyprus.

When Chantel and Dora got outside, they chatted for a while and took two separate taxies to get home. They were both tired and decided to catch up sometime the next day. But before they left, Chantel reminded Dora that she was serious about the deal they made earlier on the phone and that she really wanted Dora to start working at Champs. Life was getting more interesting for both of them, and they were having a great time together. This was part of what New York had to offer. You meet people from all over the world. Good people, funny people, odd and strange people, and people that come from many different countries to one big city.

And later when Chantel arrived at her apartment on the West

Side, Crystal was already asleep in her bedroom. Margaret was watching television in her room eating two scoops of chocolate fudge ice cream with maple syrup on top. Margaret loved desserts, so sweets didn't last very long in the apartment. She would often have to go to the supermarket to pick some more up.

Then Chantel got undressed, put on a nightgown, and laid on her bed. She thought about Spiro, and the unusual evening she just had. She also couldn't believe that she had plans with him the next day. She couldn't believe that he invited her on his yacht. It was just such a surprise to her. And she thought about the people she met that night and how they were different from the many people she had met in New York. These were the kind of people who looked like they belonged on television, in soap operas, movies, newspapers, and magazines. But this was real life tonight. That's what made it so much fun to her.

Chantel also realized that she would have to ask Margaret to take care of Crystal the following evening. She didn't like being away from Crystal this much. But Spiro had told her that he would be leaving New York soon. So she decided to make an exception for him. She also planned on leaving her office a little earlier the next day so she could spend some time with Crystal before she would leave for dinner. Then she turned out the lamp next to her bed, pulled the covers up over her shoulders, and went to sleep.

During the night, Chantel woke up from a dream. This was unusual because she rarely had dreams when she slept. In a foggy state of mind, she tried to remember what she dreamt about. She remembered seeing a large mountain with a rainbow surrounding it in the background. The mountain was covered with bright green grass and the sky around it was clear and had a rich blue color. There were also many different colored flowers on the mountain. It felt like a very peaceful dream. That was all she could remember about it. Then she went back to sleep.

CHAPTER 22

LOWERS

THE NEXT DAY WHEN CHANTEL ARRIVED AT HER OFFICE, SHE found flowers and a note with her name on it waiting with her secretary. They were from Spiro Pagonis. The note said, *Chantel, Lovely meeting you last night. I will phone you this afternoon, Spiro.* So Spiro called her a little after one-o'clock and asked her if it would still be okay to have dinner together that evening. He also confirmed they would be dining on his yacht and some of the menu. Spiro explained that it was moored at the World Yacht Marina on Forty-first Street and that his driver would take them there. Then he asked Chantel if he could pick her up at seven o'clock that evening. Chantel had already explained to him that she would be going to her apartment after work. So she gave him her address.

Later that day, Chantel had a meeting with Gordon. And after the meeting, she left the office a bit earlier than usual. She wanted to spend some time with Crystal before Spiro would come to pick her up. When she got home, Crystal was very happy to see her. Crystal's love for Chantel was growing all the time. She was also a very considerate child. Crystal understood that her mother was working very hard to take care of both of them. She appreciated this a lot and realized it often meant long hours at work for her mother. Crystal was also proud of her. She knew that she had a lot of responsibility.

After spending some time with Crystal, listening to what was happening at her new school and the people she was interacting with, Chantel told her that she was going to dine on a yacht that night with a new friend of hers. Crystal was very excited to hear this. She thought it was exciting that her mother was going to dine on a yacht and that she had a date also.

Then Chantel went into her bedroom and found a beautiful white Versace pantsuit to wear. She paired it with a brown and white silk scarf from Gucci. Then she changed her jewelry, finished her make-up, and put on a little perfume.

It was precisely seven o'clock when the doorman rang the intercom into Chantel's apartment. Margaret answered. The doorman told Margaret that a gentleman named Mr. Pagonis was waiting downstairs. Then Chantel took a light beige jacket out of one of the closets, kissed Crystal goodbye, and rang for the elevator to take her downstairs.

"See you later, my little love," Chantel told her.

"Bye Mom, have a great time. I'll miss you," replied Crystal.

When Chantel got out of the elevator, she saw Spiro standing in the lobby. He was wearing a navy blue cashmere blazer, tan trousers, a silk ascot, and a pocket square that had tiny red sailboats on it. She thought he looked very handsome. He had very distinct features. His eyes and his hair were both dark brown. And his skin had an olive tone to it. She thought he genuinely looked Mediterranean. And when Spiro saw Chantel, he smiled at her warmly and reached out to take her arm.

"Good evening, Chantel. I have a car outside waiting for us. I assume we are still dining on the yacht tonight. I am hoping so. My chef has been working all day on our menu. If I remember, we decided on things from the ocean. Not to worry, he's an excellent chef. I'm certain you will be pleased. I also asked my captain if he would take us sailing around the Hudson River, lower Manhattan, and near the Brooklyn Bridge. We will probably get good views of the Statue of Liberty on our way. Does this sound good to you?" Spiro asked her, sounding very sincere and wanting to please.

"Yes, it sounds wonderful, Spiro. I have never sailed around Manhattan before. And I haven't seen the Statue of Liberty in person either. It's a great idea," Chantel told him.

When they arrived at the World Yacht Marina, Spiro pointed out where his yacht was. There were two men and a woman standing in front of it waiting for them. Spiro introduced one of the men as Captain Alexis and the other as his assistant George.

The woman's name was Zantha. She was married to Captain Alexis. They all lived on the yacht together and were in charge of sailing and maintaining it. There were also other crew members on board who lived on the yacht with them. And Chantel later found out that there were actually two chefs that shared food preparation responsibilities. Spiro told her that they alternate the chef post every six months. The chefs were also in charge of Spiro's wine and champagne inventory and made sure that there was always enough on board for dinners, private parties, and special events.

"Captain Alexis, this is my friend Chantel Du Maurier, the lovely guest I told you I would bring tonight," said Spiro in a pleasant manner.

"Very pleased to meet you, Ms. Du Maurier. We hope you have a wonderful evening on board with us tonight," replied Captain Alexis respectfully.

George and Zantha chimed in and shook their heads in agreement. Then Spiro took Chantel's hand and led her across a little water bridge onto the yacht. The others followed behind them. Then Spiro brought Chantel to a living room area that was directly next to a large dining room. This was on the uppermost part of the yacht and had unobstructed views outside its windows of the city. It was impeccably designed and decorated with beautiful wooden furniture and paintings. There were also many candles lit around the rooms, making them look more inviting and romantic. Chantel could also hear piano music playing. Spiro had told her that he had hired a pianist to play for them that night.

"Please make yourself comfortable, Chantel. Sit anywhere you like. We'll be starting on some appetizers momentarily. What would you care to drink? I'll be having a very old red wine myself."

"That sounds good to me. I think I'd like to try some of that. Thank you," she answered.

Within a few minutes, one of the servers came in with a bottle of Chateau Lafite Rothschild. Then another server came in with several platters of cooked mussels, clams on the half shell, shrimp with crabmeat, white sturgeon caviar, and toasts and crackers. He also put a variety of unique cheeses and fruits on the table in front of them.

"Please try some of these, Chantel. I hope you like everything," Spiro told her with a big smile.

"Thank you. I can tell that you really have a fine chef, and everything looks so exquisite."

While they sipped on their wines, Alexis sailed the yacht out onto the Hudson River. The sky was clear, and the moon was already visible in the distance. There were even a couple of stars in the sky glistening high above them.

"Chantel, I'd like to know more about you. I remember you telling me that you came from Maine, now live in New York, and work at Champs. I was also quite impressed when you told me that you helped to create the Golden Doves fragrance line. I think it's one of the best in the world. And I understand it has done very well internationally," Spiro told her, glancing into her eyes.

"Yes, I always wanted to work in the beauty business and

was lucky enough to find an opportunity at Bloomingdale's with Champs when I first came to New York. I worked hard, and they kept promoting me. Then I began helping with product development and more. It has really been great. I love what I do. But there's something else I want to tell you about," Chantel told him.

"What is that, Chantel?"

"Well, I want you to know that I have a daughter. Although, I was never married. Her name is Crystal. She lives with me here in New York and goes to a private elementary school. I just thought you ought to know."

"I see. I'm sure she is as beautiful as you are. You are very beautiful, you know. I can't understand why you aren't married. But I also understand. Life can be very contradictory. I already had two wives, and neither marriage worked out for me. I also have two sons that were from those marriages. I am happy I had them though. But I no longer have much faith in marriage. While I still believe in love, I'm not so lucky in marriages. So I doubt I will ever marry again. Perhaps, that is why some people live together for years and never marry. They stay together for a long time and still seem to love one another. Maybe its better that way," Spiro said to her, pondering his words.

Chantel smiled at Spiro. She found him to be very different from many of the men she had met in her life. He also had an aristocratic air about him. It was evident that he was a strong and personable person. But she also thought there was something careful and maybe even a bit vulnerable about him.

"Spiro, you certainly have a point. There are many kinds of

relationships. But, tell me a little more about you. I really don't know anything about you except that you are Greek and own different businesses," Chantel commented.

"About me. Well, I was lucky. My family was originally in the cargo shipping business. This afforded us many things. I was born in Greece. I went to schools all over Europe. The school that I enjoyed the most was Oxford University in England. I studied economics there. Then I worked in some of my families businesses for a while and created some of my own companies. I own several homes around the world. But I tend to spend most of my time in Mykonos, Greece, Lucerne, Switzerland, and New York. I love visiting America. And I stay at the Waldorf a lot. But I'm also considering buying another place, perhaps something in the Pierre Hotel on Fifth Avenue. I'm not certain yet though. However, from time to time, I do have some business to take care of in New York," Spiro explained to her as he kissed one of her hands.

They both looked out at the luminous moon above them and smiled at each other. Then a server walked in to tell Spiro that the chef was ready to serve dinner. The server also told them that they were about to pass the Statue of Liberty.

"Let's go into the dining room, Chantel. I believe our chef is waiting to serve us. We'll also be able to see the Statue of Liberty from there. By the way, I think you have a lot in common with her. You're so beautiful and brave to come all the way from Maine by yourself. And it is amazing that you helped to create Golden Doves," Spiro told her, flattering her with the comparison.

Then they walked over to the dining room. And they looked out over the water and admired the Statue of Liberty together. Chantel was delighted to see it. They also got very close up to it and were able to admire the details of the statue. Then they sat down to eat. Seconds later, the chef walked over to them. He was a portly man with a pleasant looking face. His name was Daniel.

"Welcome, Ms. Du Maurier, we hope you enjoy your meal and will be back soon again," Daniel told her, trying to make her feel at home.

"Thank you. It's been a pleasure so far. The appetizers were extraordinary," replied Chantel, emphasizing her words.

Then one of the servers brought two more bottles of wine for them to drink, one white and one red. And Daniel served them lobster tails covered with another variety of caviar, poached salmon, smoked salmon rolls, oysters, and assorted grilled vegetables with petite potatoes. Chantel was bewildered by the presentation and variety.

"Enjoy, Chantel. I want you to be very happy," Spiro told her.

"Happy. I understand. I think you should be happy also. It is so thoughtful of you to make all this effort just for me," she said to him, appreciating all of his intentions for her.

"Look, there's lower Manhattan. It's the jungle of jungles. I'm just joking. Well, maybe not. But it is one of the most famous places in the world, even if it's not the most beautiful. Speaking of beautiful, you know, you remind me of many of the beautiful places in Europe I've been to. Many of these places have views of the sea that go on forever. You remind me of places where I felt the most peaceful in my life, removed from everything and everyone. You remind me of times when I felt an inner peace with life," Spiro explained to her.

"Spiro, I never imagined that you would be such a poet."

"I never imagined that I would meet someone like you, someone who would make me feel the way you make me feel inside. There's something so special and different about you from any woman I have ever met. I can sense it," Spiro told her, trying to understand his sudden emotions and how he was feeling about her.

"Wow, that's quite a compliment, Spiro. I'm really enjoying being with you as well. I really am," Chantel said to him, looking into his eyes thoughtfully.

After they finished dessert, they walked around the exterior of the yacht together and looked out at the water that surrounded them. They also admired the New York skyline. However, the weather was a little cool for them, so they soon decided to go back inside. Then they sat down next to each other while one of the servers brought them some cordials.

"Chantel, I really would like to see you again. In fact, I would like it if I could see you for lunch tomorrow before I go back to Europe. I will return to New York in about a month after that. I'd also like to keep in contact with you until then. Is this possible for you?"

"Yes, it's possible for me," Chantel answered, feeling like something was tugging at her heart.

They were soon going to dock. So Spiro decided that he

better kiss her before they did. So he touched her lips and led them to his. And they quickly kissed before they arrived at the pier where they first departed. They also decided to have lunch the following day at a restaurant called La Grenouille. Spiro told her that he would pick her up at her office by car and take her there.

~

THE NEXT DAY SPIRO PICKED CHANTEL UP AS PLANNED. Chantel had never been to La Grenouille and thought it was elegant. The restaurant had the most exotic and ornate flowers she had ever seen. There were so many flowers that their scents filled the entire restaurant. It was as if they were in a garden. Chantel thought the smell was incredibly refreshing and uplifting.

After they sat down, Spiro talked about Europe. He described many of the places that he enjoys there. He also told Chantel about some of the people he met throughout his life. Many of them were well-known and famous. Spiro also told her that he thought she was meant for Europe because she was so beautiful herself and that she would dazzle them all there. Chantel felt very flattered. But she didn't want the compliments going to her head either. She was too modest for that.

For the rest of their lunch together, they talked more about their lives and how they planned to keep in touch with one another. Spiro asked Chantel if she could set up Skype on her computer so that he could see her face to face when they spoke.

Chantel agreed. There was already a chemistry between them that they could feel towards one another. That was enough for both of them to know for now. And later, before Spiro left Chantel in front of her office building on Park Avenue, he held her in his arms and tenderly kissed her goodbye.

CHAPTER 23

HESS

JOHN COULDN'T WAIT TO SPEAK WITH STEVE. HE HAD NEWS that he knew would be of interest to him. Steve was in his study when his phone rang. "Steve, it's John. I have a surprise for you."

Steve ruffled through some papers he was looking at on his desk. His business affairs were continuing to go badly. The Woods store revenues were worse than ever. Steve knew he just couldn't keep depleting the funds that he had been swindling out of the store for years. He was drinking more heavily, borrowing greater sums of money without repaying people, and stalling many of his creditors. And he kept this all from Kate. She hadn't any idea how bad things were going at the Woods store and the way Steve was handling their finances.

"Guess who's in town, Steve?"

"Come on. Tell me."

"Octavian Senova, the master chess player from Russia, who happens to be an old acquaintance of mine. If I recall, you mentioned something about Max Conners and chess?" said John, hoping that Steve would connect the dots and get him excited.

Steve did get excited. But he also became angry. "That fucking bastard. This can be interesting. Are you telling me that you know Octavian well enough to get him in a game?" asked Steve.

"I bet I could. I just found out that he's staying at the Harvard Club for two weeks."

"Why the hell didn't you mention this to me sooner? I've heard of him. He's a worldwide professional of the game."

"Well, I just found out today. And, I called you. I wonder if we could get in touch with Max somehow and get him interested in a little tournament. Based on what you told me about him, I bet we just have to give him enough financial incentive. But, we need to speak to Octavian first," answered John.

"It sounds like you might know how to get in touch with Max," said Steve, thinking of how much he would love to get a win over him. He wanted a big win so badly.

John had already expected the question from Steve. So he explained to Steve that an acquaintance of his had mentioned Max's name recently and that he knew him. John also said that he heard Max had just bought an apartment in Manhattan and he's working on some large real estate development deals in New York with a partner from Los Angeles.

"Can we arrange to have lunch with Octavian tomorrow? Perhaps, we can meet him at the Harvard Club. I would like to make him a proposition," Steve asked him while playing with a brass ornament on his desk.

John was amused. He knew that Steve would probably want to set up a match between Max and Octavian. So John told Steve that he would contact Octavian and call him back. He phoned Steve later that afternoon and told him that he was able to get a lunch meeting with Octavian the following day.

THE NEXT DAY, STEVE AND JOHN WERE ALREADY SEATED AT A table in the Harvard Club dining room when Octavian walked in. The dining room had changed little throughout the years. The walls had the same wood paneling and paintings that they always had, and mostly covered with portraits of people. John welcomed Octavian over to their table. Then they all shook hands and sat down together.

"Octavian, very pleased to meet you. Thank you for coming. I have been a fan of yours for years. You must be one of the best chess players in the world," Steve said, trying to make him feel good.

Octavian had dark gray hair that was a little disheveled and smoky blue eyes that somehow exuded some kind of extraordinary intelligence. He also had a very heavy Russian accent when he spoke. But fortunately, his use of the English language was excellent.

"Thank you for the compliment. I played chess ever since I was a boy. Some of my old school mates are champion's themselves. Back in Russia, we used to play everyday after school and before doing our homework. Today, most of us simply play professionally," Octavian told him.

Steve found Octavian to be even more personable than he expected. Octavian had a powerful presence of confidence and sophistication about him.

"Shall we order?" asked Steve.

Then Steve waived down one of the waiters in the dining room. He told him that they were ready to order. And after the waiter took their orders, Steve explained to Octavian that he had a couple of disappointing dealings with Max Conners. Steve told him that he would really love it if he would play chess against Max on his behalf. Steve also told him that he was certain that he would win. But he wanted this to be a big win. So he offered Octavian a fee of a million dollars to play against Max. He would receive the money no matter who won the match. Steve wanted him to play three games of chess in a row. He told Octavian that the person who wins two of three games would get five million dollars. In this case, Steve would get the five million if Octavian wins.

"Staggering what you Americans will gamble and risk," commented Octavian.

"Yes, Octavian, it is. But I have faith in you. After all, you are a world chess master and champion," said Steve.

Octavian liked money just as much as anyone else. He had a hard time refusing such an offer. There would be no losses for him. He would still get a million dollars. Moments like these made him feel good about being a new American citizen. He knew something like this wouldn't happen in Russia or many other places for that matter.

On the other hand, Steve was again planning on betting money that he really shouldn't be. He planned to sell some of his private investments if he needed to. And he still could manage to hide all of this from Kate. And he still had considerable assets compared to most people. Kate was too busy with her own interests to notice what he was doing. She also trusted him with managing their money. All he wanted to do was to win. So he convinced himself that he was going to get back at Max once and for all.

"Certified or bank check only before the match. Then you have a deal," added Octavian.

Octavian was no fool when it came to money. He always made sure he got paid what he was due, no matter how much or for whom. Then he put a forkful of his steak into his mouth and nodded his head up and down.

"You've got it. I've been waiting for a chance like this for a while. But, I want you to beat the pants off of Max. It's his turn. Do you understand, Octavian?" Steve told him, turning red in the face with anger.

"Certainly, Mr. Woods. I haven't lost a game in twenty-five years. And I don't intend to now. After all, I have a reputation to uphold. So, again, you have a deal," Octavian replied.

As fate would have it, Max Conners also walked into the dining room with three other men. They all sat down at another table in the room to have lunch. Max hadn't noticed them. He looked calm and polished in his blue Brooks Brothers pinstripe suit and tie. But when Steve saw Max, his blood began to boil.

"I just can't believe this. There is Max, Octavian. The loser just walked in and is sitting over there. Do you see him? He just took a sip of water," said Steve, eyeing in the direction of Max's table.

"Yes, I do see who you mean, Mr. Woods. It's okay. I understand well how you feel," said Octavian.

"Now calm down, Steve. Let's see if I can lure him from his table so we can make the proposition to him," said John, raising one of his arms to signal a waiter to come over to him.

"I would like to send those gentlemen over there a bottle of Salon champagne. Mr. Conner's is an old friend of ours. Please tell him it is compliments of Steve Woods," John told the waiter.

"Certainly, sir. I'll see to it right away," the waiter answered.

Steve watched closely as the waiter brought the champagne to Max's table. Then Max looked over at their table to acknowledge them. He figured something was up. He knew that Steve Woods hated him. But he also found Steve's temper toward him amusing. Fifteen minutes later, Max walked over to their table to find out what they were up to.

"Thank you for the toast. To what do I owe this pleasure?" asked Max, looking directly at Steve.

"Please sit down for a moment," Steve told him.

"Only for a few minutes. As you can see for yourself, I have guests of my own here to attend to," said Max.

"In case you haven't met, this is John Dillard. And this friend of ours is Octavian Senova, the master chess player from Russia. We heard that you enjoy playing chess and were wondering if you would be up to a competition and wager? The stakes would be very high," said Steve.

"Hello Octavian. Yes, I have heard of you. You have quite a reputation. This is a rare treat to meet you in person. So, what is the wager, Steve?" asked Max.

"It would be five million dollars to whoever wins two out of three games. And Octavian would be playing for me. I also suggest that we have it here at the Harvard Club. And we insist on certified and bank checks only to be held by an attorney here at the club. It's that simple. The winner of two out of three games gets the five million. Or, maybe that's just too much for you to wager," Steve told him.

Max wasn't intimidated by the offer. He knew he was a much better chess player than any of them were aware of. He had played with a few chess masters in the past and held his own.

"Actually, I like this deal. You know, you must be one of Manhattan's biggest idiots, Steve. But that is precisely why I am willing to do it. Just make sure you have the money ready. I've heard that you're not doing so well lately. There are some bad rumors going around about the financial condition of your store," said Max chuckling at Steve.

Max could tell that Steve was becoming infuriated. But that

was exactly what he wanted to see. And John was getting a little nervous. He didn't want a scene in the club dining room.

"Where do you get your information from, Max, the sewer or the gutter? So when should we have this game? How about this coming Friday? We can reserve a room for six o'clock in the evening. Just make sure you bring the five million with you," Steve said to him, visibly teeming with resentment over his past losses.

Then Max got up from the table. And he looked over at Octavian who was quietly listening to everyone.

"You're on, Octavian. I do respect you. But you just might be surprised this time. Don't say I didn't warn you. See you on Friday," Max told him, before he went back over to his table with a grin on his face.

FRIDAY CAME AROUND QUICKLY. AND OCTAVIAN HAD RESTED most of the day to get ready for the competition. He knew his reputation was at stake. And even though he hadn't lost a game in many years, he realized there was always a chance that he could. But he wasn't going to lose anything himself. A million dollars was a lot of money for him to get paid for playing a few games of chess. He wasn't especially nervous or excited about the competition. He was mostly focused on the money and his standing as a player.

Steve had phoned Octavian earlier that day and asked him to meet him in the lobby of the Harvard Club at five-thirty. Octavian was a little early and waited for him in one of the club chairs. He had on a light gray suit with a thin red tie, shiny black leather shoes, and a *Wall Street Journal* on his lap when Steve and John arrived. Then they took Octavian into a private room that was reserved for the chess match. Steve and John also greeted a couple of people they invited to watch the competition. One of the men was the attorney who would be holding all the bank checks. Steve had already given him an envelope with a check for five million. And Steve also gave Octavian an envelope with his check for a million.

"Octavian, as promised, this is for you. But you can only cash it after the match," Steve reminded him.

Then Octavian sat down at the game table and waited for Max to arrive. Max was there a little after six. And he also brought a few guests with him. Several minutes later, Max sat down with Octavian at the chess table. The chess set was made by Baccarat. It was the most expensive chess set in the club, costing nearly twenty thousand dollars.

"I see you have showed up. Don't forget the check," Steve told Max.

Max took an envclope out of one of his pockets and gave it to the attorney to hold. Max knew who he was and that he was trustworthy.

"Pity. This unfortunate twit hasn't learned his lesson yet. Always in over your head, Steve," Max uttered.

John almost let out a laugh but he held it in before Steve could tell. He also had a few words with the attorney, making sure that everything was in order. John actually felt that Octavian would win the match. After all, Octavian was a very well-known chess master. John figured that Steve would finally have his revenge. Yet, John himself would never risk that amount of money on one chess game. He was well aware that Steve let his emotions get the best of him.

Octavian made the first move on the chessboard. But a little later on, it became apparent that Octavian was having a harder time defeating Max than anyone expected. Max was proving to be a much more competent player than anyone anticipated. Steve was watching closely, putting down three scotch and sodas in the meantime. So far, Octavian had won one game and Max another. They had just begun their third game. And about an hour later, Octavian lost the game, and Max had won the match.

"Checkmate," said Max, raising his king off the board in the air, laughing uncontrollably, looking thrilled at Steve and the attorney.

Completely shocked and outraged, Steve got out of his chair and tried to put his hands around Max's neck to choke him. He slammed Max down on the chess table, nearly breaking some of its pieces. Then John and another man pulled Steve off of Max and held him so he couldn't attack him again. They didn't want the police to be called in. It would be an embarrassment to the club.

"You son of a bitch. I'll get you for this," yelled Steve, at the top of his lungs at Max, watching him receive the five million dollar check from the attorney.

Then one of the security men at the club informed Steve that due to his violent behavior, he was immediately expelled from the club and had to leave right away. He told Steve that he would have to go peacefully or he would be forced to have him arrested.

"Do you understand, Mr. Woods?" asked the security guard.

"Yes, I understand totally," shouted Steve, loosening himself from being held while straightening out his jacket.

"Sorry, Mr. Woods. I tried my best," said Octavian as he looked at him. Octavian felt sorry for him, but a deal was a deal.

Steve didn't say anything more to Octavian. Then John and he left the club quietly. Steve didn't want Kate to find out about what just happened. If he was arrested, they might contact her. So he kept his composure to prevent any more of a scene. His car and driver were still outside waiting for him. When he got outside, Steve turned to John.

"You told me I was going to win. You got me into this one. You're another son of a bitch, John. Get the fuck out of my face," Steve yelled at him.

"Look, I'm sorry, Steve. I really thought Octavian would win. I really did. I lost some money betting on this match also."

"Oh, fuck off," said Steve, slamming the car door of his limo after he got inside of it.

Steve decided to go back to his office at the Woods store. He sat at his desk all night long drinking cognac until he passed out right on top of it.

CHAPTER 24

OGETHER

WHILE SPIRO WAS AWAY, HE AND CHANTEL KEPT IN TOUCH. They often Skyped together online, so they could see each other in person. Spiro also showed Chantel what his perfumery company was like using Skype. That was when he was visiting Lucerne. Other times, when he contacted her, he was sailing around the Greek Islands. Spiro and Chantel thought about each other constantly. There became a special bond between them. On their last communication on Skype, Spiro told her he was on his way back to New York. He told her that he was sailing over the Atlantic Ocean.

When Spiro arrived in New York, he once again had rooms reserved at the Waldorf Astoria. This time Chantel took the lead and asked him if he would like to visit her and

Crystal at her apartment on the West Side. Chantel thought it would be nice for him to meet Crystal in person and to see where they lived. Since he arrived late in the evening, they waited until the following day to have dinner together. Chantel prepared a meal for all of them. Margaret had only helped with some of the minor details. When Spiro arrived, they anxiously waited for him in the foyer to greet him. And when he got off the elevator, he was carrying two large boxes with him.

"Hello, Spiro. Welcome. Come inside. This is my daughter, Crystal. And this is our terrific housekeeper, Margaret. Please, make yourself at home," Chantel told him.

"Hello, Crystal. Hello, Margaret. It's a pleasure to meet you both. Now, where can I put these two boxes? One is for you, Chantel, and the other is for Crystal. I also have something for you Margaret in my jacket pocket," he said, hurrying to get his hands free.

Crystal looked up at Spiro and smiled at him. She was delighted that he had thought of them and brought them gifts. She took the boxes out of his hands and put them on a nearby table. Then Spiro took out an envelope from one of his jacket pockets and gave it to Margaret. He told her that it was a gift card for Bloomingdale's and that he appreciated her taking care of Chantel and Crystal. Margaret was very touched that he thought of her also. She thanked him and hung up his jacket in the entryway closet.

"Chantel, did you receive the wine I sent you yesterday? You should have received a few bottles of champagne. I thought we could sample one or two tonight?" Spiro asked her, hoping they'd already arrived.

"Yes, I did. Thank you. That was very thoughtful. We already have some chilled and on ice waiting for you. What's in this box, Spiro? More wine? Sounds like bottles or something fragile."

"No actually. Those are not wine bottles. It is a surprise. Why don't we wait until after dinner for you to take a look? Is that okay?" he asked Chantel, giving her a quick kiss on the cheek.

"Sure, what about Crystal? I bet she doesn't want to wait to open hers," replied Chantel.

Spiro looked at Crystal and warmly smiled at her. "Crystal, please go ahead and open yours," Spiro told her.

Crystal tore open the box. Inside of it, she found a traditional Greek outfit with shoes, stockings, and a tiara made out of flowers, ribbons, and rhinestones. There was also an ornate jewelry box made of elm wood that played the Magic Flute melody by Mozart.

"I see. It's a Greek princess outfit. Mom, can I put this on now?" asked Crystal, propping the outfit against her body with one hand, and trying to balance the jewelry box in the other.

"Of course you can, Crystal," Chantel told her.

"That's a lovely music box. It reminds me of one that I had when I was a little girl," said Margaret.

Crystal went to her room to put on her new outfit. When she returned, they all told her how adorable she looked and what a pretty princess she was.

"Princess Crystal is here," remarked Spiro, with authoritative inflection in his voice.

"Yes, I'm definitely a princess," Crystal replied, twirling around to show off her outfit.

Then they all sat down in the dining room for dinner. Margaret helped to serve so that Chantel and Crystal would have more time with Spiro. Margaret brought in some appetizers followed by duck, asparagus, and wild rice as a main course. Spiro helped to open the champagne. And after their main course, they had dessert, a combination of berries, whip cream, and chocolate syrup. When they finished dessert, Crystal went to watch television with Margaret in another room. Chantel and Spiro finally had some time alone. They closed the doors to the dining room so they would have more privacy. Spiro looked out the windows of the room and commented on the views of Central Park. Chantel stood next to him, also looking out of the windows.

"I have missed you so much, Chantel. You can't even imagine how much I miss you," Spiro told her, pulling her gently toward him.

Spiro touched her lips and hair with his fingers. Then he leaned over and kissed her.

"I also missed you, Spiro. I'm so glad you're here in person. Thank you for all the gifts. That was kind of you to think of Crystal and Margaret," Chantel told him.

"Speaking of which, it's time for you to open yours."

Then Chantel took the box and opened it. It contained many little bottles of perfume samples. They each had a number posted on them. She reached for one, opened it, and smelled it with her nose. Then she gave Spiro a curious look as if she wanted an explanation.

"Those are perfumes from my factory in Lucerne, Chantel. I thought you might like to try these samples. Perhaps, you can tell me which ones you think are the best," Spiro suggested.

"Are you serious. All of these are from your factory? Are they in production?" Chantel asked.

"No, not yet. I wanted to get your professional opinion first."

"I'm flattered, of course. But give me a little time on this. I don't want to give you hasty advice," Chantel told him, putting the bottle back in the box, touched by the fact that he wanted her recommendation.

"That's terrific. Now, I want to make plans for tomorrow night. Since I met Crystal tonight, I would like it if we could have dinner alone tomorrow. We can go anywhere you like, even for a sail. I think we need some time to ourselves."

"Mmm, that sounds good to me. Well, I really enjoyed our sail the last time. I'd like to do that again. Maybe, we can time it so we can watch the sunset?"

"Certainly, we can. If you like, we can also watch the sunrise. That would be different. Wouldn't it? How about I pick you up tomorrow at five o'clock?"

"That would be great. I'd really like that," Chantel answered.

Then the two of them spent some more time together to hold

and kiss each other. And before Spiro left, he said goodbye to Crystal and thanked Margaret for her help.

~

THE NEXT DAY, CHANTEL WAS ALREADY DOWNSTAIRS IN THE lobby of her building when Spiro arrived in his car. His driver got outside and opened the door for her. Then they headed to the World Yacht Marina and boarded Spiro's yacht as they did the last time. Captain Alexis, George, and Zantha were also there waiting for them.

"Welcome back, Ms. Du Maurier. Hello, sir," said Alexis, when they arrived.

"Thank you," replied Chantel, walking onto the yacht with Spiro.

"Alexis, perhaps we can go a longer distance tonight along Long Island Sound and around Southern Connecticut. Might be nice to travel a little bit around there," suggested Spiro.

"Yes, sir. The weather will be good all evening and tomorrow as well. There is no reason not to," replied Alexis.

Chantel and Spiro went back to the lounge where they spent most of their time together before. The sun was still shining bright, and it was warmer than a month ago. Different colors of yellows bounced in the room creating reflections around the windows. One of the servers came in with a bottle of champagne, a pitcher of ice water, and asked if it would be okay to bring them some appetizers. Spiro nodded to give him the okay. Ten minutes later, the server returned with an assortment of fine cheeses, olives, grilled squid, fried oysters, and miniature crab cakes with lemon aioli. Then they lifted up their glasses, gently touched them to cheers, and took their first sips of champagne together.

"We're finally taking off. Please, have something to eat. I'm going to request grilled lobster with shrimp tonight for our main course. Is that okay with you, Chantel?" asked Spiro.

"That would be great. I haven't had lobster since I saw you the last time. You're reminding me of Maine again," she said, delighted with the idea.

"Wonderful. Now, let me put some music on for us. I would like to select our own music tonight. Is there anything in particular that you would like to hear? I'm sure I can find something for you."

"Some soft piano music would be nice. I know you like piano music also. Maybe something New Age-like," answered Chantel.

"I will see what I can find for you. By the way, have you noticed the water looks very calm tonight? So we should have smooth sailing. I also understand a crescent moon is expected. Sometimes that can be just as beautiful as a full moon if not more."

Then Spiro sat closer to her, and they began kissing each other passionately. Chantel realized that she was falling for him. All the conversations they had together on the phone and Skype made her feel like she already knew him well. He didn't feel like a stranger to her any longer. She realized she hadn't had feelings like these since she fell for Marco. But it also frightened her a little to have these feelings for another man again. Falling in love made her feel a bit apprehensive. She didn't want to be disappointed or to get hurt again in the future. She knew that she was taking a risk into the unknown.

"Chantel, have you had time to think about the perfume samples I brought you? I'm wondering which ones you think are the best to further develop? Have you any ideas yet?" Spiro asked her, holding one of her hands and kissing it.

"I did sample them this morning. They're quite exceptional. So far, I like nine and eleven the most. I like nine for the quality of its rose oils, and I like eleven for its interesting citrus combination. But my guess is that they are not completely finished. Am I right?"

"That's right. They are still being brought to life. I thought you could help me with that. I'm wondering if I can steal you away from Champs. I'm wondering if you would be willing to come to Lucerne and help me finish developing our next line of fragrances."

Chantel was very surprised by Spiro's offer. But she was also very flattered that he thought enough of her to want her help.

"Of course, I understand you couldn't do this while you work at Champs. So, I'm offering you five times whatever they are paying you. I'm also offering you a partnership in the profits. If the fragrances do well, you could become a very wealthy woman."

"But I can't leave the United States and Crystal here. I'm sure you understand that. I'm grateful for the offer though."

"I know, Chantel. That is why I only want you to come to Lucerne for its product development. Then you can come back to New York to be with Crystal and work from here. I'm sure you have an idea by now how I feel about you. Yet, as I explained before, I will probably not marry again. But I would like to see that your career dreams are realized. By the very least, I can offer you this. It would also make me happy knowing that you would be financially taken care of. I don't want you to ever need or worry about money in your lifetime. Please think about it."

Chantel looked out at the sky and once again felt like life was being so surreal. She calmed herself to get a hold of her emotions. She didn't expect to have to make a decision like this. She was also doing well at Champs. But she knew this was an even greater opportunity.

"I know this seems somewhat strange to you. But I want to assure you that my intentions are in your best interests. If you accept, I will have my attorneys draw up a contract to protect you financially. I only want the best for you. I know that you have the talent to do this. And this will ensure that you and Crystal will be taken care of with or without me," Spiro explained to her.

Then Spiro took another sip of champagne and looked out onto Long Island Sound. A server came in and announced that dinner was ready. So they went into the dining room and began eating their dinner together. When they were finished with their main courses, they went back into the lounge to have their desserts and sip on some port wine. The sun had already set by then, and the crescent moon above them looked magical. Spiro found some more music that he thought Chantel would enjoy and played it. Then he put his arms around her.

"Would you like to dance?" he asked her softly.

"Yes, I would, Spiro. It's so beautiful tonight. Dinner was delicious. But I want you to know that I appreciate everything. And I have to give going to Lucerne some more thought. You kind of caught me by surprise, as you must imagine," she told him, looking into his eyes, smiling at him warmly.

"Only if it feels right to you. Take your time, my darling."

They danced under the moon and stars for a while, holding each other tightly. Then they started kissing more passionately and became completely lost in each other. Spiro held her even tighter, feeling more like a man in love than he had ever felt in his life. He realized how much he loved her.

"Can we be more alone than this?" he asked.

Chantel knew what he meant. She looked at him silently and nodded her head expressing approval. Then he took her hand and kissed it again. Spiro led her to his bedroom on the yacht. Then he closed the door behind them and put some more soft music on. They held each other for a while just looking out onto the water in silence. The water was still calm and reflecting the shadows of light from the moon.

"I love you, Chantel," Spiro whispered into her ear.

They sat on his bed and began to undress each other. Spiro gently traced every part of her body with his lips and hands. He touched her from the top of her head to the bottom of her feet and toes. Then she felt his body with her hands, noticing how muscular and strong he was. The passion between them became unbearable. And their bodies soon became intertwined as they made love for the rest of the night. They became completely consumed with each other's sexuality and sensuousness. They were so sexually aligned that when they came together, they each let out endearing cries of joy and had tears in their eyes. Their bodies fluttered like butterflies from the electric current they felt. And they whispered into each other's ears telling each other how much they loved one another. They felt incredible, just like they were in a different universe altogether.

"How can I ever live without you in my life, my darling? I just can't. Not now. Not ever," Spiro told her, holding her as close as he physically could.

For the rest of the night, they kissed and held one another. It wasn't until sunrise that Spiro asked Alexis to bring them back to Manhattan. During their sail, they had breakfast together in the dining room. And just before the yacht returned to the pier, Spiro had his driver meet them there.

SWITZERLAND

IT WAS LIKE A DREAM TO CHANTEL WHEN SHE AND SPIRO WENT to Switzerland to develop their fragrance line together. Spiro had been honest with her. He was paying her what he promised and gave her a contract that protected their partnership. Her career aspirations were materializing in front of her very own eyes. It was true that if the perfume line were to be successful, Chantel would become a wealthy woman. The best part of becoming wealthy though to her would be the advantages that she could offer Crystal. Margaret was taking care of her while she was away. Chantel felt at ease and knew that she could rely on Margaret. Margaret had already proved to be a trustworthy housekeeper and caretaker to Crystal. This gave Chantel a peace of mind while she was in Lucerne.

Dora had come to Lucerne with Chantel also. Dora worked with Chantel for a while now and helped her a great deal with everything she needed help with. Dora was very happy with the arrangement because she enjoyed being with Chantel and was getting paid far more money than she was at Buckleven. She was also thrilled to travel. This was Dora's first trip outside of the United States. She found Switzerland fascinating. And Chantel was grateful to have her there, especially since they were such good friends.

Chantel's feelings for Spiro had become even stronger. And Spiro was still very much in love with Chantel. He also trusted her more than any other woman he'd ever met in his life. But Chantel was much more cautious of her feelings for him. She felt like she had a different kind of love for him than she had with Marco. She thought that maybe it was because it wasn't her first love.

Spiro had a large home on Lake Lucerne with panorama views of the water. It also had stunning views of the mountains around it. Instead of staying at a hotel, they decided they would all stay there together. Spiro also had domestic help to care for them and to help with any of their needs. The perfumery and lab, where they were developing the new fragrance line, was located nearby. The lab was nestled among a few mountains that also grew many of the plants that were used in the fragrance formulas. Chantel thought the scenery was extraordinarily beautiful. She found herself admiring the views and totally absorbed in how lovely the land looked. The mountains were so high up that many of the peaks were not even visible when the clouds passed. This gave them an even more mysterious look. And the blue waters below on Lake Lucerne reflected their many colors.

Over the past few months, Chantel had learned more about Spiro's businesses. He'd already told her when they first met that fragrances were only one of the many businesses he was involved with. He had different kinds of factories in various places in Europe. The name of the perfumery was Moritz. It was a pretty good size for a manufacturing lab. Chantel was quite impressed by it and thought there must be more going on there than just fragrances being developed.

Spiro was at home in his office when Chantel heard his phone ring. He sounded somewhat agitated with the caller. After twenty minutes of speaking Greek, she heard the receiver hang up.

"Is everything all right?" she asked him, wondering what was going on.

"Yes, it will be. It's just many people need my input and sometimes have a hard time making decisions without me. Everything will be fine, my darling. Now, how was your day today? How is your progress at the lab coming along? But before you answer, please kiss me," Spiro said leaning toward her, waiting for her lips to meet his.

They kissed for a while. Then Chantel showed Spiro some samples she was working on at the lab. She carried them in a leather attaché case.

"I've brought these for you to try. I'm still working on them though, so they are not completely finished. The good news is that everything I need is there and it shouldn't take too long to have several perfumes ready for a product line," she told him confidently.

"Excellent. These do smell very good. Don't rush too much though. I want them to be perfect. But for now, let's get ready for dinner. There's a restaurant I'd like to take you to tonight. I also think it might be fun to go to the casino here in Lucerne. Let's bring Dora with us. It wouldn't be nice to leave her here alone," Spiro said, thoughtfully.

"That's a great idea. I'll go tell her to get ready to join us for dinner. She'll really like that. I'm sure."

"But Chantel, before you go. I have a little surprise for you on the table over there. Please open it," Spiro told her warmly.

Chantel walked over to the table and picked up a lavender box that was tied with a large purple velvet ribbon. Inside of it, she found a perfume bottle made out of enamel, gold, and pearls. She had never seen anything like it before.

"It's a Fabergé, Chantel. I had collected some pieces in the past and thought you would like this one. I hope you do."

"Yes, I like it very much. It's so unusual. Breathtaking actually. Thank you. You are already doing so much for me. You didn't have to do this," she told him, feeling touched inside.

Spiro walked over to her, lifted up her hair, and kissed her gently on the neck.

"It's breathtaking like you, my darling. Now let's get organized for dinner. Please tell Dora to get ready and that we'll be leaving soon. I'll tell our driver to get the car outside."

"You're far too thoughtful and generous. I hope so much that the fragrance line I'm working on will be a tremendous success," Chantel told him. Then she hugged and kissed him also.

"Do you have any idea what you might call the collection yet, Chantel?" Spiro asked.

"I'm considering naming it the Du Maurier Collection consisting of five different fragrances with their respective numbers. I would also create the related products with the same name," Chantel explained to him.

"Sounds very good. I am glad that you are planning on using your name with them just like any designer out there in the world. Let me know when you are ready and have fully decided. Then we can have some preliminary labels created."

"Absolutely. That would be great," replied Chantel.

A little while later Chantel, Dora, and Spiro left for the restaurant. When they got there, they were seated at a comfortable table that also had views of the lake. Then they enjoyed a long three-course meal together. And when they were finished eating, they decided to go to the casino.

"How about we go over to one of the roulette tables?" suggested Spiro.

"This is just like the movies," remarked Dora.

Chantel and Dora followed Spiro. He sat down at a roulette table and took out some chips he brought to play with. He also asked Chantel and Dora if they would like to give it a try. But they were not inclined to because neither of them knew how to play. They opted out to watch Spiro play instead.

"We don't mind watching, Spiro. That's fun for us also," Chantel told him.

Spiro played roulette for almost an hour. He won most of the bets he made and was satisfied with his winnings. And when he was tired of playing, they decided to walk around the casino together to watch the other players try their luck. Then all of sudden Spiro saw Max Conners sitting at one of the roulette tables. Spiro was happy to see someone familiar.

"Ladies, follow me. I see a friend of mine from the United States that I would like to introduce you both to. What a nice surprise this is, Max," said Spiro loudly, walking toward him.

Max heard Spiro's voice and turned around to look at who was calling him. He immediately recognized Spiro and smiled at him. Then Max asked the dealer at his table to cash him in so he could say hello and talk with Spiro.

"Hello, Spiro. You're the last person I would expect to see here in Switzerland. I thought you'd likely be in Greece, or London, or back in the United States at this time. It's great to see you again. Are you here on business or pleasure? I'm taking a short holiday myself," said Max, eager to hear a response.

"A little of both, Max. But mostly business I would say. Let me make some introductions. This is my dear friend Chantel Du Maurier and her assistant Dora Moore from New York. We're only here temporarily to work on a fragrance line together. Ladies, this is Max Conners. Like the two of you, he is also from the United States," said Spiro.

"Sounds interesting. Spiro is quite the international businessman, isn't he? Pleased to meet you both," replied Max, glad to be introduced to women and not men for a change.

"Good to meet you, Max," said Chantel.

"Same here, nice to meet you, Max," added Dora, trying not to sound too awkward. Although, she was happy to see another man there herself. She also thought that Max was quite attractive and hoped that he was single.

Then Spiro suggested they all sit down at a table together and talk for a while. Max quickly agreed. He also thought that Dora was attractive and wanted to find out more about her. After they all sat down together, they decided to order some champagne and pear brandy to sip on.

"This is Chantel's and Dora's first visit to Switzerland. Lucky for me, they both seem to like it a lot. Otherwise, we might have had to hop on my jet back to the United States," said Spiro, half joking.

"I'm glad to hear it. Where are you all staying?" asked Max.

"In one of my homes on Lake Lucerne. It isn't too far from here. But tonight I thought they would enjoy going out to dinner and the casino. I'm glad we came here. Or, we might not have run into you," Spiro told him, offering him a Padron cigar.

"As for me, I'm staying at the Palace Hotel. Say, I wonder, have either of you been on any excursions up to the mountains? They are even more beautiful when you see them high above," asked Max.

"I never knew you liked to travel up to the mountains, Max." commented Spiro.

"No, no excursions for me. I'm far too busy in the fragrance lab right now," Chantel answered.

"I haven't either," said Dora, thinking of how intriguing it sounded.

"I highly recommend it. I happen to have plans to go up to the summit of Mount Pilatus tomorrow morning. Perhaps, you would be interested in going, Dora?" asked Max, figuring he would give the idea a chance.

Chantel thought that it would be good if Dora went. It was true that they hadn't been on any special excursions since they got there. And Dora didn't have a male companion with her like Spiro.

"Yes, you should go, Dora," Chantel encouraged her.

Dora briefly hesitated but decided to accept the invitation. She thought it would be adventurous. And she liked to be adventurous at times.

"Okay, I'll go, as long as it's all right with you, Chantel. Can you live without me for a day?" asked Dora.

"We'll survive somehow. You officially have the day off tomorrow. Enjoy it. I heard the weather is supposed to be good also," Chantel told her.

"Well, that settles that. I'll pick you up at Spiro's in the morning. I just need his address. Here's my card with my international cell number in case you need to reach me by phone," Max told them, reaching into his pocket to get a couple of his cards to give to them.

Spiro lifted his brandy glass to make a toast to them all. He also gave Max his address in Lucerne. They were all feeling very comfortable with each other.

"So tell me, Max, how's the real estate business doing in California?" Spiro asked him.

"Actually, Spiro, I've been concentrating on some recent acquisitions in New York. I purchased two office buildings in midtown Manhattan. And, I'm also involved in some other transactions further downtown. This led me to finally buy an apartment in Manhattan. California was getting a little stagnant for me anyway. Here's another one of my cards. This one has my new business contact information in New York. What about you, Spiro? Have you been in New York a lot since I saw you last? You had some party at that time. I always enjoy being on one of your yachts. I had a lot of fun the last time," said Max.

"Yes, I have. I've got many new interests there, and this is one of them," Spiro said, pointing at Chantel. "You'll have to come to our next party to celebrate the launch of Chantel's new fragrance line. It's sure to be a smashing success."

Spiro took one of Chantel's hands and kissed it. Then Chantel blushed, and Dora laughed out loud.

"Don't be so modest, Chantel. Modesty does little for someone as ambitious as you," added Spiro.

"Often the truth. I look forward to receiving the invitation," replied Max.

For the next hour and a half, they talked more about New York and then they decided to call it a night.

~

THE FOLLOWING DAY MAX PICKED UP DORA IN AN OLD ANTIQUE silver Porsche that he rented in Lucerne. They were both dressed in fur hats, down jackets, and down pants to keep them warm. During their drive, Max told Dora about some of the places he'd been to in Switzerland, such as Geneva and Zurich. He also told her that he loved the mountains in Switzerland and tried to visit the country at least once every year or two.

Max often glanced over at Dora while he was driving. He admired her pretty, healthy, and wholesome look. He was beginning to feel more attracted to her. Her carefree attitude and the way she carried herself really impressed him. He thought she was so optimistic, vibrant, and full of life. He was already planning on seeing her again when they were both back in New York.

"It was a really nice surprise meeting you last night, a very nice surprise. Perhaps, we will see each other in New York in the future. It might be fun," Max said, trying not to sound too pushy.

Dora didn't mind though. Meeting Max in Switzerland was very unique to her. The thought of seeing him again in New York just made everything all the more interesting.

"Sure, I'd like that," answered Dora.

"Terrific. Maybe we can go to a concert or something? I often get tickets for Madison Square Garden, Radio City Music Hall, and the Metropolitan Opera. But since you're from the South, I'm wondering if you've ever been to the Grand Ole Opry in Nashville?" he asked her, curious what she would say.

"Regretfully, no. I've never made it there yet."

"No matter, I'm sure you will someday. After all, you made it to Europe, so you're bound to make it to Nashville someday. Right?" Max said, in an upbeat tone of voice.

"I hope so," answered Dora, knowing that Nashville was the last thing on her mind right then.

They rode a little longer, and when they got to their destination, they boarded a cable car to take them to an aerial cable that would bring them to the summit of Mount Pilatus. Max explained to Dora that they would see a good part of the Swiss Alps. Dora was getting a little nervous with the elevation changes though. Sensing her nervousness, Max held her hand for the first time and told her not to worry. Then Dora closed her eyes and hid her head on his chest. Max could feel the contours of her eyes, nose, and mouth. He could tell she was secretly smiling and was charmed by her.

As they continued in the cable ride, they were surrounded by some of the world's steepest mountains. Dora knew she would never forget an experience like this, even if she was nervous and had butterflies in her stomach. She enjoyed Max's company and had no idea how much he enjoyed hers.

Over the past few years, Max hadn't really taken much time out for women. Business had been his major priority over all other things in his life. However, with Dora, he began to feel alive again romantically.

By the time they made it to the top of Mount Pilatus, they were a bit exasperated from the breathtaking ride up. They decided to sit for a few minutes before they walked along the mountain trails. Then they looked out at the towering peaks around them and took some photos with their cell phones. They even asked a tourist to take a few photos of them together.

"Max, I have to be honest with you. This is a little frightening. A good frightening though," said Dora, holding onto a railing, looking around at the vastness of the geography.

Max moved closer to Dora and put his arms around her waist. "You needn't be frightened, Dora. I know we're at a high elevation, but what frightens you the most about it?" Max asked her.

"I think it's the enormousness and beauty of it up here," she answered, in a reflective tone of voice, still taking in the views around her.

"Yes, it is pretty awesome. Nothing like the skyscrapers in New York, is it? It's even better."

"It also makes me wonder about people and life on the planet. It makes me wonder what this world is really about. It seems so much larger than us, this natural beauty. It's kind of overwhelming, and even kind of scary in a good way," said Dora, reflecting on what she was seeing.

"Scary, it's not supposed to be. It's to be admired, enjoyed, cherished, lived on, and loved. That much I think I know," Max told her.

"I see. But it's still an incredible sight, nature compared to humans and human-made things."

"You deserve a kiss for that observation, Dora." Then Max leaned over her and placed his lips on hers before she even had time to think of what was happening. Their lips locked instantly, and they earnestly kissed one another. "Sorry, I just felt compelled to do that. I hope you didn't mind," Max said to her, clearing his throat.

Dora didn't complain. She blushed a little and smiled at him. Then they decided to walk along the summit for a little while longer. On their way back down, they talked about each other's work. Dora found Max's real estate business interesting. And Max liked the fact that Dora worked so closely with a personal friend of his. Max was very fond of Spiro.

"Were you ever married, Dora?" Max asked her, getting a little more personal.

"No. And you?" Dora answered and asked quickly.

"Not yet. That's a good thing, isn't it?" he added.

Dora wondered what Max meant by that exactly. But she didn't want to ask him to elaborate either. So she simply looked out the windows of the cable car and watched the sunset in front of them. There was a family of four riding with them also. They had English accents. Dora wondered if they were from London or some other city in England. Then she wondered what it would be like to be married and have a family. And she knew that she was only wondering about it because of Max. There was something about him that brought these thoughts to her mind.

When they got back to Max's car, they decided to have dinner together before returning to Lucerne. Max recommended a quaint country restaurant he knew of named Le Charme. It was conveniently located among some of the smaller mountains, so it wasn't as difficult to get to. The restaurant was very romantic. It was dimly lit with candles. And there was a guitarist playing soft music for people to listen to. They were seated at a small square table that had a bouquet of wildflowers on it, giving off an aromatic smell. Then they started flirting with each other, acting as if they were already established lovers.

"Again, I hope we'll be seeing each other again in Manhattan," said Max, wishing that Dora would be traveling back to New York soon.

"Yes, but it will have to wait until Chantel's perfume line is complete. I'm not exactly sure how long we'll be staying here yet. But we will eventually go back to New York. I imagine it won't be too long."

Max was a little disappointed by the answer. But he knew that Dora would return to New York. He knew that she lived in Manhattan and her visit to Switzerland was only temporary.

"Unfortunately, I'll be leaving at the end of the week. I have some important business that needs my attention. Otherwise, I would stay here with you longer. So, since we still have some time together, how about we make the best of it?" Max told her, taking one of her hands, holding it tightly.

Dora felt sad. Her heart felt warm and her head somewhat dizzy. She looked at Max and felt something inside for him that she didn't fully comprehend yet.

After dinner, Max drove Dora back to Spiro's home in Lucerne. Over the next few days, they went out together a few more times in the evenings. Max showed Dora some other favorite places of his in the area. They were enjoying each others company so much that they began to feel like they already knew each other for some time.

When Chantel found out about the budding romance between Dora and Max, she was delighted. She had always wanted Dora to find a really good man. She liked Vinnie. But Vinnie wasn't as sophisticated or as polished as Max. Spiro was also pleased to hear about it. He was proud of the fact that he was the one who introduced them.

Meanwhile, it took another several weeks until Chantel and Spiro decided on the final scents for the new fragrance line. Fortunately, production and packaging were going to be the easiest part of creating the products. Chantel had designed all the packaging herself. The bottles would have etchings that correlated with a particular perfume fragrance and symbol. And there would also be related products such as colognes, eau de toilettes, creams, lotions, bath essentials, and body oils. Everyone at the lab complimented the fragrances. Spiro was very pleased. The plan was to introduce the products in New York and then across the United States. Then international sales would begin after that.

During their last night together in Lucerne, Chantel told Spiro how grateful she was to him for making the fragrance line and products possible. She knew this would have been very difficult without his help. Spiro was deeply touched by her gratitude. He insisted that she was just as responsible for everything that was happening to her as he was. He wanted her to understand that. And he reminded her again that he wanted the best for her and Crystal. Then he held her in his arms.

"I love you, Chantel. Don't ever forget that I love you. You are my sweetheart, forever and ever."

"I love you too, Spiro. I always will," she whispered.

Then they went inside to the bedroom they were sharing and made love to each other. With the moonlight shining in through the windows nearby, they stayed in each other's arms the entire night. And when they woke up in the morning, they made love again before boarding Spiro's private jet back to New York.

CHAPTER 26

U MAURIER'S EVENT

A FEW MONTHS LATER CHANTEL AND DORA WERE BACK IN NEW York preparing for the Du Maurier Collection party. It was being held at the Waldorf Astoria in the same ballroom where Chantel and Spiro first met. Spiro was staying in his usual suite to attend the party and to oversee the event preparations. Chantel was with him getting ready. She decided to wear a long black and white satin dress made by Saint Laurent with a gemstone necklace and earring set from Piaget. The dress fitted her perfectly and looked spectacular on her. And Spiro was dressed handsomely in a classic black tuxedo and bow tie.

"Are you almost ready, my darling?" Spiro asked her, clearly excited and eager to go.

"Yes, Spiro. I'm ready. Don't forget. We'll have to go downstairs to use another set of elevators to get up to the ballroom."

"But first, I need a kiss from those lovely lips. Otherwise, I don't think I can get through the party," he told her, pulling her body close to his, wiping off her lipstick with a handkerchief so that he could kiss her without getting lipstick all over their faces.

The promotion party was carefully thought out. Department store owners, executives, and buyers from the entire tri-state area and beyond were invited to attend. People were coming from Barneys, Bergdorf Goodman, Bloomingdale's, Century 21, Henri Bendel, Lord and Taylor, Macy's, Neiman Marcus, Nordstrom, and Saks Fifth Avenue. There were also many others from smaller stores throughout the United States. The product line was already heavily contracted by many of them. But Chantel and Spiro wanted to get as much publicity as they could and celebrate the fragrance line arrival. Many newspaper and magazine reporters were also invited to attend. Some would be there to take photos and to write up articles about the event. One of Kitty Houghton's magazines planned on dedicating several pages to cover the party.

After they finished kissing each other, Chantel and Spiro took the elevator downstairs to the hotel lobby. Then they got inside the elevators that go to the ballroom. When they got there, Dora was standing at the entrance waiting for them. She was wearing a turquoise Christian Dior dress that contrasted nicely with the color of her reddish hair. She also had on a pair of ruby earrings from Boucheron, giving her an even more formal look. Dora grabbed Chantel by the arm when she arrived, pulling her towards her. There were samples, photos, and promotional products everywhere. There was also a small band playing popular music in the background.

"Chantel, everyone's crazy about the collection. Congratulations! You did it!" Dora told her, very excited.

Spiro overheard the praise, smiled at them, and laughed. Then he excused himself and told them that he would catch up with them a little later on. He wanted to mingle with the guests by himself for a while.

"Remember, you've been a great help too, Dora. You also helped to get this event off the ground. You've been a great support to me throughout this entire process. Don't ever underestimate how much I appreciate you," Chantel told Dora, clearly wanting her to feel good.

"Flattery will get you everywhere. And anyhow, without you I might not be wearing this," said Dora smiling, looking down on her left hand.

Then Chantel looked down also and saw a huge diamond ring on Dora's finger. She could tell it was real and estimated it to be at least seven carats.

"Are you engaged?" asked Chantel, with her eyes rolling up at the ceiling.

Dora looked at Chantel glowing. She had never looked happier.

"Yes, Max proposed last night, Chantel. I couldn't believe it. I'm so thrilled. We're in love," answered Dora.

"How wonderful! I'm very happy for the two of you. Your

ring is beautiful. We have a lot more to celebrate tonight. When is the wedding? Do you have any idea?"

"As soon as we can put a good one together. He's standing over there," said Dora, pointing toward Max.

Chantel looked over at Max. She could tell that he was watching them. He was smiling and looked very happy.

Then one of the promotional agents in the room requested everyone's attention to make an announcement.

"Everyone. You're attention, please. I am pleased to announce the fabulous Du Maurier Collection of fragrances. There are many samples and gift baskets for everyone to take before leaving this evening. A special thanks and recognition also goes to Spiro Pagonis, the co-creator and collaborator of the line. This fragrance collection is already in great demand throughout the United States and will soon be available around the world. Thank you for your support and joining us tonight for its celebration. Congratulations again Ms. Du Maurier and Mr. Pagonis on bringing us this exceptional collection. Now let us enjoy and celebrate the evening together with dinner and dancing," said the agent to all the guests in the ballroom.

Chantel was deeply moved by the announcement. She was getting the recognition she deserved. Spiro was proud of her and admired her for everything she was and everything she accomplished with him. He was also very happy to see her dreams come true. He didn't really care about the credit or the spotlight for himself. He wanted Chantel to be happy, genuinely happy. Then he went around the room and talked with people about the future plans for the line and other related products that were being manufactured.

A half an hour later, Max saw Steve Woods getting a drink at one of the service bars in the ballroom. He couldn't believe his eyes. His blood started to boil. He wondered what the hell Steve was doing there. He didn't know that he was invited. If he had known, he would have asked Spiro to remove him from the guest list. What he didn't know was that Steve hadn't been invited but just decided to show up and crash the event.

"This is some party," Steve commented sarcastically, as one of the bartender's poured him a scotch and soda.

"Yes, it is. That Chantel Du Maurier sure is a talented lady. Mr. Pagonis and her are very close. They sure make a nice pair," said the bartender, unaware that Steve was not invited to the event.

"Oh, isn't that something," replied Steve.

In the meantime, Max went to find Spiro. He found him talking with a small group of writers from one of the magazines. Max pulled him aside so that he could speak to him privately.

"I'm sorry to interrupt, Spiro. But this is important," Max told him.

"Sure, my friend. By the way, I wish to congratulate you on your engagement to Dora. Chantel already told me the great news," Spiro said, completely unaware as to what Max really wanted to talk to him about.

"Spiro, do you know that Steve Woods is here? Was he invited?" asked Max.

"Well, let me think a moment. As a matter of fact, I don't

remember seeing the Woods department store on the list. That's odd. Chantel never mentioned it to me or anyone else. I wonder how he got in?" pondered Spiro aloud, wondering why he hadn't seen his store on the list in the first place.

"Oh, so he is crashing the promotion party. Nice. Well, I can understand that. I don't think you realize how psychotic Steve Woods is. Ever since I met him on your yacht some years ago, he's been looking to get even with me. It's because I always win gambling bets against him. Most recently, he almost killed me after a chess match at the Harvard Club. I walked away with five million even though it was his idea to play. He didn't even play against me himself. He hired the famous chess player Octavian Senova to play against me. And, I still won. Then he was furious and tried to strangle me right in front of everyone watching the match. I also understand that he's a pretty bad drunk and that his store has huge financial troubles. I wish he weren't here. Please don't tell him I'm here if you run into him. I don't want anything to ruin this event," Max explained to Spiro.

Max was somewhat relieved that he had a chance to warn Spiro. He imagined that Spiro didn't know Steve as well as he did. But Max wasn't the only person who recognized Steve. As fate would have it, Chantel had just spotted him also. She didn't waste any time before going over to him where he was standing with a drink in his hand. Chantel gave him a look that could kill.

"Get the fuck out of here, you pig. Get the hell out of here! Or, I will have your ass thrown out, you bastard," she told him firmly, with her eyes looking like they could kill.

"I understand, Chantel. It's your party, isn't it," Steve said crudely, without moving yet.

But Spiro was watching from across the room. He could tell something was terribly wrong. He never saw Chantel look at anyone with so much distress or hatred on her face. He wondered how Chantel knew him. Spiro started walking over toward them to find out what was going on. But before he made it to them, Steve quickly left the ballroom.

"What's wrong, my darling? I saw you talking with Steve Woods. I didn't know that you knew him. I never saw you look at anyone the way you looked at him. What did he say to you to offend you, my love?" asked Spiro, clearly showing his concern to her, especially since Max also warned him about Steve.

Chantel didn't want to get into her past right then. She didn't want anything to interfere with their promotion celebration and event. So she caught hold of herself and her emotions to calm down.

"Offend me. Let's not talk about it right now, Spiro. I don't want anything to upset our evening. And it looks like he just left," Chantel told Spiro, hoping that he wouldn't ask her to elaborate any further.

"Good. We can discuss it later. Now let's meet some more people that you haven't met yet who are interested in putting the line in their stores. Dinner should be starting soon also. Again, I want you to know how proud I am of you. You did it, Chantel. I knew you would be a success. And for whatever Steve was bothering you about, we'll take care of that too," Spiro told her, taking her by the hand.

Chantel immediately felt better. Spiro's touch quickly melted her inside. She felt the sincereness of his love and affection for her, even among other people and in public. Chantel knew that she had a great and supportive man who loved her. Her life seemed to be blessed now. At least it felt that way until she saw Steve again. However, she knew that he was still Crystal's father. And she never told Crystal about him. But should she, she thought to herself. She hated him. How could she tell Crystal that her father denied her and rejected her when she wasn't yet born? Chantel was left to fend for herself and Crystal both. Chantel knew that Steve never had any compassion or remorse for them. She thought that he would only try to hurt them in some way again. In her mind, she was protecting herself and Crystal also.

The event continued as planned. And many photographers were still walking around the ballroom taking photos for newspapers and magazines. Much later on after dinner and dessert, the crowd of people began thinning out. Then Chantel and Spiro decided to leave and go upstairs to his suite. They invited Dora and Max to join them for a toast. A couple of cold bottles of champagne, aged cognac, and port were waiting for them when they arrived. There were also some miniature sweets to snack on. Margaret had already called and left a message on Chantel's cell phone that everything was fine with Crystal at her apartment across town and not to worry about them or anything else.

Spiro asked them all to raise their glasses to toast together. He officially congratulated Dora and Max and told them that he thought they made a wonderful couple together. Spiro was very much a romantic and really liked the thought of going to their wedding. That was one of the qualities Chantel loved about him. Spiro became even more delighted when he was asked to be Max's best man, and Chantel was asked to be Dora's maid of honor. Dora and Max spent about an hour longer with them. Then they thanked Chantel and Spiro for everything and left for the evening.

Chantel and Spiro were now alone. Then Spiro took off his jacket and tie and hung them up in one of the nearby closets. Chantel went into their bedroom to find a robe to put on. Then she went back to be with him. They embraced each other for a few minutes without saying a word to one another.

"Chantel, I can't help but wonder. What happened between you and Steve Woods? Please tell me the truth. I know you didn't want him here tonight. I realize now that he wasn't invited or on the list. And you clearly looked upset when you saw him."

Chantel didn't answer right away. She got up and looked out one of the windows at the buildings in the distance. Then she looked down at the windowsill below. Spiro could tell that she was taking some time to think about what she would say to him. He could tell that she was hesitating. He could see that she was tense. Her eyes were beginning to tear. Then she sat down on one of the sofas and started to cry.

"Spiro, there's something I've never told you about. No one knows about it except Dora. My family in Maine only knows part of what happened. I didn't tell you because I didn't know how you would react or what you would think of me. But I realize, I have to tell you now."

"Come on, Chantel, go ahead and tell me. Don't be afraid of what I think. I love you. I'll always love you no matter what you tell me."

Chantel cleared her throat. She knew she had to tell him.

"As you remember, Spiro, when I first came to New York, I began working at Bloomingdale's for Champs. It was back then that I met Steve Woods. I was very naive and went out with him on my last day at Bloomingdale's. He took me out to dinner and then over to his apartment. I didn't know he lied to me about his marriage. He got me quite drunk and may have put something in one of my drinks. I was unable to handle myself. Then he took me into his bedroom and raped me. Not long after, I found out that I was pregnant with Crystal. So I went to the Woods store to tell Steve. I thought he should know that he caused me to get pregnant. I also asked him for some help. I wasn't making a lot of money at the time. He denied Crystal as being his child and treated me like I was a common whore. And still, I decided not to press charges against him. He was so horribly cruel. Tonight was the first time I have seen him ever since. I'm sure you understand now. I'm sure you understand why the Woods store wasn't on the list. But he had the nerve to come to the event anyway," Chantel told Spiro, wiping tears from her eyes.

"My darling, now I do understand. I always wondered who Crystal's father was. I don't love you any less because of something you are plainly not the blame of. I can only imagine how difficult that was for you at the time. But I'd like to know, why didn't you press charges against him and put him in jail?"

"At the time, I was too ashamed and upset to tell anyone except Dora. My family doesn't even know that I was raped. And I was afraid of him."

Spiro got closer to her and lifted up her face to him.

"He should have been punished for what he did to you. Don't worry. I'm on your side. I'm sorry he showed up tonight. I had no idea he was going to be here. His store wasn't on the list. Security should have noticed. I gather this was the reason he wasn't on the list in the first place?" Spiro said, putting the pieces together.

"Yes. That's correct, Spiro."

"Chantel, don't worry about him. You are the love of my life. And I love your daughter Crystal also. I never want anything bad to happen to either one of you ever. The happiness you have brought me is worth more than all the wealth I have. I will always love you."

Then Spiro asked Chantel for her hand and led her into the bedroom where they got into bed together. Spiro pulled the bed sheets over her and told her to rest. He thought about what Steve had done to her. For the rest of the night, they just slept next to each other, holding each other in their arms. It wasn't until morning that they made love to one another, and Chantel went back home to her apartment on the West Side.

 EVENGE

EVER SINCE CHANTEL TOLD SPIRO ABOUT STEVE WOODS AND what he did to her, he wanted revenge on him. Spiro decided to have a meeting with some of his financial advisors at the Bull and the Bear in the Waldorf Astoria. Bill Worth and Marco Puccio would be meeting with him. Bill usually handled most of Spiro's New York affairs. And Marco had been working for Spiro in London for the past several years. The two men arrived together in navy pinstriped suits, Paul Stuart ties, and white collared shirts. It was lunchtime, so the restaurant was busy with other business patrons.

"Please sit down, gentlemen. Let's not waste any time," said Spiro, when they arrived.

One of the waiters came over and gave them all menus. Then he took their drink orders. Since this was a business meeting, they ordered club soda and sugarless ice tea.

"So tell me, Marco, what have you found out about the Woods store?" asked Spiro, eager to get information.

"Well, Mr. Pagonis, it's worse than anyone might imagine. It turns out that the Woods store has many financial problems and debts," replied Marco.

Spiro took a sip of club soda. His glass was cold and had frosted from the ice melting. "Very good. Tell me more," Spiro responded.

Then a waiter interrupted them and took their food orders.

"Once again, the store is overridden with debt. It's a wonder that Mr. Woods hasn't filed for bankruptcy. It's millions and millions of dollars in debt. At this point, he is so overleveraged and has so many legal issues that his own wealth can't bail him out. I doubt he can get much help from any more bankers. I hear he's pretty much blackballed out there in the financial circuit," Marco continued.

Their food arrived, and they carried on their discussion.

"That's correct, Spiro. I have spoken to one of Mr. Woods attorneys who happens to be an old friend of mine from Princeton. He's very frustrated with Mr. Woods. Off the record, he told me that the store has been on shaky grounds for years and that he's surprised that Mr. Woods has been able to keep it this long," added Bill.

Spiro was pleased with the information. Then he thought briefly about Max Connors and what Max had told him.

"In addition, we found out that Mr. Woods also owes a substantial amount of money in gambling debts, particularly in Atlantic City. He has some serious problems there also," Bill continued.

Then one of the bartenders came over to their table and interrupted them. His name was Ken. Spiro was also a long time favorite of the staff for years, and Ken wanted to greet him.

"Nice to see you, Mr. Pagonis," Ken said.

"Thank you, Ken. Nice to see you also," replied Spiro. Then Spiro gave Ken a look of approval and continued his conversation.

"What chance do you think we might have of purchasing the store? As you both already know, I am interested in taking it over. Perhaps, you can approach his attorney, Bill?" asked Spiro.

Bill and Marco shook their heads in agreement.

"It's not officially up for sale. But, we can try to make a private deal. He's in enough of a bind that we might be able to get him interested. But this isn't the kind of deal that you normally do, Mr. Pagonis. Are you sure you want to take over a debt-ridden store?" asked Bill, with a concerned look on his face.

Spiro took a deep breath and gave them both a sweeping look. "I understand. However, the answer is yes. I want you both to do everything possible to get the Woods store. Do you understand?" Spiro told them.

By now, Bill and Marco knew that Spiro was determined to acquire the Woods department store. Somehow, they would have to find a way.

"For personal reasons, I also would like the store to be put into a partnership. I have everything in the documents that I brought with me today," explained Spiro.

Then Spiro passed them each a copy of the documents that would explain the partnership and how he wanted the ownership set up.

"I want you to use my newly formed company Compass Holdings to purchase the store. And I do not want Mr. Woods or anyone else he knows to be aware that I'm behind this acquisition. Do you both understand?" Spiro asked them, sitting back in his chair, looking at them closely.

"Yes, Mr. Pagonis. We will work on this immediately," answered Bill.

Bill didn't really care why Spiro wanted the store. He knew that Spiro had the money to acquire it and was being asked to help him do so. Disappointing Spiro would not be a good idea. He was a very generous and prominent person to work for. Bill thought to himself that they'd figure something out. Somehow, they would get the store for Spiro. He also felt that he ought to talk to some people in Atlantic City to see if they could help with the matter. If they put more pressure on Steve, then maybe he'll let go of the store, Bill surmised.

After they finished lunch, Spiro got up from the table to leave first.

"I'm looking forward to the completion of this acquisition," Spiro told them while he headed out one of the exit doors to the escalators.

For the next several weeks, Bill and Marco, along with a

handful of attorneys worked on getting Steve Woods to sell his store to Compass Holdings. They were able to get Steve's lenders to put enough pressure on him that he decided to sell and make a deal with them. Steve Woods had no idea that Spiro Pagonis was behind it all.

CHAPTER 28

S URPRISES

CHANTEL AND DORA WENT OVER TO BERGDORF GOODMAN'S bridal salon together. Dora was getting the final fitting for her Vera Wang wedding dress. And Chantel thought it would be fun if she went with her.

"Why don't you have dinner with Max and I tonight, Chantel? Spiro is away in London and you can bring Crystal with you," suggested Dora.

"Thanks for the invitation, but I'd like to stay at home tonight. I promised Crystal that I would spend some quality time with her. I appreciate the invite though," answered Chantel, watching Dora fuss with her gown.

"You'll be missed. Well, what do you think? They just finished all the alterations. Do you like it? I want to look absolutely beautiful for Max. I only plan to do this once," said Dora, looking at herself in a large floor to ceiling mirror.

A saleswoman was also helping them and came out with Dora's headpiece. It was made out of lace fabric and petite pearls that matched her wedding dress. Dora wanted simple elegance and that was something that Vera Wang's designs had.

"You look sensational, my dear. If I were a man, I'd marry you myself. That's how lovely you look. And the embroidery on the dress is just darling," answered Chantel.

"Yes, you certainly do look magnificent in it. I think it's one of the best Wang has ever designed," said the saleswoman.

"Well, I can't think of anyone who deserves it more. I think Max is a very fortunate man to have you. He's very lucky to have such a lovely and loyal person like you. Keep that in mind. Sometimes, we tend to take ourselves for granted. He's really lucky. I think you should know that. Wow, I was just thinking. Isn't it something that we're here together after meeting in the park so long ago? I still can't quite believe it. What an adventure this has been," Chantel commented.

Then Dora twirled around in front of the mirror.

"Time sure does fly. Before you know it, maybe, I'll even have children also. But for now, can I have some help getting out of this?" said Dora, looking at the saleswoman.

"On my way. One second please and I'll help you. I hope you are happy with it?" she asked, helping Dora undo the back of the gown.

"Yes, very happy," answered Dora.

"So, I'm finally going to meet your family," said Chantel.

Then Dora changed into a bright magenta outfit that Chantel helped her pick out at Chanel a month earlier.

"Yes, they are all excited to come to New York and all. They are pretty simple people though. I'm not sure what they will make of all of this," replied Dora.

"Those are the best kind. Remember where I came from? I didn't have much money growing up, but I felt rich inside anyway. I always had love and laughter in my heart. I always had hope and promise in life. And my family has been so good to me. That's worth more than gold."

Dora gave her a puzzled look and commented, "Well, you sure are rich now. And you have a man who loves you too."

"True."

"Tell you what, Chantel. Since you aren't going to have dinner with us tonight, let's have lunch at the Palm Court in the Plaza Hotel. We can go there now. I just feel like celebrating a little with you. We haven't been there in ages," Dora suggested.

"Okay, you have a deal."

"Now, can I ask you a ridiculous question?" said Dora.

"Sure, what is it?"

Dora waited until the saleswoman left the dressing room area so she wouldn't hear the question. "How does it feel to be super rich?"

"It feels better than being poor. But having money brings a lot of tedious responsibilities with it. For example, more complicated taxes, investments, and estate planning. Otherwise, I guess it's sort of a privilege and makes life kind of easier in other ways," answered Chantel.

"Well, I imagine it would," commented Dora.

Then they laughed at themselves and how silly they were acting.

～

THE PALM COURT WAS A LARGE AND OPULENTLY DECORATED restaurant in the middle of the Plaza Hotel. It was decorated in very classic decor. When they arrived, they were seated at a table toward the rear right side of the restaurant. A waiter soon came over and gave them each tea and lunch menus. After they gave their orders, they talked for a while. Then all of a sudden, Chantel had a look on her face that was very unusual to Dora.

"What's wrong, Chantel? What is it?"

"I can't believe my eyes."

"What do you see?"

"I thought I just saw Marco Puccio leaving the restaurant."

"Are you sure, do you think he saw us?" asked Dora.

"I don't know," said Chantel, spilling some of the tea from the teacup she had in her hand onto the table.

One of the waiters noticed and came over to help her with a cloth napkin. "Are you all right, Madame?" he asked her, cleaning up the spill.

Chantel managed to calm herself down and cool the sudden heat that she felt in her body.

"Yes, I'm fine. Thank you," she answered.

Dora didn't think much of the matter. After all, Chantel had Spiro now. Marco had been history for a while.

"You're probably mistaken, Chantel. However, I am surprised how you reacted if you really think you did see Marco. Do you still have feelings for him? It's been so long," asked Dora, curious of the answer.

"Oh, let's not talk about it, Dora. I'm sorry. It just caught me off guard."

Then Chantel's cell phone rang. It was Spiro calling. Chantel quickly excused herself from the table so she could talk to him in the lobby.

"Hello, darling. How are you?" she asked Spiro.

"I'm fine, my love. But I have some very interesting news for you. I know you might be very surprised, but we just acquired the Woods store. We now own it and you are my partner. I had a few of my financial and legal people help me to take it over. One of them is Bill Worth. He is at the store now and is ready to escort you around as soon as you wish. Also, give some thought to a name you would like to call it. We'll need to give the store a name as soon as possible. In the meantime, call Bill and he'll arrange a tour for you. Here's his cell phone number. I'll be back in New York soon. I love you," Spiro told her, as he got off the phone to take an important business call.

Chantel could not believe her ears. She didn't have any idea that Spiro had any intention of taking over the Woods store. She was a bit in shock and felt a little faint. Then she went back to her table in the Palm Court. Her lunch was waiting for her and Dora had already started eating.

"The most incredible and shocking thing just happened, Dora. You might not believe this, but Spiro just bought the

Woods department store. That was what he was phoning me about. He also told me that he made me a partner. Can you believe this?" said Chantel, gasping for air.

Dora almost choked on the piece of salmon she was chewing on. "Oh, my God. How do you feel about that, Chantel?"

"Like I'm on top of the world."

"Spiro said that a man named Bill Worth would show me around the store. He said that Bill is already there. And he told me that I could phone Bill and have him meet me there when I arrive. Would you like to join me?" Chantel asked her.

"Sure, why the hell not? This is totally amazing," replied Dora.

A half an hour later they paid the check and called Bill. Then they went over to what was now the old Woods store. Bill Worth was already waiting for them at the main entrance. He was nicely dressed in a dark navy suit with a briefcase in one of his hands.

"Ms. Du Maurier, is that you?" Bill asked, making sure it was Chantel.

"Yes, it's me, Bill. And this is my friend and assistant, Dora Moore," Chantel answered.

"Nice to meet you both, Ms. Du Maurier and Ms. Moore. Well then, let's begin our tour. Where would you like to start, Ms. Du Maurier?" Bill asked her.

"Let's take a quick tour of the different departments and then go to the executive offices upstairs," Chantel answered.

Bill escorted them throughout the store. He also informed them that there would be a group of people coming to take down the Woods sign in front of the store and that there would be others redecorating. When they arrived at the executive offices, Chantel told Bill that she wanted to go into Steve Woods old office alone for a few minutes. Chantel also noticed that there were already different administrative assistants at work. Then she walked into his old office.

Chantel remembered the painful memories she experienced there long ago. The office had already been emptied out. Paintings had been taken from the walls and antiques removed from the room. Even Steve's desk was gone. It was more or less an empty shell of the past now. Chantel thought about how unpredictable life can be. It all seemed a bit idiotic to her that Steve had done what he did to her. Why couldn't he have behaved differently? Why did he have to scar her for the rest of her life? Why didn't he help his unborn child Crystal? Why couldn't he take some of the responsibility for what he did to her? Then all of a sudden, a peaceful feeling came over her. Chantel realized that what was once Steve's was now hers and would eventually become Crystal's. She thought the whole thing was unbelievable and exceptional karma.

When she came out of the office, Bill came up to her and gave her an envelope. "Sorry, I almost forgot to give this to you, Ms. Du Maurier. It's from Spiro Pagonis," he informed her.

Dora watched Chantel as she opened the envelope and read the note from Spiro. It said:

DEAR CHANTEL,

If it pleases you, these are your new offices. The store is ours now. Let me know what you wish to name it. Name it anything your heart desires.

ALL MY LOVE,

SPIRO

This new reality had started to sink in. Chantel had a hard time holding back her tears of joy. She was tremendously moved by Spiro's actions. And Dora could tell that Chantel was astonished by what Spiro did.

"Thank you for the tour, Bill. I'll be in touch with you soon," Chantel told him while shaking his hand.

Then Chantel and Dora left the store knowing that they had a lot to think about and figure out. They had a store to take care of now.

CHAPTER 29

$\mathcal{A}$ WEDDING

A FEW WEEKS LATER JUST BEFORE THE WEDDING CEREMONY, Chantel helped Dora get into her wedding gown. They decided that Dora would get ready at Chantel's apartment on the West Side because it was not far from where the wedding was going to be. It was being held at the historic Tavern on the Green restaurant. Tavern on the Green was a very romantic place to get married and to have a wedding reception. It was located just off of Central Park West and Sixty-seventh Street in the park. While they got ready, a limousine waited for them downstairs. As planned, Chantel was going to be Dora's maid of honor, and Spiro was going to be Max's best man. Dora and Max wanted to keep the wedding very intimate. So they didn't ask any others to participate in the bridal party except for Crystal. They wanted a small but quaint wedding with no more than a hundred guests including their family members.

Some of Dora's family from Atlanta would be there for the ceremony. They were all staying at a hotel on Sixth Avenue in the Fifties. And some of Chantel's family would also be attending the wedding from Maine. Claudette, Brian, and Chris would be there. And Chantel's mother Susan and her father Edward would also be there. They were all staying at a hotel nearby. And some of Max's family members were going to be there as well. Crystal was going be the ring bearer and bring Dora and Max their rings during the wedding.

"Mommy, I'm so excited! Dora, you look so gorgeous. You look just like a real princess," said Crystal, wearing a white lace dress with white patent leather shoes and a large white bow in her hair. Crystal seemed as excited as Dora, maybe even more so.

"You look quite magnificent yourself, Crystal," Dora said, while she adjusted her gown.

Chantel smiled and laughed at them both. And for the occasion, she'd decided to wear a black and white silk dress made by Ralph Lauren with pearls from Mikimoto. The pearls gave a simple and sophisticated look to her outfit. Dora decided to wear diamonds. She put on a stunning set of diamond earrings with a matching necklace from Chopard. They were presents from Max. Margaret was also well dressed for the special occasion and quite excited about it. She loved weddings and warned them that she might cry. This made them all laugh in unison.

"I hope I don't cry myself," Dora told them, now feeling butterflies in her stomach.

"It's okay if you do, Dora. But try not to so your photos turn out well. Are we almost ready everyone? Let's not forget those important rings from Tiffany's and the pillow they will rest on during the ceremony. Crystal, the usher from rehearsal will guide you when it's time to go up to give Dora and Max the rings," said Chantel, trying to get them better organized.

It was twelve-thirty when they were all ready to leave. The ceremony was timed to begin at one o'clock sharp. Max and Spiro were supposed to be standing with the minister when they arrive. And the guests should have been seated by then. Then Chantel made one more adjustment to Dora's veil, kissed her on the cheek, and wished her good luck.

"Is everyone ready to go now?" asked Chantel, grinning with a smile.

"Yes, let's go," answered Dora.

Then they all took the elevator downstairs together. Margaret helped with Dora's dress while Chantel helped Crystal into the limo. The wedding rings were kept inside a blue satin bag from Tiffany's with a color-coordinated pillow. They were also held down with two silver pins to keep them in place.

When they arrived at Tavern on the Green, their driver dropped them off at the front entrance. Lovely flowers adorned the grounds. There were daffodils, tulips, and an assortment of exotic plants in bloom. Dora's mother Stella and one of the ushers was waiting for them under the entrance awning. And a photographer, who was already standing by, starting taking pictures. He was from Kitty Houghton's wedding magazine *Celebration*. Chantel was a big fan of Kitty's magazines and had recommended that they see if one of her photographers might want to cover part of the wedding while taking personal photos for them. Kitty thought it was an excellent idea. And Dora and Max were thrilled because it would help them with their wedding photos.

Stella walked over to her daughter Dora and gave her a big hug and kiss. She had a cotton handkerchief in her hand just in case anyone needed it.

"Ready Dora, you look so lovely. Everyone is ready inside and waiting for you to walk in. We also have the pianist already playing music. We just need to give him a cue before you go in. Max is so excited, and Spiro has been so good to him. They're both terrific men. You two ladies are very lucky. Very lucky, indeed," Stella told her.

"Are you ready, Crystal?" asked Chantel, checking her makeup one last time before putting a hand mirror away in her purse.

"Yes, Mom. I'm so excited!"

"Okay, we're ready to give the cue. Let's go you all," Dora told them.

Then they all walked back into a private room that was reserved just for the matrimony ceremony. Afterwards, they would go into another private room being held for the wedding celebration and meal. Five-courses were planned that included a custom-made wedding cake.

When the pianist saw Dora in the entryway, he began

playing Clair de Lune by Debussy. Then they proceeded inside with Crystal walking in first, followed by Chantel and Dora. Crystal was given a little white chair decorated with white fabric and flowers to sit on while she waited for the minister to ask for the rings. Max looked extremely happy. And Spiro looked very cheerful also. They both smiled at Chantel and Dora as they entered the room. Then the minister began the marriage ceremony. Dora and Max exchanged their wedding vows, put on each other's rings, and kissed each other at the end. While Margaret and Stella were drying their eyes with handkerchiefs, everyone in the room clapped. Then they all proceeded to go into the dining area for the wedding celebration.

Dora, Max, Chantel, and Spiro were seated at the same table together. The room was exquisitely decorated with white satin fabric, flowers, bows, and mood lighting. A small band started playing music that was pleasing to the ears. During dinner, Chantel thought of how ironic it was that Dora was the one getting married. She had been in love with Marco and felt she had to leave him. And now she had Spiro who told her that he would never remarry. She loved Spiro also. But she knew that he wasn't going to propose to her. No matter how much he loved her, she knew he wasn't getting married again. This made it a more unusual relationship than a traditional marriage. Yet, at the same time, she was genuinely happy for Dora. Dora was her best friend for a long time, and Chantel wanted the best for her. Chantel was pretty happy with how her life was going anyway. Many of her dreams had come true. She became a very successful businesswoman. And Spiro was very generous, kind, and loyal to her. She was very much aware of how much he did for her.

After the main courses, the wedding cake was served. It was a beautiful tiered white cake with pastel icing and flowers hand carved on every tier. When they finished eating cake, Dora and Max had their first dance together as husband and wife. They chose a romantic French song to dance to. Dora's mother was so happy that she began to cry again. So Chantel went over to comfort her.

"It's a good happy, I hope?" asked Chantel, watching Stella wipe away her tears with a handkerchief.

"Yes, it's a good happy. I can't believe this day is finally here. I was hoping that Dora would eventually get married to someone. It would be great if she would have some children also," said Stella, smiling at Chantel.

"Well, it's never too late. Maybe she will," Chantel said, smiling at her.

Then Spiro came over and asked Chantel to dance. "I'd like it if you can stay with me tonight. Do you think your family would mind? I miss you so much, my darling. I already have a bottle of cold Dom Pérignon waiting for us," Spiro whispered in her ear.

"Well no, I don't think they'd mind. You spent time with them last night. And I miss you too. The romantic mood of the wedding makes me want to be alone with you even more," Chantel told him.

Spiro gently touched the side of Chantel's face near her forehead. Then he held her body even closer to his. It was easy to see that they loved each other even though they weren't married or even engaged. There was a feeling in the air when they held one another. People could sense it. They could sense the happiness and love between them. Spiro had never felt such complete contentment with a woman before. And he was getting aroused holding her so close next to him. His body could feel the curves of her breasts, hips, and thighs. He already started to fantasize that they were alone together and making love. But for now, he knew he'd have to wait until they were alone together.

"Let's go spend some more time with Dora and Max before they take off for their honeymoon," Spiro suggested.

"Yes, let's do that," Chantel said while looking deep into his eyes.

So they mingled some more with Dora, Max, and the other guests. And then Dora and Max announced that they were ready to leave and thanked everyone for coming to the wedding. Their limo was waiting outside to take them across Central Park to their apartment. It was located on Park Avenue and East Sixty-six Street. The apartment was very large. It had five bedrooms, four baths, and a spacious terrace. The terrace was completely private from their neighbor's views. It had huge brick walls surrounding it on all sides. They could sunbath in the nude there without anyone ever seeing them. It was one of the most private penthouses in the city. Dora liked the privacy and the fact that she could put potted plants on the terrace. She actually liked gardening and hadn't done any since she moved to New York. It was more space than they really needed. But she thought that if they have children, it would be perfect for a family in the future.

So she was content with it for now and wanted to give it a chance. Dora was grateful that she had just married a man she loves and who could afford such a lovely home.

But before Dora and Max said their farewells to Dora's parents, they spent a few moments with Max's family. Then they went over to her mother and father just before they left.

"So long, Mom. So long, Dad. We'll be in touch with you. We're flying to the Cayman Islands just as soon as we change and get our luggage. Our flight takes off during sunset. We timed it that way. I hope you all enjoyed yourselves. I love you," Dora told them.

"Yes, it was a pleasure meeting you both. I hope you visit New York often in the future. Next time you should stay with us in our apartment," said Max, giving Stella a kiss on the cheek and shaking Dora's father's hand.

"That would nice. Well, you two have a great honeymoon. Be careful of the stingrays down in the Caymans. I understand they're pretty friendly but be careful anyway. You never know," Stella told them.

"Love you, Mom, Dad. We'll be careful. Also, we will probably be back in New York in about ten days. Max has an important business deal he's working on and needs to be back by then," said Dora as she got into the limo.

"Love you too. Stay in touch and let us know how you are doing," Stella told them.

"Good luck," said her father to the both of them.

Then Dora and Max got into their car and headed across Central Park to the East Side. There was a funny just married sign printed on a piece of cardboard hanging from the back. The photographer from *Celebration* was still there and kept taking pictures of them until they disappeared across the park.

Chantel left with Crystal and Margaret. She told Spiro that she would meet him in the evening so she could spend some more time with her family. Susan, Edward, Claudette, and Chris were planning on going to Chantel's apartment for a visit. A little later on, Chantel explained to them that she would be staying at Spiro's that night. Crystal was used to this by now, so it wasn't a problem or even slightly embarrassing. Margaret also knew that this was not unusual. Margaret liked and respected Spiro. She knew that he was loyal to Chantel even if he hadn't proposed marriage to her. Then they all spent some more time together until Chantel left to meet Spiro.

IT WAS EARLY EVENING WHEN CHANTEL ARRIVED AT THE Waldorf. She quickly walked through the hotel lobby and took the elevator upstairs to have dinner with Spiro. When she got there, Spiro answered the door in a t-shirt and pair of shorts. He wasn't usually this casual. But Chantel liked it, especially after a formal wedding. She also changed before she left her apartment and wore a short sleeve blouse with a pair of linen pants. Dinner was waiting for them in several silver trays that were kept warm with tea lights underneath them. There were also some candles lit and spread out around the dining and living rooms.

"It smells good. What are we having tonight?" Chantel asked him.

"Bouillabaisse, salad, potatoes. We also have some caviar and cheeses over here. And if you want dessert, we have fresh berries and chocolate," answered Spiro, lifting one of the tray tops where the caviar and cheeses were arranged.

Then Spiro gave her a glass of cold champagne.

"To us, Chantel. Let's toast to our love. We had quite a day at the wedding. I'm so happy for them. But tell me, how did you feel about it?" Spiro asked her.

"I felt okay. I'm very happy for them also," she answered.

"But that's not what I mean. Did you feel like you should be the one getting married?" he asked her, watching her facial expressions carefully.

Chantel took a sip of champagne. Then she gave Spiro a look as if she understood what he was asking her. Then she looked up at the ceiling like she was thinking about what to say next.

"Look, I know you don't want to get married again. You already told me that. You have always told me exactly the truth. I know that you love me. And you treat me like you love me. And I love you. That's what really matters, isn't it?" Chantel told him.

"To me, that is what really matters. I love you more than I have loved any other woman. I just can't commit to marriage. I'm sorry. But you know that I only want you and no other woman. I would do anything for you but marriage. I just don't want you to feel hurt or cheated in any way," Spiro said to her.

Chantel went up to him and gently touched his face. She looked deep into his eyes again. When she did this, it felt like a magnet drew them together. It was a feeling so strong and so real that she almost had to convince herself that she wasn't dreaming.

"Spiro, I never felt cheated by you or with you. You are my love. I know this relationship is a little different, but we're a different kind of people. We also make our decisions and paths together. It just so happens that our two paths are so compatible that there is no need for marriage in the first place. In the second place, I will always love you no matter what. And I'm pretty happy with the way things are. If I were married to you, you would still be traveling the world. Maybe you would even be traveling more. So, I just think to myself that I have to be grateful for what we do have. Not every woman or man finds a love like ours. That's what is most important. And we're together often, often enough so that I don't miss you too much for too long," Chantel explained to him.

"I see my love, Chantel. I see. I'm glad you feel that way. I don't want to lose you. Now, let's have some dinner before it gets too cold," said Spiro.

They dimmed the dining room lights a bit and sat down to eat together. They talked about the wedding, who danced with who, who looked funny, and who looked sort of sad. Spiro was also glad to meet Chantel's family. And it was a long time since either of them was to a wedding, so it felt like a special novelty. After they finished dinner, they sat down together on a sofa in the living room. Spiro put some music on. Then they started kissing each other and soon ended up in the bedroom.

"You are the most important woman in my life," Spiro told her as he took off his shirt and watched her get undressed.

Spiro pulled down the sheets on the bed. Then they got into bed together. Spiro started kissing her feet and toes. Then he kissed her along her legs and between them. Chantel kissed him too all over his body while he watched her in ecstasy. Then he kissed her breasts and her lips again before he got on top of her. They made love for a few hours and fell asleep. When they awoke the next morning, Spiro wanted to make love to her again. So he started kissing her all over her body. And Chantel started kissing him also. They were completely absorbed and impassioned with each other as they made love. It was as if they were the ones on a honeymoon.

CHAPTER 30

A GREAT LOSS

It was a Sunday morning, and Chantel was sipping on a coffee reading *The New York Times*. Margaret had just finished making blueberry pancakes for everyone, so they sat down together to eat. Margaret had asked Chantel about Spiro. Chantel told her that he was still on a business trip in London working on a business deal. Chantel also mentioned that Dora was back from her honeymoon with Max and settled into their apartment across town.

"Mommy, can we go to Central Park today? I'd really like to go for a walk and stop at the playground and the zoo. Maybe we can also go to the Boathouse and get an ice cream or something," asked Crystal, fussing with her fork and knife and the pancakes in front of her.

Crystal loved the park. And it was a pleasant sunny day. Chantel could understand why Crystal wanted to get outside and go for a walk.

"Sure, we can go. Let's finish our breakfast and we'll go," answered Chantel.

After they finished eating, Chantel took a quick look at the mail. There was a letter from her sister Susan. She had sent some new photographs of their family for Chantel and Crystal to see. Chantel planned to show them to Crystal later that day. Then she opened an envelope that had some real estate listings of homes in Montauk. Chantel was thinking about purchasing a summerhouse. She didn't tell anyone about it yet because she wanted to see what she could find first. She was planning on maybe surprising everyone some day. Then she went to find Crystal to see if she was ready to leave for the park.

"Are you ready to go, Crystal? I'm all set. Margaret, we'll see you later. Thanks for the delicious breakfast," said Chantel, searching for her sunglasses and wallet inside her purse, making sure that she could find them.

"Yes, Mom. Here I come," answered Crystal, following her mother to the foyer next to the elevator.

Central Park was already crowded with people. That was expected on the weekends, especially when the weather was warm. They decided to walk over to the zoo first. It was one of Crystal's favorite places. Crystal liked to watch the sea lions get fed. The zookeepers fed them little fish in exchange for a trick or two. The sea lions also made funny noises, communicated with the zookeepers, and always wanted more food. After they watched the sea lions, they took a walk past the park bench where Chantel and Dora first met. Chantel reminisced about the past a little. Then they walked around the zoo to the park's merry-go-round where Crystal went for a few rides. Crystal spotted a few girls she knew from school and said hello to them. They were also enjoying the park with their parents. Then they went to a large playground just off of Fifth Avenue and Seventy-second Street. The playground was close to the Boathouse where Crystal got two scoops of chocolate chip ice cream. Then they sat on a park bench together and watched people row their rowboats in the lake. Chantel also thought about the time she was there with Marco long ago. The memory she had was more like a distant dream of the past than reality now.

When they got back to their apartment, Crystal told Margaret about everywhere they went and everything they'd seen. Chantel was happy because she had some quality time with her daughter. She always enjoyed taking Crystal for walks in the park.

Later that evening, Chantel read a storybook with Crystal called *The Secret Garden* by Frances Hodgson Burnett. It was originally published in 1911 and has since been a children's favorite. It was also one of Chantel's favorite books when she was growing up. Her mother Susan had given her a copy and used to read it with her, especially when the weather was bad, and they were both stuck in the house. Chantel always enjoyed books like it. Some of the characters in the books that she read growing up also inspired her. She especially liked books that had characters that overcame adversity or obstacles.

Then the telephone rang. It was Spiro. He informed Chantel that he was coming back to New York the following day and that he missed her very much. He told her to give Crystal and Margaret his regards and that he looked forward to seeing them all soon. Spiro also told her that he planned on taking them on his yacht for a sail around Manhattan. He said that he already had Alexis take his yacht back to New York ahead of time. Spiro wanted to fly back on his private jet. And Chantel was thrilled to hear that he was returning so soon.

"I miss you too, Spiro. I love you. See you tomorrow," said Chantel over the phone.

"I love you, Chantel," Spiro repeated before he ended the call.

That evening they decided to order in Chinese food to give Margaret a break. They also decided to watch a movie together. Before Crystal went to bed, they all had an old-fashioned pillow fight, laughing with every strike. That reminded Chantel of her childhood days in Maine. She and Claudette would do the same thing until her mother would come in to break up their fight and tell them to go to sleep.

THE NEXT MORNING CHANTEL GOT UP AND DECIDED TO MAKE A cup of tea. Margaret was already in the kitchen. And Chantel had plans to visit her new store and to see how things were coming along. She decided to name the store Du Maurier's. Spiro was pleased with the idea. He thought the name sounded very good for a store. Chantel had contractors gut out the entire seventh floor where the old executive offices were to create new ones. Dora was going to have an office next to hers on the same floor. And there was still other construction going on throughout the building. Then Crystal woke up and came into the kitchen to join them. When Crystal found out that her mother was going to Du Maurier's, she asked if she could go with her.

"Yes, you can come with me. But tonight I will probably spend time with Spiro when he arrives back at the Waldorf. Okay?" Chantel told her, preparing her in advance.

"That's fine, Mom. I understand," Crystal answered.

After they both had something to eat, they left to go to the store. The weather was pleasant and warm again. So, they decided to walk. Along the way, they passed some street entertainers doing dances that looked like they were quite difficult to do and required a lot of practice. Then they walked into Du Maurier's and took a look around. Chantel observed the customers that were spending money at the counters. She could tell that many were tourists. There were always tourists buying merchandise, but even more on a warm day during the summertime. And the executive offices were not finished yet, so there was no one there to see. Only some of the department managers worked on the weekends, making sure everything was going okay and that customers were happy with the salespeople. After a while, they left the store and walked through the park again like they did the day before.

While they were out, Margaret received a phone call from a

man who was looking for Chantel. She could tell he was very nervous and upset.

"This is urgent. I would like to speak to Ms. Du Maurier, please," he told her.

"What is this in regards to? Ms. Du Maurier is out with her daughter. Can I help you?" Margaret asked him.

"My name is Antonios Kapese. I'm a relation to Spiro Pagonis. He is my stepbrother from Greece. Spiro left London earlier today in his private jet with his pilot. We found out that his jet was in a severe storm and was struck by lightning. We know it went down into the Atlantic Ocean. We know because Spiro and the pilot communicated with the nearest airport before the plane started to dive. The jet was on fire. It's likely the engine began to malfunction. They were already too far from land to have an emergency landing when the plane began to descend into the ocean. We have sent authorities confirming this, flying over their last known coordinates, looking for the plane. It is highly unlikely that they survived. Spiro wanted me to contact Ms. Du Maurier immediately if anything ever happened to him," Antonios explained to Margaret.

Margaret was in shock and almost fainted. But she was still able to write down his contact information for Chantel. Antonios also told her that he would call back later when he had more details. After their call ended, Margaret picked up the phone to call Dora and Max. She felt panicked. Max answered the phone.

"Max, this is Margaret. I need to speak to Dora right away."

Max told Dora that Margaret wanted to speak to her. He

could tell from Margaret's voice that something had happened and that she was very distraught.

"What's wrong, Margaret?" Dora asked when she got on the phone.

"I just got a call from a relative of Spiro's named Antonios Kapese. He told me that Spiro was in a plane crash over the Atlantic Ocean. He said they were looking for Spiro's jet, that it had been struck by lightning, which started a fire and probably damaged the jet's engine causing it to dive," she told Dora, starting to cry.

Dora couldn't believe her ears. She realized what this might mean. "Where's Chantel, Margaret?" Dora asked.

"She's out with Crystal. She took Crystal to Du Maurier's earlier. They are probably in the park now and will soon be back. I'm not sure how to tell her all of this. I would have called her cell phone, but I needed to speak to you first. You're her closest friend. I also thought Max should know," Margaret said, trying to keep calm.

Dora turned to Max and told him what had happened. Then she asked him if they could go over to Chantel's apartment to give Chantel some support. Max agreed. They both arrived before Chantel and Crystal returned and wondered how Chantel would handle the news. They were worried the most about her.

"Margaret, please give me a glass of brandy to calm my nerves," Dora requested.

"I'd like one also," said Max, looking very upset.

Margaret went to get them brandy and took some for herself. Twenty minutes later they heard Chantel and Crystal come inside the entrance of the apartment. When Chantel saw Dora and Max there, she became disconcerted.

"Nice surprise. But what's the occasion? Or should I ask what's wrong?" said Chantel, noticing their somber facial expressions.

Dora took a moment to respond. She gave a signal to Margaret to take Crystal into her room. Chantel could tell that they didn't want Crystal to hear whatever it was they were there for or whatever it was that they were about to tell her. Then Margaret took Crystal into her room. Margaret explained to her that Dora and Max needed to talk with her mother alone. After Crystal went into her room, Chantel sat down in a leather chair facing them.

"Okay, what's going on that you don't even want Crystal to hear about?" she asked them.

"Margaret called us at home after she received a call from one of Spiro's stepbrother's named Antonios Kapese. He informed her that Spiro's jet was hit by lightning and went down into the Atlantic Ocean. We immediately thought it would be a good idea to come here to give you some support. We're afraid he might not have survived. It sounds like there was no place for an emergency landing," Dora explained to her.

Margaret was back and explained to Chantel that she was frightened and had to call someone she knew for help. She also told Chantel that they were looking for the plane and that Antonios would call back when he had more information. Chantel felt a sharp and sudden sorrow overwhelm her. She started to feel ill.

"Do you mean to tell me that Antonios didn't say whether he was alive or not? This is horrible. This is horrifying," Chantel said, choking when she asked the question, her eyes beginning to tear.

"I'm afraid all we can do is wait to have the answer. We wanted to be here with you when Antonios calls back," Dora told her.

Chantel saw the brandy bottle on the table and poured herself a glass. She looked bewildered. And it wasn't for another three hours until Antonios phoned back. This time he had an answer to give them.

"Yes, this is Chantel Du Maurier. Is this Antonios? Did they find Spiro? Is he all right?" she asked him, afraid of what she might hear.

Antonios could hardly bear to give her the bad news. He explained that the jet went down while Spiro was on the phone with the nearest airport. However, it was too far from where they were for an emergency landing. He told her that Spiro reported that the jet was hit by lightning and that there was a fire damaging the engine. His jet went down while he was giving them the coordinates of where they were. Then the line went dead. Antonios also told her that they did find the area where the jet went down, but only fragments of it were found. And they couldn't find any bodies from the wreckage, and highly doubt that Spiro or the pilot survived.

"I'm so very sorry to bring you this terrible news. If it is okay, I will be traveling to New York in a day or two to visit with you. I will also contact Captain Alexis for a service and ceremony. Spiro left instructions on many things in the event that something ever happened to him. So, I must see you. In the meantime, I hope you will be all right. I can imagine how difficult it must be hearing this unfortunate news. I loved him also. If there is anything I can do for you in the meantime, please do not hesitate to contact me. Again, I'm so sorry."

Chantel was silent for a few moments. She was taking in everything Antonios had said to her. She never expected anything like this to happen to Spiro. And she knew life would never be the same without him. He had become her lover, her confidant, and most intimate friend. She knew that he was one of the most important people that she ever met in her life and now he was gone. The floor under her felt like it was falling in. Her heart felt a tremendous pain that was difficult to accept or deal with so quickly. Tears welled in her eyes.

"Yes, I understand Antonios. I'll see you then," she told him, hanging up the phone.

Chantel looked over at Dora and Max and told them that Antonios confirmed that Spiro had died. She also told them that Antonios would be in New York in a couple of days. Then she ran into her bedroom, threw herself down on her bed, and began to cry.

"Damn it. Why did this happen to such a great man?" said Max in anger, realizing that he lost one of his best friends forever.

Dora went over to caress him. She started to cry herself. Then she went into Chantel's bedroom and sat down beside her. Chantel was holding a photo of Spiro close to her chest. Then

Chantel and Dora held each other, knowing what a tragedy his death was.

A FEW DAYS LATER, ANTONIOS ARRIVED FOR THE SERVICE AND farewell ceremony he immediately planned on Spiro's yacht. There were only about twenty people invited to attend the sail. Captain Alexis, Zantha, and George helped them to get on board. They planned to sail out to Long Island Sound and the Atlantic Ocean near Montauk. The itinerary included a Greek Orthodox priest who would give a sermon, a memorial with photos and film clips of Spiro, and personal statements from people he knew and loved him. Chantel asked to speak. She had brought a typed letter she wrote to read out loud to everyone. When Chantel took the letter out of her purse, she noticed the sky was an intense sapphire blue with flickering pink hues showing in the distance. The view reminded her of the times when she and Spiro had sailed on the yacht and the happy times they had together. She knew she would always cherish those memories in her heart. Then the priest on board began the sermon. And afterward, Chantel read her letter to Spiro.

DEAR SPIRO MY TRUE LOVE,

I will always remember our time in this world together. You brought me so much joy. I will always love you forever and for eternity. Without you, my life would have been so much different. You helped me to be the best I could be in this lifetime. You supported my dreams and loved me in ways no one else had ever before. My love for you will always be as deep as the deepest part of the ocean, the earth, and for distances as far as the universe goes, and even beyond that. Crystal and I also want you to know how much we appreciate what you did for her as well. You made our lives so much better. You were so generous and kind to us. With all the love in our hearts, we thank you so much for everything that you did for us. And we will miss you tremendously. May God be with you always and may you rest in peace with love and light all around you.

Love always,

Chantel and Crystal Du Maurier

Then Chantel and Crystal took several large bouquets of flowers from the deck and threw them overboard into the water. They watched them drift away from the yacht in different directions. Then Max got up and spoke about Spiro. He described how great a man and friend he was. Antonios spoke last. Then Antonios invited the guests to have some drinks and food in the dining area. Antonios also arranged to have a pianist play some of Spiro's favorite songs as they sailed.

Before Chantel left the yacht that day, Antonios told her that he had some important papers for her to see, some that concerned the department store. He explained that one of Spiro's financial associates would be arriving from London soon to meet with her and Bill Worth to help with Spiro's estate. Antonios told her that he had to go back to Europe. He also told Chantel that the yacht would be at her access for some time until they sort everything out. Chantel thanked him and told him she understood and would meet with Bill and the associate from London.

Later that day, when Chantel got back home to her apartment on the West Side, she told everyone that she just wanted to be alone for a while and to have some time to herself. She went into her bedroom and cried all night until she fell asleep. She didn't come out of the bedroom until the very next day.

$\mathcal{M}$ARCO

A WEEK AND A HALF LATER, CHANTEL RECEIVED A PHONE CALL from Bill Worth. He wanted to set up a meeting with Spiro's London associate who also handled many of Spiro's business and personal affairs. Chantel had asked them to come to her apartment to speak with her. She left Du Maurier's early to meet them there. Margaret was out with Crystal when they arrived that day at four o'clock in the afternoon. And one of the doormen rang upstairs on the intercom to let her know when they arrived.

"Thank you. Send them up, please," Chantel said to him, looking into a mirror and adjusting her hair.

When they got off of the elevator, Chantel opened the door to her apartment for them to come in. She couldn't believe her eyes. The person that was with Bill was Marco Puccio. She took a deep breath, stunned to see him there, and welcomed them both inside. Then Chantel brought them into the dining room where she had some coffee, tea, and pastries put out for them to have. Bill had no idea that Chantel and Marco had met before in the past.

"Ms. Du Maurier, this is Marco Puccio, the associate of Spiro's that Antonios told you about," stated Bill, adjusting his tie and fidgeting with his briefcase for papers and pens.

"Pleased to see you again," said Marco, just as surprised as Chantel was. Marco had to see for himself that this was the same Chantel Du Maurier that he'd met and fallen in love with years earlier.

Marco thought Chantel looked more beautiful than ever. He thought she looked even better than he had remembered.

"You two have met before?" asked Bill.

"Yes, Bill. I know you might be wondering how we know each other. But, we met several years ago when Marco was an intern at Buckleven Swaith. In fact, I met Marco long before I met Spiro. What a coincidence," Chantel told him, feeling the serendipity in her life again.

"That is a coincidence," echoed Bill.

Then they sat down at the dining room table and started looking at papers.

"Chantel, as you know, Antonios sent us here to help you review some of these important papers and to settle some financial matters. Everything is from the instructions of Spiro's wishes and estate. At the time that Spiro acquired the

Woods store, he also prepared documents in the event of his death that the entire store ownership would be passed on to you. He made it clear, that in the event that something happened to him, you would inherit the store entirely," Bill explained.

"What? Are you certain? What about his family in Europe? What about them?" she asked, with an apprehensive tone of voice.

"Yes, we are quite certain. Spiro's wealth was so great, he left them many other assets that are mostly in Europe. We have all the information here in these documents that we will also need you to sign and validate for his other estate attorneys. All of these papers were found in one of his private safes in London where I worked for him and were not to be opened by anyone unless he passed away. Even Bill and I weren't able to see their entire contents until a couple of days ago," Marco explained to her.

"Oh, my God," responded Chantel.

"Spiro said that if you choose to keep the store or sell any part of it, that would be at your own discretion. In any case, we are here to help you with the necessary financial and legal issues you need to know about. We suggest that you take a day or so to read through the papers, some of which have signature pages. If you have any questions, we will help to answer them," said Marco, handing Chantel a stack of documents while looking over at Bill for acknowledgment.

Chantel glanced at some of the papers. But she couldn't help but wonder what Marco's affiliation to Spiro had been. She had never heard Spiro mention Marco's name, or that they knew each other.

"Marco, did you work for Spiro? I mean for a long time?" Chantel asked, trying to understand the connection they had.

"Yes, I've been working for Spiro in London since I graduated from grad school. I've been managing many of his vast assets and holdings. So, Antonios thought it would be a good idea for me to come over to the United States. We are also working on some other assets here as well," Marco told her.

Chantel was intrigued. She raised her eyebrows and shook her head side to side.

"I understand. It's just that I never heard him mention your name before. I had no idea that you two knew each other all this time," she said kind of confused.

"Many people around the world worked for and with Spiro, Chantel. This is actually not at all that unusual. And I might add, Spiro was very fond of Marco," said Bill.

Then Bill asked Chantel if it would be okay if Marco had use of an office at Du Maurier's while he was still in New York. Chantel thought that might be a little uncomfortable for her, but answered yes. She knew she could always work from home if she wanted to.

"Just to remind you, Chantel, you have access to Spiro's yacht for a while if you want to use it or take it somewhere. In the meantime, we'll be looking out for your and the store's best interests," Bill told her.

"Thank you. This is still a difficult time for me. But I see I have your support and help. I'll go through the papers," Chantel told them.

Then Chantel escorted them both to the entrance door of her apartment. She and Marco looked at each other for a few moments in silence. And when Marco left in the elevator, Chantel felt a whole new spectrum of emotions go through her.

CHAPTER 32

ATE

DURING THE NEXT FEW DAYS, CHANTEL REFLECTED ON everything that had happened to her since she came to New York. She couldn't believe how Marco resurfaced in her life. She never imagined that she would see him again, especially under these circumstances. The entire experience surprised her a lot. It also stirred up feelings and emotions inside of her that seemed somewhat confusing and a bit unsettling.

Chantel also decided that there was still unfinished business between her and Steve Woods. She didn't want to keep the fact that Steve was Crystal's father a secret any longer. She felt that she would have to tell Crystal the truth someday, especially as she got older. Chantel thought that it would be a good idea to tell Kate Woods about it also. So she got Kate's phone number from Bill Worth and phoned her. She told Kate that she was the new owner of the old Woods department store and that she wanted the opportunity to speak with her alone. As per Chantel's suggestion, they agreed to meet at a restaurant named Avra on East Sixtieth Street for lunch two days later. Kate got there first and waited for Chantel to arrive.

Kate was very nervous. She didn't know what to expect from Chantel. Then she ordered a glass of chardonnay, waited, and wondered what this was all about. She now knew that her husband had many problems and was afraid of what she would find out next. She wondered what else he could have done and what other trouble he might be in. Losing the store was enough. Ten minutes later, Chantel arrived and found her way to the table where Kate was sitting.

"You're Kate Woods. Am I right?" Chantel asked her, acknowledging her presence.

"Yes, I'm Kate," she answered, nodding her head up and down.

"I'm Chantel Du Maurier. Thank you for coming. I wouldn't have bothered you, but I have something important to tell you that I think needs to be said in person. But first, would you like to order something to eat?" she asked Kate while she ordered a glass of Pouilly Fuisse.

"Okay, I'll order something," answered Kate cautiously.

They both ordered lunch specials from the menu. Kate felt quite uncomfortable but was very curious to find out why Chantel wanted to see her.

"So what is so secretive that you had to see me in person, Chantel?"

"It's about your husband, Steve. There's something very important that I believe you ought to know about him. I met your husband several years ago after I first arrived in New York. I'm from Maine originally. It was then that I worked at Bloomingdale's."

Kate gave Chantel a disconcerted look. She wondered why on earth Chantel was bringing up something from several years ago. Then Kate took another sip of wine. In the meantime, their food arrived, and they began to eat. Then Chantel took out a photo of Crystal.

"One day back then when I was celebrating a promotion from the company I was working for, I met your husband in Bloomingdale's. He told me that he was looking for a perfume for his mother and that he was celebrating something also, something like gambling on horses. Anyway, we went out to dinner together that night. During the evening, he told me that he was in the middle of a divorce. So I didn't think that he was in a relationship with another woman. And later that evening, he took me over to your apartment on Central Park South. Then he raped me. As a result, I became pregnant with my daughter Crystal. This is a picture of her. When I told him that I was pregnant, he laughed at me and told me no one would take me seriously. At that time, I didn't have a lot of money and was still struggling to take of myself. He refused to help me in any way," Chantel divulged to her.

Kate didn't want to accept what she just heard. It was like a nightmare to her. She wanted to believe that Chantel was crazy or something.

"Are you kidding me? How do you expect me to believe you? How dare you? I must have been out of my mind to meet you here today. Somehow, you got the store. Now you're telling me that my husband is the father of your child?" Kate said furiously.

"Yes, I'm telling you the truth. I'm not telling you this to hurt you or to even hurt Steve. I'm telling you this because I want to tell my daughter the truth one day. So, I think you need to know the truth also. Even though it's very painful, I just don't want to keep this a secret any longer. Only Spiro Pagonis and a good friend of mine ever knew about it," Chantel explained, hoping that Kate would begin to believe her and understand her reasons.

"I see. Spiro Pagonis. That's how you got the store, isn't it? I later found out that he had something to do with it. When I heard of his death, I wondered why we weren't told about it ourselves. We read about it in the newspapers. Then we saw your name with Spiro's. I wondered why Steve didn't say anything when he read about you in the papers," Kate told her, putting two and two together.

"You are right about Spiro. But I am being truthful about what I am telling you. Here is a copy of my daughter's birth certificate. As you can see, I put down Steve Woods, your husband, as the father. I put that down even though he wasn't at the birth or took any responsibility as being her father. I just think you ought to know the truth. I also want my daughter to know the truth someday," Chantel said, giving Kate a look that told her how serious she was about what she was saying.

"If I decide to believe this, what do you want from me?" asked Kate, collecting her thoughts.

"I only ask that you don't hold it against me. I was much younger and quite vulnerable at the time. I didn't expect him to do what he did. I didn't press charges because I was afraid to. That is the truth." Chantel paused. "You can keep the picture and the copy of the birth certificate."

Kate put the photo and birth certificate inside her purse. She could also see that there was a resemblance between her husband and Crystal. Then she took several deep breaths to help calm herself down.

"Okay, Chantel. I'm beginning to believe you. I have to tell you it was brave of you to meet me and to tell me about this. I realize now that you only want the truth known. And I can understand why you want Crystal to know one day. It must be hard for her not to know who her father is or was. I understand my husband is not perfect, but I never expected to hear anything like this. That bastard!" Kate told her, starting to cry and feeling horribly betrayed.

"I'm sorry about this, Kate. I'm truly sorry."

"No, I get it. I definitely get it. That bastard. He'll get his. I'm going to kill him. It's time to take him to divorce court," Kate said, slamming her purse on the table.

"I completely understand, Kate. Again, I'm sorry if it hurts you to know. That was not my intention. I swear."

"I understand, Chantel. Look, I've got to go. I've got to get that lying bastard. You should have pressed charges. Then he'd be in jail where he belongs," said Kate, grabbing her purse to reach for her wallet.

"Don't worry about the check. I'll take care of it," Chantel told her.

"Thanks, Chantel. And I'm glad you told me. Good luck with the store. I wouldn't have wanted to run it by myself anyway," said Kate, as she got up from the table to head back to Greenwich, Connecticut.

KATE KNEW THAT STEVE WAS OUT PLAYING GOLF WITH A FEW friends that day. So when she got back to Greenwich, she immediately rode over to the country club where she would find him. She got one of the caddies to drive her to where he was on the golf course. Then she got out of the golf cart with a golf club in her right hand. While Steve putted a ball, he saw her out of the corner of his eyes. He wondered what she was doing there.

"Steve Woods. You lying, cheating, bastard!" Kate screamed at the top of her lungs.

Then Kate swung the golf club and hit Steve directly on the forehead. His head started to bleed. He was dumbfounded. The other players just stood back and looked at them in shock and disbelief. Kate swung at him a few more times until Steve finally got the golf club out of her hands.

"I hear you have a daughter, Steve. Funny, you never told me about that. You're a fucking cheating loser. Do you hear me?

You fucking bastard! I met with Chantel Du Maurier today. Does that name ring a bell to you? She told me everything that you did to her. She even gave me a photo of your daughter Crystal with a copy of her birth certificate. It wasn't enough that you lost our store. You had a daughter I never knew about also. And now, Chantel Du Maurier is the one who owns our old store. Did you know that she knew Spiro Pagonis? Now I understand how she ended up with the store. They had a romantic relationship. Spiro obviously loved her and wanted to get revenge on you. You stupid bastard," Kate yelled at him with a stare that could kill.

"Come on. This is crazy. This is ridiculous," he told her.

Kate laughed at him. She began to really hate him for the first time since they met. She was furious about the store, but infidelity was unforgivable.

"You're lucky I didn't break anything on that thick head of yours. You loser. I'm going to file for divorce. By the time I get through with you, you won't have a cent left to your name. If you're lucky, maybe you can get a job at Bloomingdale's yourself. You fuck. Your life is about to become a living hell. The first thing I want you to do is to pack your suitcases and get your belongings the fuck out of my house in Greenwich and the apartment in New York. Then be prepared to hear from my attorney who will get everything you have left. You bastard!" Kate screamed again and laughed at him while the other men listened in the distance, paralyzed with fear.

CHAPTER 33

$\mathcal{E}$XPLANATIONS

EVER SINCE MARCO HAD SEEN CHANTEL AGAIN, HE COULDN'T keep his mind off of her. He thought about her every day and what he might say to her about the romance they had years earlier. But it was a bit awkward for him knowing that Spiro had a relationship with her. He also knew that he had to be professional about the work he was doing for Spiro's estate. He had business responsibilities to Chantel and the department store's organization and finances. Marco also imagined that Chantel was probably still mourning Spiro's death. Yet he wanted to know what happened in the past. He still didn't understand what happened between them. He didn't know for sure why Chantel ended their relationship. What made this even more frightening to him was that his love for her had never died. While he thought about all of this, the phone rang in his room in the Plaza Hotel. It was Bill Worth.

"Marco, how are you doing? I'm wondering if you could have dinner with Chantel and I this evening? I know it's short notice, but it's the soonest time I could get her to meet. I think we need to talk about the future of the store and what she intends to do with it. We have lawyers waiting on her decisions that we need to answer. She agreed to meet downstairs in The Palm Court at eight o'clock. Can you make it?" asked Bill, sounding impatient because he wanted to get things settled.

"Yes, of course. I will make it. That's what I'm here for. I'll be there at eight," answered Marco, actually relieved to hear they had a meeting.

Then Marco took a shower to freshen up and put on a new suit that he had custom made in London. Before he left to go downstairs, he took one last look in a mirror, straightened out his tie, combed his hair, and put on a tiny bit of cologne. When he arrived downstairs, Bill was already seated at a table in The Palm Court. Then he walked over to his table and sat down to join him.

"Hello, Marco. Chantel just called me on my cell phone and is going to be a few minutes late. So tell me, how is your stay here at the Plaza so far?" asked Bill.

Marco took a piece of bread from a basket on the table and spread a little herbed butter on it.

"Well, to be honest, I didn't realize how much I missed New York until now. And the hotel is fine. The staff is very attentive and pleasant," answered Marco, taking a bite from the bread in his hand.

"Yes, it's a great city. But so is London. I can understand why you've been working there over the past several years."

Then Marco thought it might be a good idea to tell Bill about his past with Chantel. "Bill, there's something I'd like to share with you."

"What's that Marco?"

"As you recently found out, Chantel and I met several years ago. In fact, I met her not long after she moved to New York from Maine. I was an intern at Buckleven Swaith at the time. Just before I went back to finish my MBA, we met at a holiday party at Cipriani's. At the same time, Dora Moore worked at Buckleven and brought Chantel to the party with her," Marco told him.

"That's very interesting, Marco."

"Yes, but there's more. We quickly dated and I fell in love with her. I thought that she loved me also. But for some reason, she suddenly changed her mind and didn't want to see me again. I still don't understand the reason why. It just didn't make any sense at the time. I'm curious. Are you aware of any marriages she might have had in the past?" asked Marco, looking confused and taking a sip of wine to clear his throat.

"No, I'm not aware of any marriages. But it is obvious that Spiro loved her also. He left her the store and helped her with her career and everything. You've seen the papers he had drawn up in the event something happened to him," answered Bill.

"I understand that part. But they met much later."

Then Bill ordered his second vodka martini and put the olives from the first one inside of his mouth.

"In any case, Bill, I'm hoping that I might have a chance to speak with her alone tonight after we go over her business affairs. I'm wondering if you could do me a favor?" asked Marco.

"Sure, what is the favor, Marco?"

"Around the time that we finish our business conversation, can you quickly make an excuse that you have to leave? It's just that I finally have a chance tonight to ask her what happened between us. I just need to know what happened. I want to know the reason why she decided not to marry me," explained Marco.

Bill was somewhat touched by Marco's call for help. He and Marco were also friends and he wanted to help him out. Bill was also the sentimental type and this sort of thing got to him inside.

"Sure, I'll think of something. No problem. But business comes first. There are still a lot of things to be decided on with the store. And we still don't know all of Chantel's plans," said Bill.

Just at that moment, Chantel walked into the restaurant. Marco was grateful that he already had a chance to talk to Bill before she arrived.

"Sorry, I kept you both waiting. I needed to review some more of the papers," Chantel told them as she sat down at the table.

Even though this was still a tough time for Chantel, she looked lovely. She had on a brown and white silk dress with a matching scarf designed by Givenchy. Marco didn't think she looked a day older than he remembered her. In fact, there was a new confidence he saw in her that made her look even sexier than before.

"When you're ready, Chantel, can you tell us what you would like to do with the store? And have you signed any of the papers that we gave you the last time we saw you?" asked Bill, with a polite and respectful tone of voice.

Then a waiter came over to their table and temporarily interrupted their conversation. He wanted to know what Chantel wanted to drink. She decided to have a glass of white wine. Then the waiter gave them all menus and said he would be back in a few minutes to take their orders. Bill suggested that they put in their orders before discussing business. He told Chantel that he just remembered that he had something important come up at home and that he would need to attend to it as soon as possible. So they ordered dinner as soon as the waiter returned.

"Yes, I have signed some of the papers that you gave me. There were a few that I didn't sign because I would like to make some suggestions to them. I have decided that I will continue to keep the store for now. I also have the option of bringing in a new partner if I want to. Or, I can sell it in the future if I decide to do so. But for now, I'll try to keep it on my own. Dora will help me. Also, I want to keep the name Du Maurier's and add some new and diverse merchandise to create a larger product line under my brand name. Oh, and, here are the papers that I've already signed," Chantel told them, pulling the papers out of her briefcase looking calm and collected.

"Thank you. And here are some more from the attorneys.

Sorry, we realize there are a lot of papers to read. But at least we know better what your immediate and definitive plans are. We thought you might need a little time to think it over before you made firm decisions and all," said Bill, starting the main course he ordered.

"Yes, I'm thinking of perhaps expanding from my perfume products into fashion as well. I'm going to meet with some fashion designers to talk about those possibilities. In the meantime, let's continue the store designs, the newer renovation, and move forward. The sooner we can do this the better. I understand we are also within our given budget. If we keep moving quickly with the interior designers, contractors, and decorators, we will get a lot more accomplished sooner rather than later. I see they are all working on it though," said Chantel.

Bill had been working with a couple of design teams. He explained to Chantel that they already had new designs for a lot of the departments that were not renovated yet. The Du Maurier sign was also put on the building. And the new shopping bags for merchandise had also been given to all the departments in the store. The outside of the store looked much better than it did before. It was newer and fresher looking. Chantel loved how it looked and had received many compliments.

"Fortunately, we've been pleased with how the renovations have been coming along so far. But the store has a lot of square feet so it will take some more time and planning," commented Bill.

"That's terrific. In the meantime, I'm going to take a short trip to Bermuda for a few days. I will be sailing there on Spiro's yacht but will keep checking my phone and computer for messages. I'll also be staying at the Fairmont in Southampton Parish. I want to spend some time there on land. But again, I'll have my computer with me and you can also contact me by phone," Chantel informed them.

Marco thought about how strange this was. In a way, Chantel seemed like the same person he remembered. But at the same time, she seemed very different. Her life was certainly very different than when he met her. He thought she also had a new worldliness about her that she didn't seem to have when he first met her years ago. He also wondered how she felt inside. He couldn't quite tell what emotions she was feeling. In a way, he just wanted to hold her and tell her that everything would be okay. He wanted to tell her that he was there for her no matter what. But he wasn't sure about that also.

"Not to worry, Chantel. We have a number of people to help with the store. It'll just be a bit of a jumble for a while. So, it's good for you to get away for a few days. You've been through a lot. And, as you said, we can always contact you by phone," Bill said to her.

They all agreed that everything would be fine. Chantel seemed pleased. So they talked a bit more about her fashion ideas and new designs before Bill announced that he had to go. He told them not to worry about the check either. Chantel thanked him as he got up from the table, leaving her and Marco alone together. Then Marco looked into Chantel's eyes and felt a little nervous about what he wanted to say to her.

"Chantel, it's been quite a while. Hasn't it? I've often

thought about you and how you were doing. It's amazing seeing you again after all this time," said Marco, looking at her carefully.

Chantel blushed. She knew inside that their meeting again was somewhat remarkable. But it happened and became their new reality.

"All the time Spiro was alive, I never knew that you two even knew one another. Well, that's certainly a coincidence, isn't it? Anyhow, you look very well, Marco," Chantel told him in a soft tone of voice.

"So do you, Chantel. And you have a daughter named Crystal also. I saw a photo of her when I was in your apartment. She is beautiful. But did you ever marry anyone?" asked Marco.

"No, I never married. Spiro is not Crystal's father either. I'll explain that another time. I really don't feel like talking about that right now," she answered, feeling a moment of sadness as she thought about his question.

Marco felt butterflies in his stomach, but he needed to know what happened in the past. He spent years wondering about it.

"Chantel, I hope I don't make you feel self-conscious, but I just need to know something. It's been bothering me for all the years I haven't seen you. When we met, I fell in love with you, and I thought you loved me also. But I still don't understand what happened or why you stopped seeing me or talking to me," Marco said to her, hoping he would finally get an answer.

Chantel sighed and took a deep breath. It was hard for Marco to read her feelings. He waited for an answer or a response of any kind and took another sip from his glass of wine.

"I'm sorry. I regret what happened," Chantel said, looking sincere.

"If you really can't talk about it right now, I understand. But, it's going to drive me crazy until I know what happened. I really thought you loved me. I felt your love," Marco told her.

Chantel took another deep breath and had a hesitant expression on her face. "I guess there's no sense in not telling you now. I still owe that to you. I just couldn't tell you at the time," she said, clearing her throat.

"Don't worry. It's okay. Go ahead. I'm listening."

Chantel looked down at the table and memories of the past began to flood her with emotions she long ago tried to forget and suppress from her memory. She took one of the flowers from a vase on the table and felt it slowly with her fingers. It looked as if she was trying to calm herself with it.

"Do you remember the holiday party you took me to at your mother's house on Long Island?" Chantel asked him.

"Yes, I remember."

"Well, that evening your mother invited me inside one of the rooms in the house. She said she wanted to tell me something. I, of course, never told you about it, or what she had said to me. Luna told me that if I ever married you, she would make our lives miserable, especially yours. She also told me that she would disinherit you as a son," Chantel informed him feeling nauseous inside.

"What the hell? You're not joking, are you?" Marco asked her stunned.

"Marco, that's what happened. I was afraid that she really meant it. After that I didn't want to ever see her again. I also didn't want her ruining your life, or mine for that matter. I had very little materially back then, and she told me that she wanted you to marry someone from a family that had a lot of money. I didn't know what to tell you. I didn't want her to hurt you or me. I could tell she was very serious," explained Chantel, wiping a tear from her cheek.

Marco couldn't understand why his own mother would do this to him. But he believed that Chantel had finally told him the truth. Then he thought about the reality of the situation and the harm that his mother had done to them. He realized then that his mother still had hurt them both. She ruined their happiness of being in love. He realized that his mother meddled in his love life and scared away the only woman he ever romantically loved.

"And, what about you? You never married all this time, Marco?" Chantel asked him.

"No, I never did. I met a few women. But I never felt as strongly as I did about you," he answered with sadness in his voice.

"I'm really sorry, Marco. I never meant to hurt you. I was a lot younger and felt more vulnerable back then. I was afraid of how she would be. I thought I was helping you by leaving you. I did love you," Chantel told him.

"You did love me. I see. At least I know the truth now. And

what about Crystal? Do you feel like telling me about her now?" Marco asked, trying to compose himself.

"That's another story altogether, Marco. I was raped not long after I met you. I was raped by Steve Woods and became pregnant with his child. But he denied everything. It wasn't until Spiro found out about it recently that he went after Steve and quietly acquired the Woods store. I didn't know anything about it until after he bought it. I understand no one knew who was really buying the store. Spiro kept it very secretive from people and the press. After I told Spiro what Steve did to me, he hated him with a vengeance. So that's my story," Chantel explained to him.

Marco put all the pieces together. Now he really understood why Spiro went after the store. He knew it was a bit unusual at the time. Spiro wanted it so he could take it away from Steve and give it to Chantel.

"I understand now. I worked on that acquisition. I also hear that you became very successful even before you met Spiro by creating fragrances at Champs. It's remarkable how much you have accomplished. I can understand why Spiro loved you. I really get it. I also hope you are very proud of yourself and all of your success."

"Thanks. So tell me more about your life, Marco," said Chantel.

"Well after I finished grad school, I went to work for an investment firm in London. Then I met Spiro and he offered me a position to manage many of his holdings and investments, particularly overseas. Ever since then, I've been living and working in London with occasional visits to the states," Marco told her.

"Were you in the states recently? I could have sworn that I saw you here in The Palm Court one day as you were leaving. But it was in the split of a second, and I wasn't sure."

"Yes, I was in New York more recently for the store acquisition."

"That makes sense. And what about your family?" Chantel asked, curious to know what happened to them.

"My mother sold her home in Southampton and moved to West Palm Beach. She got tired of the cold winters here in the Northeast. My sister went to live with her. I haven't seen them much because I've been living in London."

After they talked some more and finished their desserts, they asked about the check. As Bill had told them earlier, it was already taken care of. Then Marco asked Chantel if he could escort her home. She agreed if only to be polite to him. She felt sorry about what she had finally told him.

When they got outside, Marco waived down a taxi and told the driver to take them to Central Park West and Seventy-second Street. But before he let her walk inside her building for the night, he talked with her some more.

"Chantel, no matter what, I want you to know that I'm here for you and to help you with all of your business concerns. But I especially want you to know that I'm here for you period. If there's anything at all I can help you with, don't hesitate to ask me," Marco told her, taking her hand and holding it gently.

"Thanks. I really appreciate it, Marco. It's good seeing you again after all this time. I'm also happy that you've been doing so well for yourself. Spiro certainly had good taste. I didn't ask you though, do you like living in London? I guess you'll be going back sometime soon after our business is complete."

"Well, I'm not sure about that yet. I wasn't planning on Spiro dying on us. And, I've met you again. Should I stop or keep going?" Marco asked.

Chantel laughed. She suddenly remembered how much fun they had in the past. "I'm not sure," she answered, smiling at him, gazing deep into his eyes.

"Perhaps it's not too late, Chantel. I mean for us. I'm hoping there might be a possibility. Maybe you can at least give it some thought," Marco added as he admired her in the moonlight, finding her even more beautiful than ever.

Then Marco leaned over and kissed her quickly on the lips. It felt like a magnetic charge went through the two of them at the same time. They both shivered from the electric surge they felt. But it was a familiar feeling to them also. It was a feeling they both experienced together years earlier.

"Good night, Chantel. Sleep well," said Marco as he watched her walk toward the entrance of her building.

"I'll try my best. Good night to you also," she told him while she turned back to glance at him one more time.

CHAPTER 34

NFINITY

TWO DAYS LATER CHANTEL BOARDED THE YACHT INFINITY TO sail to Bermuda. She took a couple of suitcases and a taxi from her apartment. Margaret would take care of Crystal while she went away. She met Alexis at the marina wearing a faded pair of blue jeans, a lacy white blouse with mother of pearl buttons, a beige straw hat, and Armani sunglasses. The weather was sunny and warm, and there was a nice breeze from the water.

"Good morning, Ms. Du Maurier. It's a pleasure to see you again. I have the master suite ready for you," Alexis told her when she arrived, greeting her with a big smile.

"Alexis, I prefer to stay in one of the guest quarters. I'm sure you understand," Chantel told him, feeling too sad to sleep in the same bed that she and Spiro had slept in and made love to each other before.

"I understand, Ms. Du Maurier."

"Please, Alexis, call me Chantel. Let's be more casual. I've known you for a while now. You don't need to be so formal with me," she told him, walking onto one of the decks as he helped her with her luggage.

Meanwhile, the crew prepared to leave, and Chantel found a comfortable lounge chair to lay down on. Chantel remembered there was a wet bar with a fridge nearby if she wanted something cold to drink. Then one of the crew came up to her to ask her if she wanted anything, or if she was hungry.

"Not yet, thank you. I'll wait a couple of hours," she answered softly, closing her eyes behind her sunglasses, taking a deep breath to feel more relaxed.

The crew was soon ready to depart, and Infinity left World Yacht Marina. There were a couple of people strolling along the piers that waved to them as they pulled out further into the Hudson River. Chantel didn't notice. But Alexis' wife Zantha did. Zantha usually waved to people when they arrived at or departed from different ports and marinas.

Chantel laid in the lounge chair barely moving at all. And the skyscrapers of Manhattan were further and further away. She began to think about her life and how incredible it had been so far. She realized that she was fortunate in many ways, even though there had been problems in her love life and Spiro dying and all. She also felt hopeful of the future. In many ways, she felt grateful. She thought things could always be worse if not better. She also thought about Manhattan. She knew that some people loved it while others were somewhat intimidated by it. But Chantel always felt that Manhattan was a place of possibilities. A moment later, one of the crew interrupted her train of thought.

"Ms. Du Maurier, there is a phone call for you. It's Dora Moore. Would you like to take it?" he asked.

"Yes, I'll take it, thank you. Hello, Dora, what a nice surprise," said Chantel, adjusting her hat and glasses to better position the phone.

"Don't you even say goodbye to your old Southern friend?"

"I'm sorry, Dora. I asked Margaret to tell you for me. I was kind of in a hurry. It's been so busy for me lately, as you know, with the store and all the decisions I've been making," Chantel explained.

"Sure, but you wouldn't believe who called me last night? It was Marco Puccio. Somehow, he got my phone number. It was probably through Bill Worth because he explained that he was involved with Du Maurier's and has recently seen you. You didn't tell me about this. So that's what happens when you have meetings outside of your new office. Well, anyway, he asked about your trip to Bermuda and seemed to be fishing for just about any other personal information. He did this while he pretended to want to say hello to me. But I know better than that," Dora said, chuckling in the background.

Chantel looked up at the sky and rolled her eyes. Then she scrunched her lips together side by side.

"I was wondering if you started seeing him again and just haven't told me?" asked Dora.

"No, it's been business only," replied Chantel.

"Well, you might want to consider it. It sounds like he still cares a lot about you. I'm curious. How do you feel about him?"

Chantel smiled and shook her head. She wasn't ready to satisfy Dora's curiosity. "You know, Dora, you still haven't changed. And I don't think I ever want you to," she said laughing.

"Well, have a good trip. Just think about it. I know you loved him once. Sometimes when a person loves someone, they love that person forever, even when they're not around for a long time. Anyhow, talk to soon. If you need me, you know where to find me," Dora told her.

"Thanks, Dora. Love you."

"Love you too. Bye."

After Chantel hung up the phone, Alexis came to see how she was doing. He wanted her to feel most welcome, especially since Spiro was no longer there.

"How are you doing, Chantel?" Alexis asked her.

"Just fine, thanks. I've always loved this yacht. I have so many fond memories here," Chantel told him.

"I'm glad to hear that you are comfortable. We want your trip to be as pleasant as it possibly can. But another reason why I came to see you is that I have a letter for you. I was asked to give it to you after we got further out into the ocean. It is from a gentleman named Marco Puccio. I have met him before in Europe but never had seen him in New York. In any case, he came by early this morning before you arrived and asked me to give this to you," explained Alexis, handing her the envelope.

Chantel took it from his hand. She looked down at it inquisitively, wondering what was in the contents. Then Alexis asked if she would like to dine with him that evening and if that would be agreeable to her. He didn't want her to dine alone and thought it would be good if she had some company. Chantel agreed and told him that she thought it was a good idea.

"Very well, Chantel. If you excuse me now, I need to attend to some more navigation. I will also be checking in with the kitchen. In the meantime, George will be serving you lunch when you're ready," Alexis told her, nodding his head and smiling.

A few hours later, Chantel started to get hungry and went inside to have lunch in the formal dining room where she and Spiro used to eat together. She had a large salad, some trout, vegetables, and a small fresh berry tart and sorbet for dessert. There were also assorted chocolates on a tray, but she didn't have room for them.

Then Chantel decided to go into her cabin to see what Marco had sent to her in the envelope. She wanted to read it in private. When she got there, she lied down on her bed and propped a pillow to hold her head up. Then she opened the envelope and began to read the letter. It said:

DEAREST CHANTEL,

By now you are probably in the midst of the ocean surrounded by water. Forgive me if I invade your personal space or privacy. But you are a love of mine I cannot forget. I think about you all the time, especially since I've seen you in person again. I always thought of you all these years. You are still so gorgeous and stunning a woman. But you have only been a dream to me since I've known you. I am hoping that there's a chance that you will be more than a dream but a reality for me, for us, once again, giving us a chance at love, to love one another, and to live out love together for the rest of our lives. At least, I'm hoping you give us that chance one more time. I hope that you consider this seriously. I know that you've been very hurt by others in the past. I know that you've lived through tragedy and loss. But I want to help to make you happy and hope you take a chance. I know you can make me happy. I didn't know if I would ever see you again in this lifetime. And because of that, I have always felt a void in my heart since we parted years ago. It's been cold, empty, and painful. God knows I've tried to love others, but it is you that I truly love. It has always been you. I hope that you understand this letter is from my heart and soul. I would marry you in an instant if you would marry me. I'd live anywhere in the world with you. I just want to be with you. I want to be with you forever. Please think about this.

LOVE,

MARCO

Tears poured down Chantel's face. She couldn't believe that Marco would even write such a letter after all this time they were apart. She couldn't believe how passionately he expressed himself in words. She genuinely felt them. They resonated inside of her. She realized that life had brought her another opportunity of love with him, even though she wasn't expecting it. Then she put the letter close to her mouth and kissed it gently with her lips. And for the rest of the afternoon, she decided to stay in her cabin. Then she opened the door to a private outdoor balcony and spent the rest of the day just looking out at the ocean.

Several hours later Chantel heard a knock on her cabin door. It was one of the crew to inform her that dinner would soon be ready and that Captain Alexis would be waiting for her. A few minutes later, Chantel took a light sweater from one of the closets and went to the dining room to have dinner with Alexis.

"Pleasant evening, isn't it, Chantel?" said Alexis when she arrived.

The weather was a little chillier but still lovely and comfortable. And the views of the ocean, now at sunset, were as serene and peaceful as Chantel could ever remember.

"Yes, Alexis. It's perfect sailing weather. And I'm glad we are dining together. It's great to have company," Chantel told him.

"I thought it would be. It's my honor and pleasure. And our chef has once again prepared an exquisite menu for tonight. I hope you will enjoy it. We'll be starting with fish soup followed by red snapper and much more. We have an idea of what you like," Alexis said opening a bottle of red wine.

"Sounds great. Thank you," replied Chantel taking a glass of the wine.

A few minutes later, another one of the crew arrived to serve them dinner.

"So tell me, Alexis, how did you become captain aboard

Spiro's yacht? I always wondered about that. But please tell me if I'm being too personal. I just always wanted to know."

"Not at all. I don't mind. At first, I started out in the navy, like many sailors. And after I left the navy, I began sailing on commercial ships. Then I began sailing on private yachts for their owners. I met Spiro when I was working on another yacht. Spiro really wanted to hire me and offered me much better compensation. So, I took the position. Ever since then, he has treated me very well. But now that he's gone, I'm not sure what my future will be like. His stepbrother Antonios is working on giving me another position on a different yacht. I'm still not sure what is going to happen to Infinity yet," Alexis explained.

"What about your wife, Zantha? Have you been married a long time?" Chantel asked him.

"Well, Zantha and I have only been together in recent years, a couple of years before you met Spiro. But I was married once before also to another woman years ago," Alexis answered.

"Come to think of it, I should have asked. Is it okay with Zantha that we're dining together?"

"Yes, it's fine. She's quite busy tonight with some paperwork and orders for the yacht."

"I see. I understand. So you were married before, Alexis. What happened to your first wife, if you don't mind me asking?"

"Chantel, she died. It was a tragedy that happened a long, long time ago. It is only recently and since I met Zantha that I can even talk about her without feeling like there's a stone in my heart."

"I'm sorry. Perhaps you don't want to talk about it now. It's none of my business really."

"No, it's okay, Chantel. Her name was Maria. She was a very beautiful and delicate woman. It happened off the coast of Valencia, Spain. One night we took a small boat out onto the water. We also had a lot to drink that night. When we went back to land, Maria and I socialized with some of my comrades. A couple of hours later, no one could find Maria, and we noticed that the boat had disappeared. When we went to look for her, we found her drowned in the water not far from the boat. We figured she took the boat out by herself and must have fallen into the water by accident. The grief and guilt I felt lasted for years. I hated myself after that. I never felt worthy of another woman's love until Zantha. Zantha helped me to open up my heart and feelings to love again. I'm very grateful that she came into my life," Alexis told Chantel wiping sweat from his forehead and a tear from one of his eyes.

"My God, that's awful. How terrible that must have been for you. But at least Zantha came into your life later and helped you heal from the loss."

"Yes, I blamed myself for a long time."

"I'm sorry. I'm truly sorry," Chantel said.

"It was quite a struggle inside for me. Life was, I mean. But you must understand, Chantel. You had a huge loss yourself with Spiro suddenly dying. You know what loss is, even if you are not responsible for it," Alexis told her.

"Yes, another tragedy," Chantel agreed, shaking her head.

"Yet you, Chantel, are still quite young. There is still time for you to love again. Please forgive me. I'm not trying to be disrespectful to Spiro or you. I just learned, that no matter what, you can't change what happened in the past, no matter how much you would like to. And there's no point in living a life in the past and without love. I learned that the slow and hard way."

"I see, Alexis. I really appreciate you sharing this with me," Chantel said, deeply touched by his story.

"You are welcome. Just remember, love never ends. I came to understand that it is eternal and infinite. There is no reason to keep your heart closed to love no matter what happened in life before. It's something to keep in mind."

Then for the rest of their dinner together, they talked about current events and books that they each had read. They also looked out onto the stars and admired them. A new closeness of friendship emerged between them that hadn't existed before.

A FEW DAYS LATER, CHANTEL WOKE UP TO THE SOUNDS OF Bermuda longtail birds singing and views of Hamilton Harbor. She could also see some of the island's lighthouses in the distance. So she got dressed and finished packing her luggage. When she got on deck, she saw Alexis holding a pair of binoculars in his hands looking out at the harbor.

"So, I see we are here," Chantel told him enthusiastically.

"Yes, we are. We'll be docking in just a few minutes."

Chantel looked out in the distance and admired Hamilton. There were cruise ships, yachts, and various sizes of sailboats scattered all along it. She was happy to be there. It felt refreshing to her to finally have a change of scenery.

"Chantel, there will be a car and driver waiting for you when we dock. The driver will take you to your hotel. If you need us for any reason, we'll be here until you want us to take you back to New York. Please enjoy yourself and have a very good time. Again, just call us if you need our assistance for any reason," Alexis assured her.

"Thanks again, Alexis. I hope you and the crew get to enjoy your time here as well," replied Chantel just before they docked.

Captain Alexis was flattered by Chantel's kindness. He always admired her for her genuine and warm personality. He watched closely as the crew helped her with her luggage to the car waiting for her. Then he waved goodbye to her while the car drove off to the hotel.

CHAPTER 35

HANCES

IT TOOK A LITTLE OVER A HALF AN HOUR DRIVE FROM THE CITY of Hamilton to Southampton Parish where the Fairmont was located. The hotel sat high on top of a big hill and had striking views of large coral rock formations and the Atlantic Ocean. When she arrived, Chantel was checked in quickly. She had a spacious suite with a very large balcony and French doors to the outside, giving her panoramic views of the ocean. Her suite was also furnished with a coffee table and chairs that she could lounge on. And there were candles placed in sand-filled hurricane vases throughout the space. It was decorated in pastel colors with some impressionist paintings on the walls. There was also a small kitchenette for food and drinks.

Soon after she arrived, Chantel decided to take a walk over

to the Gibbs Hill Lighthouse. It was fairly close to the Fairmont. She thought the walk would do her good and give her some exercise. When she got to the lighthouse, she bought some souvenirs to bring back to Crystal and Margaret. She also had something to eat and sat out on one of the chairs outside to get some sun. There were many families and children there, mostly tourists from different countries. The children were chasing one another around the lighthouse grounds, laughing with joy in their eyes. A little later on, Chantel went back to the Fairmont to change into her bathing suit. She decided to take the hotel trolley down to the beachfront. When she got there, she noticed an entrance to Horseshoe Bay. She remembered that Horseshoe Bay was one of the most beautiful beaches in Bermuda. So instead of staying on Fairmont's grounds, she decided to see what it looked like for herself.

And when Chantel got to Horseshoe Bay, she rented an umbrella to provide some shade from the sun. She loved the sun, but she didn't want to get too bad a burn too quickly. The beach itself was crescent-shaped, much like a horseshoe. Chantel thought it lived up to its reputation and that it was truly picturesque. The color of the water was very pale blue. It was extremely clear so you could see to the bottom of the ocean below you. And the sand was the softest sand Chantel had ever felt under her feet. She thought it was like walking on sugar, or close to it. Chantel laid out her large towel and stood up her umbrella. Then she went for a swim. She felt very refreshed after that. Then she laid down on her towel and took a short nap on the beach. After she got up, she went for a walk along the bay and swam again. Then she went back to the Fairmont. In the interim, she decided to treat herself to a cocktail at a restaurant named Cabana. The bartender made her a delicious strawberry vodka martini. Then she went back to her suite to take a shower.

By dinnertime, Chantel was feeling hungry again. So she went downstairs to the hotel lobby to the Jasmine Lounge to have something to eat. After that, she went back to her suite and called Crystal and Margaret to let them know that she missed them both and that she was okay. They were very happy to hear from her and told her how much they also missed her, but to have a good time. Then she watched some television and fell asleep for the rest of the night.

THE NEXT MORNING, CHANTEL WOKE UP AND DECIDED TO GO into Hamilton to do some shopping. She bought some Bermudian jewelry and perfumes that she liked and wanted to bring to New York. After her lunch in the city, she took a taxi back to the Fairmont and went to Horseshoe Bay again. She swam for a while and sunbathed for a few more hours. Then she went upstairs to take a shower and wash up for dinner. When she came downstairs to Jasmine's for a cocktail, she decided to sit at the bar this time. She overheard many of the customers at the bar talking about places in the United States. Many patrons were vacationing there from the states. Then a small band began playing music in the restaurant. The musicians played many songs that were familiar to Chantel. She was enjoying herself and asked the bartender for another cocktail. Then she heard a man's voice from behind her asking her if anyone was sitting in the chair next to her. She thought the voice sounded familiar but made nothing of it. But when she looked over her shoulder, she saw Marco.

"Hello, Chantel. I guess there's no one sitting here?" Marco inquired again.

Chantel was incredibly shocked. She didn't expect to see Marco in Bermuda and wondered why he was there.

"No. No one is sitting there. Please sit down," Chantel answered.

Then Marco sat down next to her and ordered himself something to drink.

"Chantel, I know you might think this is odd. I hope you're not upset that I'm here. But I thought it might give us a chance to spend some time together. I'm sure that Captain Alexis must have given you the letter I wrote to you by now," said Marco.

"Yes, he did, Marco. I was very touched by it. It was a lovely letter. But I just don't know how to feel about it yet. I lost you for another reason years ago. Then Spiro. Sometimes, it's hard to take another chance."

"I understand, Chantel. I only hope that you're not upset that I came here to be with you. I won't bother you if you don't want me to. But I was wondering, since you are here alone, and so am I if you would like to go out to dinner with me this evening. I know a really great restaurant not too far away called Henry the VIII. It is very popular with the locals here in Bermuda and has some live entertainment also. I'd love to take you there if you would like to go," Marco suggested while taking a sip of his drink.

Chantel thought about it for a moment. She felt flattered that Marco flew to Bermuda to see her. She thought that simply being in Bermuda was special. But being there with Marco made it even more special.

"Okay. Even though this is unexpected, I don't see why not, Marco," Chantel answered.

A little later on and after they finished their cocktails, Marco got a taxi to take them over to Henry the VIII. It was located by itself on a little hill that overlooked the ocean. Once they ordered some wine and their dinner selections, they settled down and began talking about their lives. Marco told her about how confused he was when she left him years earlier. He told her that he never imagined that the cause was from his own mother. He realized that back then he was so much more naive about such things. Chantel also opened up about how she felt back then and told him how hard it was for her also. She knew that she was naive about a lot more things as well. Then they changed the subject and talked about other topics that interested them. Marco told her that he was looking for a more permanent position in finance in Manhattan again. Chantel was pleased to hear that. And by then, they were also feeling a lot more relaxed and comfortable with each other again. The combination of the salt air breezes, the wine, and the food started making them both feel good. And during their meal, a band started playing, and many people got up to dance.

"Chantel, would you like to dance?" Marco asked her.

"Sure, Marco. Let's dance," Chantel answered blushing.

Then they got up from their table and went onto the dance floor. It was a slow song, so they put their arms around each other again for the first time in years. When Marco felt the contours of Chantel's body, it excited him. But he tried not to show it. Chantel also felt warm and sensual with her arms around his shoulders and her breasts pressed against his chest. But before the song finished, Marco placed his lips on hers and kissed her gently on the dance floor. Chantel just looked at him and said nothing. Then they went back to their table to finish their dinner and have some after dinner drinks. They talked some more. There was a feeling of ease that came over them. Then Marco asked her if she wanted to go snorkeling the next day at Church Bay. Chantel agreed to go. So they decided what time they would meet each other.

THE FOLLOWING MORNING, CHANTEL FOUND MARCO IN THE hotel lobby waiting for her. She had already had breakfast in her suite upstairs and was ready to go. Marco got a taxi to take them over to Church Bay. Church Bay was located below a bunch of little cliffs. It was a much smaller beach than Horseshoe Bay, but it was very well-known for snorkeling and seeing fish up close in the water. It was a little windy when they got there. This made the waves a little rougher than they usually would be. It also made it more of a challenge and fun getting into the water. When they finished snorkeling, they took some photos together with their cellphones. Then they headed back to the hotel to relax for a while.

That evening they decided to go to the Ocean Club for dinner. It also had great views of coral rocks and the ocean. After dinner, they decided to sit out by the water on the lounge chairs on the beach. They put the chairs as close as they could so that they could hold one another and watch the waves brush up against the shore in front of them. By then, it was evening. And when they got too chilly, they decided to go back to the hotel. Marco asked Chantel if she would like to stop in at Jasmine's or his suite upstairs. Instead of going to his suite, Chantel suggested that he come to hers. She told him that he could bring some champagne with him or that she could order some for them herself.

"I'll bring the champagne, Chantel. In fact, I'll talk to room service and see you soon. I have something I want to bring with me and to show to you," Marco told her.

Chantel went upstairs to her suite and waited for Marco. She decided to light the candles in the hurricane vases that were placed throughout the rooms. Then she put on some music. Not long after, Marco knocked at the door. He had two bottles of cold champagne, a bouquet of flowers, and a box of truffle chocolates with him.

"For you, Chantel," he said, as he walked inside.

Feeling warm and sentimental, Chantel smiled at him. Some past memories also came into her mind. Then she got some champagne glasses and put the flowers in a small vase she found in the kitchen. Marco opened one of the bottles and sat down outside on the balcony. Then she joined him. They sat close to one another. Marco bent over to kiss her. They kissed each other for a long time. Then both of them started to relive their feelings from the past. It became apparent to both of them that there was still a strong bond between them. After a while, they just held each other quietly and looked out at the sky, the moon, and the stars together. It was as clear a night as any, and it was beautiful.

"Chantel, as you know, I don't want to make you feel uncomfortable or anything. I've said that before. But I want to show you something. This is for you," Marco told her, reaching into one of his pockets and taking out a jewelry box that looked very much like the one he gave to her years earlier.

Chantel looked at the box. Then she opened it. It was the very same engagement ring that he wanted her to have years ago. Then she started to cry.

"I'm sorry, Chantel. I didn't want to upset you. I just want you to know that the offer still stands. I meant what I said in my letter. If you would consider a relationship with me again, if you would consider marrying me again, I'm here," Marco continued, holding her in his arms.

"I believe you, Marco. But I need to think about it. For now, let's just be together. I'm enjoying simply being alone right here and now," she told him.

Marco understood and put the ring back inside his pocket. Then they started kissing each other earnestly. Within a few more minutes, they were in the bedroom and began to undress each other. They felt each other's bodies as if they were doing so for the very first time. They kissed every inch of each other with their lips. Then they made love. They felt an overwhelming ecstasy they remembered from the past. Their bodies were bound to each other. They made love as long as they could until they fell asleep next to each other.

THE NEXT DAY CHANTEL AND MARCO TOOK A WALK TOGETHER along Horseshoe Bay. They talked about their return plans to New York. Chantel asked Marco if he would like to go back with her on Infinity in the next day or two. Marco was extremely happy that she had invited him to go on Infinity with her. He knew this meant that she was probably giving their relationship another chance. Whether or not she had agreed to marry him yet, he was sure that this meant there was another chance for both of them.

"Of course I will, Chantel. I'd love to," he told her, putting his arms around her.

"That's wonderful, Marco," Chantel replied, knowing from that moment on both of their lives would be changed forever. This time there was nothing to stand between them or their love for one another.

ABOUT THE AUTHOR

MIMI FLOWERS is an emerging author. She was born in New York City and attended New York University undergraduate school and Walden University graduate school. She holds a Master's degree in Psychology and is a Certified Life Coach. Find her on Facebook at fb.me/mimiflowers.me and Twitter at twitter.com/mimiflowers_

Please contact or visit her at:
www.mimiflowersbooks.com